MAKING IT UP

SAPPHIRE FALLS NEXT GENERATION

ERIN NICHOLAS

ABOUT MAKING IT UP

Keeping their hands off each other was never part of the plan… but neither was falling this hard.

Rescuing Mia Hansen from the middle of a field during a storm is my job. I'm a conservation officer, not a hero. And definitely not a guy who gets caught up in trouble. At least not anymore. I have a past, but I'm a rule-follower now. And I especially don't need the kind of trouble that comes with a sweet smile, killer curves, and a library card.

But Mia is definitely going to be a problem for me. The irresistible, late-night-fantasy kind.

Because she's also the daughter of the only man in this town I don't like and can't trust. Getting involved with her would be a mistake. A reckless, hot, completely unforgettable mistake.

She keeps finding reasons for us to bump into each other. And I keep letting it happen. Call me what you want—but when she's grinning like she knows exactly how to unravel me, I'm not walking away.

Now we're sneaking around like we're starring in her dirty fanfic—which, of course, I read. Multiple times.

We said this would be short-term. Just fun. No strings. But Mia's wiggled her way past my defenses, and I'm starting to think the biggest danger isn't her dad finding out...

It's falling for the one woman I should have stayed away from.

CONTENT NOTES

This is a fun, steamy, small-town rom-com! However, your mental health is important, and I want you to be aware that both the hero and heroine have been adopted and have tragic pasts with parental deaths that they remember. It is discussed briefly in a couple of places, so if this is something that could be painful for you, please be aware and proceed with caution, or skip this story all together.
Please take care of yourself!
xo Erin

(oh, I also spoil the movie Twisters...sorry)

CHAPTER 1

DAVID

THIS IS REALLY the last thing I need tonight.

The list of things I don't need is long, but this...*she*...is the last thing.

I realize that's not a very charitable point of view and I would never say it out loud, at least not to the woman sitting out in the middle of a field as a huge storm is rolling in on top of her, but I'd definitely say it to my co-workers or my brothers.

It's been a long fucking day. I've already had to deal with a handful of annoying people, I just dropped off a pissed-off mountain lion that I spent most of the day with, Mother Nature is gearing up to be a bitch tonight, and I have no patience left for one more stupid person who doesn't take storm warnings seriously.

But here I am. Doing my job. Being the good guy.

I really just want a beer and a baseball game. But the storm's going to ruin the TV reception anyway, so...

I pull my truck in behind the silver Ford Fiesta.

A fucking Fiesta. In a field of grass that comes up to the

door handle and soon-to-be mud that could easily cover half the height of her tires.

What the fuck is she doing out here?

She's seventeen miles from town, it's nearly ten p.m., it's dark, and the thunderstorm that's bringing torrential rain, sixty-five mile per hour winds, and golf ball-sized hail, with possible tornadoes—because of course, will be here in about twenty minutes.

And she's not by the side of the road or somewhere logical. She's in the middle of a goddamned field. On private property, but far enough away from the house that no one would see her or know she's here for, possibly, days.

Now that the mountain lion that's been roaming lately and making Bill Carter's horses twitchy, and Bill twitchy, has been relocated, I can pull all the traps. I'd love to let that wait until tomorrow, but because of the pending rain, wind, and hail, I have to ensure a fox, raccoon, or stray cat doesn't accidentally spend a stormy night in one. So I've been out for the past two hours.

Good thing for this woman. She'd be spending the stormy night out here alone if it wasn't for how crappy my day has been.

I pull in behind her and put my floodlights on.

I swear to God, if she's out here fishing or camping or something, I'm ticketing her and hauling her ass into town immediately. I'm not listening to explanations or excuses tonight. Nice Guy David signed off about six hours ago.

She gets out of the car and turns toward the truck as I get out. She lifts her hand, shielding her eyes from the bright lights at the top of my truck, the wind whipping her long dark hair around under the ball cap she's wearing.

I take her in as I climb out. She's in decent boots and blue jeans. At least she realized she needed sturdy footwear to walk around out here. But she's only wearing a short-sleeved tee and that ball cap otherwise. It's early August so a lack of layers makes sense. It was over ninety degrees today. Typical. But I hope to God she's smart enough to use sunscreen and cover her arms if she's messing around in tall grass and weeds. There's poison ivy and poison oak, wild parsnip, sumac...

I draw a breath. An allergic skin reaction on this woman is probably the least of my worries right now.

We're about fifty yards from the river to the east and about a mile off the access road that led her into this field. We're four miles from the gravel road to the west and it's another four miles to the paved highway beyond that. And north and south of us is nothing but rolling prairie dotted with trees here and there.

We're pretty much in the middle of nowhere.

And it's dark. Even darker than ten p.m. would typically be. The clouds have blocked out what had been a nearly full moon and there isn't a streetlight, a house light, or even another headlight for fucking miles.

I stomp toward her. "What the fuck are you doing out here?"

"Wow," she says, planting her hands on her hips as the wind continues to whip her hair around her face. "Hi. I'm fine. Well, maybe a little dehydrated. Starving. Definitely bored. But mostly fine. Thanks for asking."

Great. Dehydrated. Starving. She just put a couple of marks on the Things To Worry About and Things That Will Make Her My Problem lists. Yes, I have two different lists going. Things To Worry About and Things That Will Make Her My Problem. I was hoping to keep from putting anything on either of those.

Other than the pending tornado of course.

Fuck.

The wind molds the T-shirt she's wearing to her body and I note that she's slim and her skin is pale—and not covered with red marks or rashes from poison plants—but her arms are muscular.

Hey, I have to catalog if she's injured or holding a weapon, seems to be having a medical incident, or is under the influence of any substances. I swear to God if she's drunk or high...

Deep breath.

The fact that I also note her curves and that her hair has long, loose curls is secondary to all of that. We're out in a fucking field in the middle of nowhere with an approaching storm. I'm not going to ask her out.

Plus, she's the type to be out in a fucking field in the middle of nowhere with an approaching storm. She's not my type.

Hell, as far as I know, she just robbed the bank or she's a serial killer hiding out here to stay off the radar.

Okay, I would have heard if the bank had been robbed or if there had been any suspicious deaths.

Chances are she was out here fucking around and got stuck.

So, she's got a great shape and isn't very bright.

Which means now I need to worry about her rather than getting *my* ass back to town before I'm pelted by hail or swept up by a tornado.

Or worse, my new truck is.

"So you're fine?" I ask dryly.

She shrugs. "My naked moon dancing is completely ruined but hey, there will be another full moon, right?"

"You were going to..." I sigh. I don't care. She's trespassing. And there's a fucking tornado coming. That's all that matters. "This is private property."

"Bob Sanders," she says with a nod. "He knows I'm here."

"Bob is cool with naked moon dancing?"

Bob Sanders is seventy-two, has farmed this land for sixty of those, starting back when he helped his father as a kid, and goes to church every Sunday. Bob's raised five children and twelve grandchildren on this land, buried his parents and his wife of forty-eight years on this land, and has let many kids learn to hunt and fish on this land. I don't think Bob's down for naked moon dancing on this land.

"Bob doesn't ask me a lot of questions," she says.

"I'm going to have to talk to him about that." I take a step forward. "After I lecture you about not coming out this far by yourself this late at night."

"Because I'm a woman? "she asks, stepping toward me.

I frown. "Because you could get a flat tire." I gesture toward her car. Now that I'm closer, I can see her back driver's side tire is flat. There is a jack next to it and a spare tire lying on the grass, but it's clear she didn't have level ground and couldn't get the car jacked up to change it.

Still, it seems she tried.

That's something.

"And...forget your phone?" I pose it as a question because I assume there's a reason she hasn't called anyone.

She holds a phone up and wiggles it. "Died."

"Exactly. So you shouldn't be this far out by yourself."

"I have to come this far out to get good prints."

I frown. "Prints?"

"Animal footprints. Or pawprints. I'm doing a project."

I take another step forward, frowning. She was out wandering around by herself looking for animal prints? "What kind of animals?"

"All kinds. Rabbits, raccoons, foxes, coyotes."

"Mountain lions?"

Her eyes widen. "That would be amazing."

"That would *not* be amazing," I say. "Mountain lion prints are made by mountain lions."

She waits a beat, as if waiting for me to go on.

I don't need to go on.

"Well..." she finally says. "Yes. Obviously."

There's a loud crack of thunder overhead just then and we both jump. I scowl up at the sky. She's not at risk from a mountain lion right now *thanks to me,* but she is about ten minutes away from possibly being thunked in the head with a big piece of hail.

"We need to get out of here," I say, turning on my heel.

"Wait, what? You're not going to change my tire?"

I turn back. "I am definitely *not* going to change your tire."

"Why not?"

"I appreciate you thinking I'm some kind of super hero here, but the ground is too soft and uneven for me to use that jack too."

"So how am I going to get my car back to the road?"

"I'm guessing by towing it."

"Are you going to tow it?"

"I am not."

"Why not?"

I sigh and stalk back to where she's standing. "Because it's late, I don't have a chain with me, it's about to get really fucking wet and windy, and, maybe most of all, I don't want to."

Her eyes widen. Then she glances back at her car. "I can't just leave it out here."

"You should have thought of that before you drove it out here."

"I didn't *mean* to get a flat tire!"

"You should still always prepare for anything. Does anyone even know you're out here?" I ask, that suddenly occurring to me. "Why hasn't anyone come out here looking for you?"

"I..."

She trails off and it's clear she doesn't want to answer me. Which is an answer all on its own.

"You didn't tell anyone," I say flatly.

"I didn't think I needed to."

"Why didn't you keep your phone charged?"

Fine, so she could have hit something with her tire. I've had a flat or two—or four—being off-road in these fields and hills, and a couple of times just sticking to main roads. It happens. But I always had a phone *and* my radio with me.

"It's not the battery," she says. "I dropped it a couple of days ago and it just shuts off sometimes now and won't come back on just because I want it to. My new one's in the mail."

Huh. Well... "You probably shouldn't come this far out all alone without a reliable phone."

Her eyes narrow. "Well, thanks. That's a super helpful observation."

Yeah, okay.

Thunder booms overhead again and lightning streaks across the western sky.

"There's a storm coming in," I tell her.

She looks up, seeming annoyed. "The rain is going to wash the prints away."

"You didn't find any?" There had to be a few, especially if she went down by the river.

I shake my head. I don't love the idea of her down by the river by herself, no one even knowing she was out here. What if she'd slipped? Banged her head on a rock? Fell down the bank and broke her ankle? Been bitten by a snake?

What the hell am I thinking? There aren't any venomous snakes here. I mean, there *could* be. I've seen a lot of things in my time. Nature is never completely predictable. But the chances of her coming across a snake that would hurt her are slim. If we were further west or southeast then...

I shake my head. What is going on with me? We're *not* further west or southeast. We're here. Where there are no poisonous snakes, where the riverbank is not particularly steep, and where there are no big rocks. The river is a little deep right now. We've had some decent rains this summer. But the current isn't particularly strong right here and if she's any kind of swimmer at all she would have been fine even if she'd fallen in.

Probably.

She's muscular but thin. And maybe she doesn't know how to swim at all. And anything can happen in nature, even if you're *totally* prepared. Which it's clear she is not.

I grind my back molars together.

"I did, but when I tried to take photos, my phone..." She sighs.

"Didn't work," I guess.

"Right."

"The animals will be back. There will be more prints." Except for the mountain lion, but she doesn't need to know that. There are plenty of deer and small, furry, harmless animals out here for her to study.

What is she? A teacher? A college student? She looks young. Maybe a biology student.

"Yeah, but that means I have to come back out here and there's a conservation officer who's ticked at me now and might not like that."

I'm still wearing my uniform, so she knows I'm here *officially*. That isn't making her all that compliant though.

"He *won't* like that," I snap. "Jesus, don't you have any friends?"

It's dark, so I shouldn't notice something like a flash of

vulnerability cross her face, but I could swear there's *something* there. And I want to know what it is.

I fist my hand and take a deep breath. I don't have time for this. I can't fix *everything* I come across today. She's not my problem. Not really. Only as long as she's out here with no other help. If I get her to town, I can get her off my To Do List.

Not that she's on my *To Do List*. Not like that…

She's on those other two lists I've got going.

And I need to get her *off*. No, I don't need to *get her off*. Not like that…

I shove a hand through my hair and take another breath. It's been a *really* long day. "We'll talk about it tomorrow. After the storm. Grab your stuff. Let's go." I turn on my heel and start for my truck.

"Let's… go?" she asks.

"Yes. I'll take you into town. You can get someone out here to tow your car tomorrow." Someone *else*. Not me. I don't need to do it. This isn't my problem.

I'm going to have to keep repeating that to myself.

I'm proud of myself as I don't even turn back to see if she needs help getting anything out of her car and into my truck.

It's going to take us twenty-five minutes, maybe more, to get to town, and then it'll take twenty minutes for Derek to make me a pizza. Unless I call ahead. I pull my phone out and start to dial, but before I can press the second number, my phone starts beeping.

Fuck.

The signal is very familiar. It's a weather alert. And I'm pretty sure I know what it's going to say before I even read the words.

Sure enough—Tornado Warning.

There's been a tornado sighted in the area.

"Come on," I call over my shoulder. "We need to move."

"Can't I just call someone with *your* phone?" she asks.

I turn back and stomp toward her. I'm not getting a pizza now if there's a fucking tornado warning. Derek and everyone else at the bar are going to be taking shelter—at least they better fucking be—and now I'm remembering this woman saying she's starving. When did she last eat? How long has she been out here? Does she like pizza? Okay, everyone likes pizza. What kind of pizza does she like though?

Who fucking cares?

"No. You can get your ass in my truck and let me drive us *both* to safety. A *tornado* touched down six miles away. And it's about to—"

The rain starts all at once.

Not a few drops as a warning. Not even a light sprinkle to warm up.

It's dry one minute and the next it's like I'm standing underneath my showerhead.

Except this is *cold*.

"Dammit!" I bend, throw her over my shoulder, and stalk back to my truck.

"Hey!"

"You had your chance," I grit out. I wrench open the passenger door and pause. "You could have gotten in *before* you were all wet," I point out. Then I plop her onto the dry seat of my new truck.

"But I—" she splutters.

I slam the door. I go to her car, duck inside, grab the bag that's resting on the passenger seat, glance around for keys, realize it doesn't matter if we lock it up, slam the door extra hard, and stomp back to my truck. I get in, toss the bag into her lap, and throw the truck into gear.

I check my phone as we bump over the ground toward the access road.

She's got one hand braced on the ceiling and one on the dash.

Yeah, the ride is a little rough. Too bad.

"Fuck," I mutter as the notifications show the tornado still on the ground and coming this way.

Of course, it is. Why would it *not* be?

The rain makes seeing out the windshield a challenge. But there's nothing out here to run into. I just head generally west. We bump, dip, and jerk along until we hit the access road and I make a quick decision. I turn right instead of left.

The road is smoother than the field and she decides to speak. "Where are we going?"

"Are you worried about me kidnapping you *now*?"

"Uh...now that you mention it," she says. "At what point in the kidnapping does the kidnapper tell the victim she's being kidnapped?"

I glance over at her. "You don't think it's kind of obvious right away?"

"Sure, if the guy comes up behind you and grabs you and stuffs you in a van or the trunk of a car or something. But what if he—or she, let's not be sexist—offers you candy or cookies first? Or like flirts and dances with you. Or—"

"Rescues you from a tornado?"

"Yeah. It might be hard to pinpoint when the kidnapping starts."

"I'm not kidnapping you." I shake my head. "The last thing I need tonight is a captive. I don't have the energy for something like that."

There's a beat of silence and then she laughs.

And the sound punches me in the gut. It's so pretty. Light. Happy. Addictive. I feel myself smiling as I look over at her.

"So I shouldn't worry about my safety with you because you're *tired*?"

I nod. "It's been a long damned day."

"But on a normal day, when you're well rested and in a good mood, you're a likely kidnapper?"

I actually huff out a soft laugh. "Nah. That really seems like a lot of work even on the best day."

She settles back in her seat, smiling. "Well, it remains that you're taking me somewhere without my consent."

"If there wasn't a fucking *tornado* approaching, I would have let you use my phone," I tell her. And it's true. Having her with me while worrying about sheltering through a storm is not ideal. It's another person to be responsible for and I'm good at that...in very small increments of time.

Like long enough to say, "You need to put out those campfires and clean up this site, so you don't start a wildfire. You have thirty minutes" or "I'm giving you this citation because of the reckless way you were driving that snowmobile. You could have really hurt somebody. I don't want to ever see you doing that again, got it?"

I hand her my phone now. "Call someone and tell them where you are. You're going to shelter with me, but I can take you to town after the storm passes."

She doesn't take the phone. "No, that's okay."

I frown. "You wanted to use my phone a few minutes ago. Call someone."

"I'm fine. I mean...*now* I'm fine. Now that I'm with you."

I look over at her again, but it's too dark to see a damned thing. I wish I could see her face. She's okay now that she's with me? What the hell? Who is she? Why is she out here? Okay, getting animal prints, but why all by herself?

"You should call someone. Surely they're worried."

She sighs heavily. "Fine." She takes my phone and a second later, I hear, "Hey, it's me." She pauses. "I know. My phone died." Another pause. "I *know*. I told you I ordered one." Pause.

"*Anyway*, I'm fine." Pause. "It's...David Bennett's phone. I got a flat and he stopped and is giving me a ride." Pause. "Yes, David." Pause. She sighs. "Yes." Pause. "Okay, I will. Love you too. Bye."

She hands me the phone back.

"Everything good? "I ask, taking it.

"Yep. My sister now knows and she'll tell everyone I'm fine and...it's all good."

"Great."

I pull into a driveway two minutes later. The house is dark, but I know the back door will be unlocked.

"Is this your house?" she asks as I park and turn the truck off.

"No. I live about eight miles from here. Too far with this tornado coming. Let's go."

Yeah, I live far from town. On purpose. And I could show her a ton of animal prints on my land. Including mountain lion. The damned thing walked into the trap I set on my property, not Bill's.

But I'm not risking driving further right now.

I push the door open and round the truck to get her. She's already out and I instinctively grab her hand as I start for the back of Tim's house. We run but are soaked by the time we step onto the back porch.

"This isn't your house but we're just going inside?" she asks as I let us into the kitchen.

"Yep."

"Is it a friend?"

"Kind of." Tim and I are *friendly*.

Tim and his wife Donna are out of town this weekend, but I know he'll be fine with us staying here considering the circumstances. I'd text him and ask, but it's late and I'm sure he's already in bed.

I flip on the lights and pull up my weather notifications and messages.

The tornado warning is still in effect. The rain is still coming down in torrents and...yep, there's the hail. Pinging off the roof, the sidewalk...and my new truck.

I blow out a breath.

Then I turn and look at the woman I rescued.

And realize in a heartbeat that hail damage and insurance claims are the least of my problems.

Goddammit.

This woman is beautiful. Even soaking wet and wind-blown.

And I'm going to be stuck with her here for the next couple of hours. At least.

And, matching right up with the crappy fucking day I've had, I do know who she is.

This is Mia Hansen.

The daughter of the man I consider my one and only enemy.

CHAPTER 2

MIA

DAVID CASTILLE BENNETT is incredibly good-looking. Even when he's scowling. Which he's been doing a lot since he picked me up tonight.

He's never scowled at me before.

Of course, he's never smiled at me before tonight either.

We've never made eye contact at all before tonight that I can think of.

If I've ever been this close to him, it was years ago, when I was much too young to appreciate it.

But just a couple of weeks ago, I noticed him working with his dad, brothers, and some other guys setting up booths and the dunk tank for our annual summer festival, and even from about fifty yards away, I noted David's muscles, bronze skin, and tattoos.

And I appreciated the hell out of them.

Just David's though, interestingly. He wasn't the only guy there without a shirt on. He wasn't even the only good-looking guy there. But he was the only one who pulled my gaze.

And now here he is.

Up close.

And scowling.

I tip my head, studying him. His intense brown eyes, his windswept, slightly curly on top and around his ears brown hair, the scruff on his jaw, the hoop earring in his left ear, the bit of ink on his forearms peeking out from under the rolled-up sleeves of his shirt.

I take it all in. I mean, I might not get another chance.

We've both lived in Sapphire Falls for twenty years and this is the first time we've ever had a one-on-one conversation.

There are several reasons for that. He's quite a bit older than me, we have absolutely nothing in common other than where we grew up, and maybe most importantly, he and my dad don't get along.

This means that if David is ever in attendance at any family get-together that includes my parents and his—no, we're not related but our parents' friend group acts more like siblings than friends—David and my dad stay far apart. I don't know all the details other than David was somewhat of a hellion in high school and his early twenties. Which means he ran into my dad, the town cop, a few times.

"Hey, Mia," David finally says. "I didn't realize it was you."

He looks, and sounds, less than thrilled. Exactly how a woman wants the hot, rugged man who just rescued her to react to realizing who she is.

"Would you have left me out in the field if you had?" I ask.

"Of course not." He seems truly offended I even asked that.

I was kidding. Guys like David don't leave people stranded out in fields. Not late at night, not alone, and certainly not in a storm.

No, I don't know him well, but he wears a uniform. He's law enforcement. Sure, it's adjacent maybe, but he takes care of people and animals for a living.

Do I have a romanticized idea of what his job is? Maybe. Is it based almost entirely upon my hero worship of my father, a man who also wears a uniform and a badge, who takes care of people and yes, animals at times, for a living? Yes. Is it also deeply ingrained in me to be drawn to men like that because my father swept into my life and literally rescued me when I was an impressionable young child? Absolutely.

But hey, at least I'm aware of all of that, right?

"I was joking," I tell David. "I know you wouldn't have left me out there."

He's still glowering at me. "How long were you stuck out there?"

I am not going to tell him it was five hours. Again, I know guys like him. The protective, in charge, take-care-of-everyone-and-everything type. I've lived with and looked up to one of those for twenty years now.

Do I think my father walks on water? Pretty much.

I know, rationally, that he's not perfect. But my instinct, my default setting, my knee-jerk reflex is always to think that Scott Hansen is right.

And honestly, so far, that instinct has served me well.

And even if my dad and David don't get along for whatever reason, I can already read all of the same things all over David. They might both hate to know that, but they're kind of the same guy.

And that could end up being a problem for me.

Because I really like guys in uniforms.

And as independent as I try to be, people taking care of me crashes right through my I-don't-want-to-burden-anyone walls every time.

I really do appreciate when people respect my walls. They're thin walls. More decorative than an actual barrier of any kind. They're more like those really pretty room dividers made of light wood and paper, to be honest. There to represent that I want to take care of myself and sometimes I need to be given that space. My friends, my little brother, and my mom are wonderful about not knocking my dividers over.

But then there's my dad and my sister. They take care of me, running right through those pretty paper screens and...I don't hate it. It's always done with love and sometimes having someone say, "I see your room divider and I understand it, but I just really don't want anything between us" is nice too.

So, a guy in a uniform who makes a living out of taking care of people coming in to rescue me? Yeah, I'm going to get stupid over that.

And that's probably going to be a problem.

"I wasn't out there too long," I say noncommittally.

He stomps to the refrigerator and jerks the door open. "You didn't tell your dad you were going out to Bob's to look for animals?" He comes toward me with a bottle of water. He twists the top off and hands it to me.

I take the water and gratefully gulp down a few swallows. I had water in my car, but not enough for several hours.

"I wasn't looking for animals. I was looking for animal *tracks*," I tell him after I swallow. "I was planning to make molds for a display at the library to go with the summer adventure reading program we're doing with the kids. We're studying all about Nebraska. We talked about the settlers for two weeks. Another week we talked about the rivers and lakes in the state. Last week was native birds. This week it's mammals." I pause.

I realize I sound very excited about the program. Because I am. I love this stuff. I love books. I love research. I love imparting knowledge, even in little bits. But give me a *project*, an entire summer of once-a-week activities to create, and a rapt audience of little, open minds to help fill up, and I'm in heaven.

I know the rivers-birds-mammals thing sounds nerdy, but this guy is a conservation officer. This is right up his alley. He could probably teach all of the units without opening a book. Not that I condone not opening books. But this is his day-to-day.

I should ask him to come speak to the kids.

He could come to the library in his uniform. He'd talk for about an hour with that deep gravelly voice.

He'd probably be so cute answering all the questions from the little kids and it would be adorable watching them fawn all over him when they learn that he is outside with wild animals every day.

And I'd be in even bigger trouble because smart guys and guys who are good with kids are also big weaknesses for me.

Okay, so I have a few weaknesses.

Growing up as Scott and Peyton Hansen's daughter after my very rocky start might have made some of my standards crazy high. It's not my fault.

I clear my throat as David continues to just stand there watching me. "And I'm thirty years old. I don't tell my dad where I go." Okay, I don't tell my dad where I go *all the time*.

"Especially when you know damned well he would have told you that was a terrible idea."

See, David thinks that scowl is intimidating, but I just find it really hot.

"Drink more," he orders me, looking down at his phone, muttering something under his breath that sounds like 'of fucking course', then moving to a cupboard.

"It was for work," I tell his back. He's pulling bread, peanut butter, and jelly out of the cupboard, clearly very at home here. "I don't need to run my work activities past my *father*." I cross my arms, trying to look cool and composed. "Or past anyone. Even Nebraska Game and Parks."

"He would have told you about the incoming storm." David grabs a plate from another cupboard and opens a drawer to pull out a butter knife. "And that there's a mountain lion prowling around that area."

Of course, he would have. But it had been cloudy and mildly windy when I'd gone out there. I'd fully intended to be back in town before dark. I should have been cuddled up, safe and sound, on my couch with a book before the storm even blipped on the local radar. The flat tire wasn't something I'd planned on, *obviously*. But even if I'd thought 'hey, I might get a flat tire' I wouldn't have worried or let that stop me. I know how to change a stupid tire. My dad made sure of that. In fact, if I'd called Chief Hansen, and told him I had a flat, the first question he would have asked would have been, "why haven't you changed it? "

So there was no need to tell my dad about my plans.

As for the...

I feel my eyes widen as the rest of David's words register. "There's a *mountain lion* prowling around out there? "

"Yep." He turns to me and hands me a plate with a sandwich on it. It's cut diagonally. And there's a banana lying next to it.

"Oh." My voice is soft. I'm distracted. By gruff men making me sandwiches. And mountain lions.

That would have been not a great situation. I think quickly. What would I do if I ran across a mountain lion?

"Yeah, oh," he says, a smug tone to his voice.

I frown as he turns away and starts across the kitchen. I notice he's already put all of the sandwich stuff away again.

"I would have made myself really big, waved my arms, made a lot of noise. Mountain lions try to avoid humans. I could have scared it off. I could have thrown stuff at it. Like..." I think about the contents of my car. "Water bottles." I don't have much in my car. There are books, of course. Lots of books. But I shudder thinking about throwing books out into an open field at a wild animal. What if he mauled them? I look down. "My boots."

David has turned back and is frowning at me. Again. "How do you know all of that?"

"I got it right?" I ask. I know I did. I want to hear him say it.

"Yes. Besides getting back in your car, locking the doors, and calling for help."

"Right. Of course. I would have gotten back into my car and locked the doors." We both know I couldn't have called for help. No need to bring up my not-working-right-all-the-time phone again.

"How do you know how to scare off a mountain lion? Did you just guess? "

I put a hand on my hip and give him a little smile. "I have a superpower."

He narrows his eyes. "What's that?"

"I'm a librarian."

He doesn't respond.

"I know *lots* of seemingly random facts. Lots of trivia. I read a lot. I look things up for people all the time and I remember a lot of it. And we did a class a couple of years ago about what to do if you come across various common wild animals around here. It started because a little boy had started feeding a stray dog in his backyard and then his dad realized it was actually a wolf."

David is just listening.

Come to think of it, David probably knows that story. He might have been called to pick the wolf up for all I know.

"So," I go on. "His dad brought him into the library to look up facts about wolves so he'd be able to recognize one in the future. If he ever needed to. And then as we talked, I decided we should offer a class for kids to recognize local wild animals and what to do if they happen to see one in their neighborhood or hurt alongside the road. That was the first time I did a class involving animal tracks."

"Would have been a short class," David says. "Since the entire instruction for if you see a wild animal in your neighborhood or hurt alongside the road is: 'Call Game and Parks'. Right?"

"That was part of it," I assure him. "But we wanted the kids to feel comfortable identifying the animals and what to do if they were out playing and saw a hurt squirrel or a bird with a broken wing."

"They should still call us," David says stubbornly.

"It's okay for the kids to know more about the animals than that," I insist.

"Is all of this *book knowledge* why you felt comfortable walking around finding animal tracks all alone *miles* from town?"

He's really hung up on this. I also don't like the way he says 'book knowledge'. As if that's not really *knowledge*. "Yes, I learned about animal tracks and where to look for them from *books*. As hard as that might be to believe," I tell him.

"So why can't you just show kids photos of the animal tracks in *books*?" he asks.

"Libraries have a lot more resources than *just* books," I say. Though books are my true love and, obviously, the main attraction. "We offer classes and tutorials, WiFi access, help with filling out forms, movies and music, maps, we even recently started a lending library where people can borrow tools and pots and pans, and things like that."

David continues to frown—he's going to have terrible wrinkles by the time he's forty—but now it's clearly in confusion.

"Why would someone need to borrow pots and pans from the library?"

"If they're baking a cheesecake for the first time and don't have a spring-form pan," I say, as an example. "Or they've decided to try to bake bread, but don't have a loaf pan. Or they'd like to use a crock pot and don't have one. Or they want to make crepes and need a crepe pan. Or they want to try making a bundt cake. Or they want to try using a wok, but don't want to buy one. All of those things are expensive if you're just learning and aren't sure you want to keep doing it. It's a great way to learn and practice."

His brow furrows, but then he nods. "You got me."

"I did?"

"I was going to say that they could borrow a Bundt pan or a loaf pan from literally ninety percent of the homes in Sapphire Falls, but I'm thinking woks might be harder to find."

I laugh. "And honestly, the loaf pans, crock pots, and Bundt pans are probably all being used and can't be loaned out."

Then the most surprising thing of all happens.

David smiles.

And yeah...he's definitely going to be a problem for me.

Scowling David is hot. Sandwich making David is sweet. Smiling David is...panty-melting.

I take a deep breath and look away from the smile that makes me want to *really* study his mouth. "Look, if it weren't for the flat tire, I would have been fine," I tell him. "I went out, found some tracks, realized my phone wasn't working, and was going to head back to town. It was still plenty light, the storm was way off—"

"It was still *plenty* light when you realized you had a flat?" he demands.

Oops. That gives him a pretty good idea how long I'd been stuck out there. "Yes. But I was fine."

"Sitting around for *hours* alone? "

"Yes. I got some...work...done."

He lifts a brow. "What kind of library work did you get done sitting alone in your car without a working phone? "

I wrote three thousand words on my fanfiction in the note-book I always keep tucked in my glove box, as a matter of fact. It's not *work*, in the make-money sense of the word. Or in the I-do-it-because-I-have-to sense. It's actually pure joy.

"I was fine," I tell him, instead of telling him I write fanfic-tion about a series of romance novels by one of my favorite authors.

Her books are steamy and fun, but there's a group of us that want more from the stories beyond the happily ever afters she writes. So we have a fanfic forum.

There are a few people who write murder mysteries in her small town that the cop and firefighter she created solve with their friends. A few that have introduced paranormal charac-ters. That started out as an off-shoot of the books one of the characters in the series writes, but it's expanded beyond that. For instance, there's a wizard in town no one knows is a wizard and none of us are sure if he's a good guy or a bad guy yet. I love reading those.

And then there's the group of us who write the very, *very* steamy side of town.

Yes, there's a secret, invitation-only sex club in this little town and there are all kinds of fun things happening there.

That's where I spend most of my time.

"I could have easily spent the night out there," I tell David, stubbornly keeping my imagination from thinking that I need to add a Game and Parks officer as a visitor to the club.

I see the muscle in his jaw tick.

"How?" David demands. "No food? No water? A tornado

could have tossed you and your car. Hail could have shattered your windshield. Lightning could have hit you—"

"Isn't being *inside* a car when lightning strikes really safe?" I stupidly interrupt. But I can't *not* comment, because I'm right. "The electricity is directed through the metal and into the ground, *around* whoever is inside. One instruction people are given during thunderstorms and in the presence of lightning is to get *in* a car." I pause. "We do storm preparedness training at the library in the summer and winter. Tornado season is wild but winter around here can be really dangerous too."

As if he doesn't know. I realize I'm poking the bear.

Why? I'm not really the type to do that.

But *god* he's hot when he's protective and upset about the idea of me being in danger.

He takes a step toward me and I suck in a quick breath.

"What about when you got *out* of the car?" he asks.

"Why would I get out of the car if it's raining and there's *hail*?"

"You don't think you're going to need to pee all night? "

"I..." Okay, he has a point. Dammit.

Satisfied that he shut me up, he goes on. "There are also wild animals. Poison ivy and oak. No one even knew you were out there. Tell me how you were *fine*."

I'm familiar with what David is doing thanks to another man I know who wears a badge. My dad does the worst-case scenario thing constantly too. I think it comes with these jobs. Or maybe these jobs draw people like this. People who instantly think of all of the horrible things that could happen and then make it *their* responsibility to keep it all from happening no matter that they're dealing with full-assed humans with free will. Or Mother Nature.

"Look, it was a flat tire. Shitty things like that happen. Worst-case scenario—" Yes, I've learned to point out the *real* worst-case scenario to my father, so his imagination doesn't get ahead of things, especially when it comes to my sister, my brother, and me.

Okay, mostly me.

My dad absolutely sees me as needier and more fragile than my siblings.

He knows it. He knows I know it. He tries not to. But even talking to a family therapist, talking to my mom, talking to *me*, about it hasn't gotten him fully over that I wasn't his to take care of for the first ten years of my life and that he didn't get to be my protector until I was in foster care and he and my mom could adopt me.

"I would have spent the night in my car safe from wild animals, hail, *and* lightning. Then I would have walked the *four* miles to Bob's house in the morning when I had light," I tell David.

He looks at me with an unreadable expression. "You mean if the tornado didn't get you."

I don't roll my eyes, but I want to. "Yes. If the tornado didn't get me."

"Speaking of that tornado, we should go down to the basement." He turns and starts across the kitchen again.

I sigh.

Scott Hansen never says, "You're right, I overreacted" either.

Yeah, David is just like my dad.

CHAPTER 3

DAVID

OF COURSE, Scott Hansen's daughter is great.

Really great.

That's very annoying.

It would be a lot easier if the asshole's kids were assholes, but they're not. I'm going to assume they get their good personalities from their mom.

I don't know any of them well, but I've been around Peyton, Scott's wife. She co-owns the bakery in town, and well, there's no way I'm avoiding that place, even if Scott does have ties to it. Peyton is warm and funny and because my parents love to sit around with their friends and tell stories, I've overheard enough bits and pieces to know that Peyton gives Scott a hard time.

I like that about her.

But I *can't* like Mia. We can't be friends. We absolutely, definitely, no question about it can *not* be more than friends.

She's making it very difficult to just not think about that at all though.

His *librarian* daughter—how did I forget she was the librarian? Maybe because I'm not really a library kind of guy—is gorgeous, funny, smart, and easy-going.

When we got to the basement, I told her to get comfortable while I did a few things around the house to make sure it was secure for the storm.

When I'd come back downstairs I'd found her stretched out on Tim's old couch, propped up with a pillow, her boots off, and a blanket over her lap. She looks right at home.

And she took off the ball cap she was wearing. Now her long dark hair is spilling around her shoulders. It's mussed from, well, everything, but I take in the waves, the coppery highlights, the way she doesn't seem bothered by the fact that it's messy.

I also notice the empty plate. She ate the whole sandwich and the banana and drank the entire bottle of water.

My first thought? *Good girl.*

But, *fuck*. I can't say shit like that. I shouldn't even think it. Or feel it.

But I really fucking like taking care of people and I love it when they just listen to me and follow my directions. It is always a good idea to do what I say, and the fact that Mia Hansen realizes that definitely has my attention.

I like fixing problems. I like helping people.

It's only peanut butter and jelly. Don't make this into something bigger.

But she'd been stranded out there alone, in the dark, for hours—my whole body tenses whenever I think about that— with a storm coming. Now she's here, safe, warm, dry, fed... because of me.

You're welcome, Chief Hansen.

I shouldn't be thinking things like that either. I didn't rescue her because of him. Hell, I hadn't even known who she was. And it would probably be best if he didn't know I was the one who helped Mia out tonight.

Kept her safe.

Looked out for her.

Took care of her.

I shove a hand through my hair and cross the room to drop into the recliner perpendicular to the couch.

This isn't about Scott. Definitely not.

She smiles at me when I look over. "Are the tater tots almost done?"

"Ten more minutes."

Despite the sandwich and banana, she had *enthusiastically* agreed we should raid the freezer and make a frozen pizza *and* tater tots.

I love a girl who likes to eat and doesn't turn her nose up at perfectly good snack food. Tater tots are one of my favorites. Another point for Mia Hansen. A point she absolutely does not need to accumulate.

Then she happily took the turtle I handed her without even blinking.

Yes, I handed her a live turtle. Well, I handed her the turtle's aquarium with him inside.

You can't leave the pets upstairs during a tornado. That is a dick move. And yes, I handed him over to test her.

But her eyes lit up, she took Rex without a word other than 'ooh', and now she's lying on her side on the sofa with a turtle on the floor next to her, watching him and tossing him bits of lettuce.

From the recliner, I can see the TV and pretend to watch this show about elephants while holding Tim and Donna's rabbit, Murphy. And steal glances at Mia. I'm also keeping track of the weather alerts on my phone. Kind of.

Okay, mostly I'm stealing glances at Mia.

Who seems equally enamored with the show about elephants and the turtle beside her. Though she keeps glancing my way as well.

She's probably just watching the rabbit.

How does uptight, rule-follower Hansen have a laid-back daughter like this?

"Do you want to hold Murphy?" I ask. I should go check on the food in the oven upstairs.

Her smile is quick and wide. "Sure!"

I start to stand. I know the pizza isn't done, but if she wants to hold the rabbit, then who am I to deny her?

I take a step toward the couch but a second later, the room is plunged into darkness.

"Fuck," I swear.

"You okay?" Mia asks.

"I'm...the power went out."

She giggles. "Yeah. I noticed."

"That's not a great development."

"Means the storm is close."

"Yeah. And our pizza isn't going to be fully cooked."

There's a pause, then she groans. "Or the tater tots."

Yep, I like a girl who has her priorities straight.

I fumble with my phone and manage to get the light on with one thumb. It's incredibly bright in the completely dark basement.

She hasn't moved. She doesn't seem upset by the sudden power outage.

"Are *you* okay?" I ask anyway.

She tosses a bit of lettuce to Rex. "I'll be honest, I was *really* craving tater tots. But I'm fine otherwise."

I hand her the rabbit. She immediately cradles him against her chest.

"I'll go get something else." I start across the room with my phone light leading the way.

"No, David! You don't have to," she protests. "You've been up and down taking care of the house, the pets, me ever since we got here. The storm is close enough to knock the power out. You should stay down here!"

But she's still hungry.

"I'll just get some chips or something. Donna always has cookies."

"No." She pushes up, bracing her hand on the sofa. "Sit down. I'm fine."

"But—"

"David," she says firmly. "Sit down." She points at the recliner. "You need to be safe." She's giving me a stern look.

I lift a brow. "Wow."

"What?"

"Is that your librarian voice?"

It's...hot.

Dammit.

She grins. "Yeah. I mean, usually my librarian voice is this one. 'Oh, let me help you with that. Let's go over here and look for books about trains,'" she says in a sweet, lilting voice. With an equally sweet smile.

That is also hot.

Dammit.

"But sometimes I have to get bossy," she says, her smile growing wider.

I move back to the recliner trying very hard *not* to picture her with her hair in a bun with a pencil stuck through it, glasses on her nose, and her wearing a cardigan.

The librarian-hot-teacher-nerdy-girl type is *not* my type.

So, why do I want to ask her how many cardigans she owns? And why am I hoping the answer is *several?*

"Of course, I usually use it with adults," she goes on,

settling back against the pillow on the couch again, Murphy against her breasts.

Lucky rabbit.

See, I really have to stop all of this. With another woman, thoughts like that would be okay. With Mia Hansen? It's so, so fucking bad.

Her long hair spreads out over the patterned pillow and I realize I like it like this too. Bun, under a cap like earlier, long and loose...it's all good. Beautiful.

Dammit, dammit, dammit.

"When you have to use your bossy librarian voice, it's usually with adults?" I ask, needing a distraction. I turn my phone light away from her. Not looking at her seems like a really good idea.

"Yeah."

"Why?"

"Because adults are way more often assholes than kids are."

I choke on a laugh. "I can't argue with that. At all."

I glance down at my phone to check the radar. "The tornado warning has lifted. Thunderstorm warning still in place for the next hour."

"Okay."

She sounds perfectly content.

"Are you all right if I turn my flashlight off? I want to save my battery."

"Sure. I don't mind the dark."

I kill the light and settle back in the chair.

I assume it's my imagination but I swear I can hear her hair moving against the pillow and can smell her body spray even from here. That whole 'lose one sense and the others become heightened' thing, I guess.

Or you're becoming a little obsessed with her.

Probably because she's completely off-limits and you're a not-quite-fully-reformed rule-breaker.

But I'm really fucking trying to be fully reformed.

Making other people follow rules helps. Kind of.

I try not to dwell on the rules I think are stupid and a waste of time. Rules are mostly good. We need rules. Rules keep things civilized.

It's completely quiet in the basement for nearly two minutes besides the sound of Rex moving in his aquarium.

Two minutes doesn't sound like a long time until you're sitting in a dark room with no sound or distraction.

It's a *really* long time.

"Did you know that Blanding turtles are endangered?" Mia eventually asks.

I give a soft chuckle. "Um, yes, I know that."

She laughs too and the sound is even more...something...in the dark. Something I shouldn't put a word to.

"Yeah, I guess you would know that, wouldn't you?"

I just smile.

"So how does Tim have one as a pet?" she asks. "And with a conservation officer's knowledge?"

She not only knows turtle facts, but she can identify the various types? Be still my Game and Parks officer's heart.

"I found Rex injured by the road. Tim has done a lot of wildlife rehabilitation, so I brought him over here. He didn't think Rex could make it if he was re-released, so he became a part of the family."

"Ah," Mia says. "That's really nice."

We lapse into a long silence again. It's not completely awkward, but I'm very aware of her and that's not completely comfortable either.

"What kind of music do you like?" I ask, opening my music app. It will use my battery too, but I don't care now.

"Whatever," she says. "I like all kinds."

Of course, the gorgeous, bright, easy-going librarian likes all kinds of music.

I choose a general contemporary country channel and lower the volume so it's background noise.

"So," she says.

I ready myself for a fun fact about rabbits. That I probably already know.

"So?"

"What's the deal with you and my dad?"

Okay, not fun facts about rabbits.

I clear my throat. "What do you mean?"

She laughs. "Come on, David. Everyone knows you and my dad don't like each other. We're stuck here together, no power, no TV, can't play cards, so we should talk."

"We could talk about just about *anything* else."

I don't know if I want to get into this with her. Then again, maybe I should. I like her. If she was anyone else, I'd be flirting with her and would probably ask her out once the power came back on. Or maybe before the power came back on. Maybe I'd join her on the couch. Before the power came back on.

But she's not anyone else, and maybe I need to tell her that the next time I see her, I'm going to pretend I don't see her. Or that I'm going to at least give her nothing more than a smile and a quick, "Hi", and that's going to make me seem like a huge asshole. I should at least explain to her why.

"Nah," she says. "Let's talk about my dad."

I sigh. "Okay. Let's talk about the amazing Chief Hansen."

"Wow, the heavy sarcasm on the word 'amazing' is noted."

"I realize I'm the only person who knows your dad who doesn't think he's amazing."

"I'm guessing you have your reasons."

Now I wish we had some light in here. That's not really what I expected.

"I do have my reasons," I agree. "We go way back."

"Tell me about it."

I blow out a breath. "I was an angry kid who acted out a lot and he was the one who got called when that happened," I say, trying to keep it simple.

"Acted out how?"

I settle back into the chair. There are *so* many stories. "Fighting. Underage drinking. Drinking when I was of age, but well past the limit of..."

"Common sense and rational action?" she supplies.

I chuckle. "Yes."

"What else?"

She sounds interested and I think I know what this is.

The good girl is fascinated with the bad boy.

Well, I can certainly entertain her if that's the case.

"There was a stolen combine once," I say.

She gasps softly. "Those are *so* expensive, David."

I nod, though she can't see me. My eyes have adjusted somewhat to the dark and I can make out her shape on the sofa, but not much else. "We didn't keep it. Or wreck it. We just took it joyriding. And half of Mrs. Wilson's garden did not survive. But the combine was fine. And I replanted her garden. My parents insisted."

"Still..."

"It was very stupid," I say, nodding again. "There was a lot of shit like that. Stolen beer. Stolen cigarettes. I stole a car from a kid in Carterville who I didn't like. He got it back, of course, but not before I made him tell his brother that he'd slept with his girlfriend." I take a breath. "I was the first guy a lot of guys punched. I was the first guy a lot of girls slapped. I got a lot of people drunk the first time. I got a lot of..." I trail off. It's got to be the dark making me forget who I'm talking to as I rattle off my offenses.

"A lot of what?" she asks. "Come on."

"I just did a lot of stupid stuff and got a lot of people in trouble with me. I think that's what frustrated your dad the most. The way I influenced other people."

I hear her move on the couch. The springs creak and her clothes rustle against the fabric of the cushions. "Come on. What were you going to say? You got a lot of..."

Fine. Maybe if I'm just blunt she'll stop poking. "Girls naked for the first time."

"Oh," she responds.

I bark out a short laugh. "You sound disappointed."

"Well, I just assumed that. I was expecting you to say you got people arrested for the first time or taught them to pick locks or hotwire cars or something."

"No. I didn't teach people to do illegal things."

"You just did the illegal things."

"Right."

"Interesting."

Is it? "You just assumed I got a lot of girls naked?" I ask, not quite ready to move past that for some reason.

"Of course."

"What's that mean?"

"You're exactly the guy most girls would want to lose their virginity to in high school," she says as if it's obvious. "The good-looking hometown bad boy. You had that dangerous edge, but you were from here, from a great family, so the girls knew you weren't going to hurt them or anything. You were just really hot and experienced and fun and sexy. I'm sure they all talked about you. Probably said you were really good at it and treated them well. Then, of course, other girls were willing to take their clothes off for you."

I'm staring at her despite the dark. The sweet, good girl librarian is so matter-of-fact about the fact that I was a man-whore in high school. And okay, a few years after high school. "You seem to know a lot about this."

"I read a lot."

"You read a lot," I repeat.

She laughs. "Yes. Bad boys have *always* been appealing. Not to every woman but to a big majority."

"I was a *criminal*," I say. "Please tell me *you* were smarter than to go for a guy like me."

Wait, am I trying to convince her that all of those girls were *wrong*? That I was a bad choice?

Yes.

I had been trouble. Not fun trouble. Not 'oh, he drinks beer and swears and my daddy hates him so I'm going to rebel and sleep with him'. No, I had been actual trouble. I had more or less dared Scott Hansen to put me in jail. For real. I had *wanted* him to intervene, to stop me, to keep me from getting worse.

He hadn't.

He'd kept giving me second chances. And third chances. And fourth.

I'd spent the night in the jail cell downtown four times. One night each. That was it. I'd never been officially arrested, despite stealing and mouthing off and putting other people in danger.

The asshole had kept saying he knew I could do better. That I had potential. That I was going to figure my shit out.

"No, I lost my virginity to Ryan Wilkins."

I blink. Again, she's so matter-of-fact, I have to shake my head. "Doesn't he work at the bank?"

"Yes, he's a loan officer. Funny thing, I actually tutored him in math," she says.

"So, not a bad boy."

She laughs. "No. Though I assume bad boys can be bad at math, and guys who end up working at banks when they're thirty could have drunk and smoked and stolen combines in high school and then changed their ways."

Right. "Yeah. I suppose." I hesitate. My next question is absolutely none of my business. But damn, I really want to ask it. And self-restraint is not one of my strengths. Still. "So things didn't work out with Ryan, I take it. Was he your only one?"

Yes, I just asked Mia Hansen if she's only slept with one guy. Am I stereotyping the librarian as a near-virgin? Yep.

Am I surprised when she laughs and says, "Well, no"?

Not really. Because I'm already learning that Mia is not exactly who I think she is.

And I like that.

"Ryan and I didn't even date. I was tutoring him and one night it was late, we were alone at his house, one thing led to another, and I decided it was time to lose my virginity. But that's all it was."

I don't think I've ever met a woman this pragmatic about *everything*.

"But I did like it," she goes on.

And I choke on air. There's nothing else to choke on. I'm not eating or drinking, but I'm suddenly coughing for no reason.

"So, I dated Cody Jenson that summer. And we had sex a few times."

I've stopped coughing, but I'm still not breathing normally.

But that's not my biggest problem.

Nope. My biggest problem is that I like Mia Hansen. A lot.

And I'm now wondering about how she likes her sex. Is she a hard and fast girl? A slow and sweet girl? Lots of foreplay? Dirty talk?

"Then I went to college. Cody and I broke up, of course."

Of course? I don't know why that's of course, but the way she says it, I'm not going to ask because apparently it should be obvious.

"I dated a couple of guys in college but didn't really like them enough to have sex with them, so it's been a while. I did date a police officer I met at a fundraiser in Omaha my dad took us all to for a few months. And of course, I fell for him."

I *really* want to know what 'a while' means, but I'm distracted by the 'of course' and the eye roll I swear I can hear in her tone.

"So I slept with him. But that didn't last. It was long distance and he didn't want to move here and I didn't want to move there, so it fizzled. And...that's it. It's been a while."

Yeah, she said that before. I need a definition here.

There's a long beat of silence and I realize that I now know Mia's entire dating and sexual history.

Wow.

"What do you mean 'of course' you fell for him?"

"I have a thing for guys in uniform," she says simply. "Because of my dad and the way he saved me and became my foster dad and then adopted me. It's natural and not a huge problem since I'm aware of it, but it *is* kind of cliché."

Again, I'm just blinking.

"It's why I want to know what your issues are with him," she goes on. "I have my dad up on a pretty high pedestal and since you and I are becoming friends and I really like you, I thought I should know what happened between you."

I open my mouth to...I suppose tell her that we can't become friends and that she shouldn't like me...but she keeps going.

"But it sounds like you know all the stuff you did was problematic and you don't strike me as the type of guy to blame *him* for that," she says. "You enforce the laws and rules now, so you have to respect that he had to do that, right?"

Yes. She's right. My problem with Scott isn't that he picked me up or broke up the fights or made me apologize or make amends.

It was that he wasn't harder on me.

And that...he was too hard on me.

I swallow. "It's complicated."

"Tell me why. You're a grown man now. Thirty-something. You're a law enforcement officer. Tell me what's complicated between you and my dad."

I can see that she's changed positions again. She's now sitting cross-legged in the middle of the cushions.

Fuck.

I'm going to have to do this.

I like her.

I *really* like her.

And she thinks we're becoming friends.

That's a fair assumption. After tonight, I'd be friends with anyone else. So, I have to be honest with her here. I'm a good guy. Now. I *am* a grown man, and I know what's going on in my head and heart. And I can't have this woman thinking I'm a dick.

"Delaney and Tucker, my mom and dad, are actually my aunt and uncle," I tell her. "I mean...they were. They're my mom and dad now. Just not, biologically." Though they've been my parents longer than the people who gave birth to me were.

"I knew that you and your brothers were adopted," she says. "I mean, I've heard about that."

"Yeah. My mom was Delaney's sister. She, uh..." I clear my throat. Jesus, it's been twenty-nine years, but this is still hard to talk about. "My mom was killed in a shooting at a convenience store when I was eight."

I sense that Mia goes completely still.

"Then my dad died a couple of months later. Of, um…" I clear my throat again. "Brain cancer. That one was more expected, of course. But I lost one parent really suddenly and one very slowly and…well, that all really sucked."

"Oh my God, David," she says quietly. "I didn't know the details. I'm so sorry."

I shake my head. "Thanks. We had Delaney, though. Through all of that. She was there. And she was the one who brought us here. We'd spent summers here because my dad was from here and he and Tucker were best friends. We came here that summer after they died and…never left. Delaney and Tucker fell in love and adopted us, and this has been home."

Mia's quiet for several long moments.

These moments don't feel as awkward as the others.

"I came here to stay with Scott and Peyton the first time when I was eight," she says, her voice quiet and a little rough now. "They were my foster home at first."

I frown. I knew she was adopted but I'd never asked about the details. I stay quiet. I know she'll keep talking. And I want to hear this.

"My parents were alcoholics. Not abusive, exactly, but neglectful." She stops and swallows. "I was left alone a lot. I had to feed myself. Get myself to school. Things like that. One of my teachers finally connected the dots and called CPS. I was removed from the home, and my parents went to rehab. I stayed with Scott and Peyton. And…I loved it." She stops. "They were amazing. I was shy and quiet, and I didn't want to get comfortable because I didn't think it would last, but I couldn't help it. They made me feel loved and safe and…happy."

She stops and I feel every muscle in my body tense. I can feel something bad coming.

"After their rehab, I went back home. And it was so hard. I missed my parents, but I didn't want to leave Scott and Peyton and Harlow and Austin. I couldn't stop crying for days. I felt so bad because I knew I should be happy to be home with my mom and dad. But I kept hoping something would happen so I could go back to Scott and Peyton's." She swallows. "I thought —and wished, honestly—that Scott would show up every single day. I remember how he looked the day they took me away from him. I've never seen anyone look that torn up."

Holy shit. I scrub a hand over my face.

She keeps going. "My parents relapsed about six months later, and one night, they were driving drunk with me in the car and got pulled over. I was taken back to Scott and Peyton's. I was...so relieved to be there. And I felt so guilty about that. I remember Scott crying when they picked me up." She stops and takes a deep breath. "Every night after that, I wished that I could just stay with them. That they could convince my parents to let me stay. Or that my parents would just want to give me up."

I hear her sniff and my chest tightens.

"And then, a week later, Scott and Peyton came into my room in the middle of the night, woke me up, and told me that my parents had been killed in a car accident. They'd been..." Her voice cracks. "They'd been driving drunk. Wrapped the car around a pole." She takes another breath. "And I felt...sad, of course. But also relieved again. Because that meant I didn't have to leave Scott and Peyton again for sure. I have never gotten over that guilt."

"Jesus, Mia," I finally say. My voice is pretty scratchy too.

"I know. I mean, I've worked on it in therapy and mostly forgiven myself. It was a normal reaction. I was a kid. It's okay.

But I still feel bad about it." She stops. Then says quietly, "I'm not telling you this to make you like Scott more. I'm telling you because no one's perfect and life's messy and...it's okay."

Mia Hansen and I have a lot in common.

I can't get past that thought that keeps pinging around in my head.

We both lost our parents about the same age. We both came to Sapphire Falls around the same age. We're both adopted.

The silence is now much more comfortable. We both need the two minutes of saying nothing.

But finally I tell her, "I wanted to be a cop."

"Because of what happened to your mom," she guesses.

Correctly.

"Yes." I feel the familiar mix of rage and anguish tighten my chest. "They never caught the guy. My mom and another guy were dead before the cops even got to the store."

"I'm so sorry, David."

"Thanks. But I'm telling you this because...this is why I don't get along with your dad."

She shifts on the couch. "Okay."

"So, yes, I was trouble as a kid. A lot of trouble. I pushed boundaries, I acted out. I was testing Delaney and Tucker. I wanted to know that they were going to be there for me no matter what. I also had a little 'who gives a fuck' in me as I grew up and really understood how fucking unfair what happened to both of my parents was."

"I get that."

I nod. "And, I wanted someone, my parents, my teachers, your dad, to step in and say *enough*. You've stepped over the line. We care enough to stop you if you can't stop yourself. All of that is true."

"You *wanted* my dad to be harder on you?" she asks.

"Yeah. That's what my therapist and I finally figured out." I sigh. "I needed to know someone gave enough of a shit to lock me up to save me from myself."

"And he never did."

"No. Tucker and Delaney, and my brothers did. Essentially," I tell her. "They sat me down and said if I didn't get my shit together, they were done. Cutting me off."

I sense her surprise. "They had an intervention."

"Yep. And it worked. I said fine. I went to therapy. And then, several months and sessions later, I went to your dad's office and told him that I wanted to be a cop."

"Oh," she says softly. "And?"

"He said he thought I'd be a terrible cop."

"Oh shit," she whispers.

"Yep. He said that I wanted to be a cop because I was angry at the system. I wanted to make up for what had happened to my mom, to make things right. Which he understood, but being angry wasn't the right motivation. Angry cops are bad cops."

"So what did you do?"

"I went to college and got a natural resources degree and a criminal justice degree, I applied to the police academy and became a cop."

I can't see her smile, but I sense it.

"And then?"

"I went to Colorado and worked for Colorado Parks and Wildlife for three years. Came back and worked for Nebraska Game and Parks out west for a couple of years. Then came back here." I shift in my chair. "This is where I wanted to live and work. But I knew your dad would never hire me. So I did what I could to make sure I was excellent at my job and would have fantastic references so I wouldn't need his and so anything he might say to anyone hiring me wouldn't matter. He could talk about me being a problem kid but the people who know me *now* and who have worked with me in this job would have opinions that mattered more than his."

"So you gave up on the cop thing though?" she asks.

"I could still be a cop if I wanted to be," I tell her. "But I do love Game and Parks. Turns out that being outside, working independently, working with the animals, all of that really suits me. So it worked out."

"And you did it all in spite of my dad."

"Yeah."

"And you resent him for what he said. For keeping you from what you really wanted."

"Yeah."

"And for not giving a shit about you as a kid?"

This time she poses it as a question.

I take a breath and blow it out. "Yeah. I mean, I know that I wasn't his only job or even his top priority. And my family stepped up, as they should have. But, I guess, I've been disappointed in him all this time. Even back then before I really knew why, but certainly now as an adult and as someone who is in a position to be a role model and to influence kids like I was. I just...can't respect him."

She's quiet for a very long time.

And something in my chest is aching.

Which is stupid.

This is perfect. No way could Mia ever be interested in someone who doesn't respect her father. Her hero. The guy who saved her.

This will end any talk of a friendship between us.

Which will end any further chance of tempting me to make it more.

"I understand," she finally says.

Just then the lights flicker back on. The various fans and appliances kick on and start whirring.

And I blink at the beautiful, surprising, interesting woman who I happen to have a hell of a lot in common with.

She gives me a soft smile.

"I'm really glad you came to my rescue tonight, David."

And, oh...I am so very fucked.

Because I'm really glad I came to her rescue tonight, too.

CHAPTER 4

DAVID

WHAT AM I DOING?

Last night I managed to get Tim and Donna's house put back together, a note written telling them I owed them a pizza, a bag of tater tots, and a pot of my chili for letting me shelter at their house, even though they hadn't known it.

Then I'd managed to get Mia back to her house and safely inside without anyone seeing us, and without saying anything else I would regret. Like, *tonight was surprisingly awesome.* Or *I'm really sorry we can't be friends.* Or *fuck it, I really want to be more than your friend no matter what.*

I'd even managed to fall asleep and sleep through the night. Sure, it had taken me an hour despite how exhausted I was. Yes, I had replayed our conversation over in my head, three times. Fuck, I hadn't known anything about her childhood or how Scott and Peyton had come into her life. And I kind of wish I didn't know now.

It makes me like her even more. Worse, it makes me kind of like Scott Hansen, a little.

Maybe even more than a little.

I can picture him watching Mia go back to her parents and being torn up about it. It definitely caused the crack in the resentment I have for the guy.

Which means I should stay far away from her.

But instead, completely in character for me, I'm doing the opposite of what I should do. I am walking up the path to the Sapphire Falls community library and planning to go inside and very much see her again.

I pull the door open and stride inside, vowing to just get this over with. I have something to give her, and I need to tell her about her car.

I stop just inside the doors. I think I've been in the library maybe twice in my life, and both times were because I had to come. Once for something with school that I don't remember at all, and once with my mother. That I do remember. My brothers and I had ridden our four-wheelers around the farm, and we were wild and chaotic as usual. Jack had accidentally ridden his too close to the chicken coop and had ended up tipping over, crashing through the fence and into the back of the coop.

I had taken the blame, and when I asked my mom what the big deal was—sincerely, because my mom had built the coop and I knew she could rebuild it because she could build or fix anything—she brought me down to the library and told me to research how to build a chicken coop. Then made me do it. She'd let me borrow her tools, and she paid for the supplies, but I'd have to do it myself.

Jack did end up helping me since the whole thing was actually his fault, but yeah, that was the other time I'd been to the library.

"David? "

I turn at the sound of my name. "Charlie?" I stride toward

my brother. "What are you doing here?" And what am I going to tell him I'm doing here?

"Checking out books," Charlie says with a chuckle.

Right. Of course. That is probably what ninety percent of the people who come in here do. Unless, of course, they're looking for a Bundt pan. Or a wok. I hide my smile.

"I guess I just wasn't expecting to see you here."

Though now that my surprise at seeing him has passed, I realize Charlie probably comes here a lot. My brother is a huge bookworm and always has been. He's probably been inside this library hundreds of times. He often came as a kid. "So are you a regular here?" I ask.

"Pretty much. Come in probably once a week," he says.

"So you know Mia?" I ask.

"Of course. I see her here a lot. But we also…"

Both of my eyebrows arch. "You also what?"

Charlie shakes his head. "Nothing. We exchange book recs. She knows what I like, so she'll hold new releases for me."

"And you also…" I trail off. There was more to that and now I *need* to know. "What were you going to say?"

He peers at me. "What are *you* doing here?"

I shake my head. "No, not until you tell me what you and Mia do together."

Is that a stab of jealousy I feel?

Fuck. It is.

My brother knows Mia pretty well. He sees her on a regular basis, and they share something in common that's important to both of them. Books. Something I'm not that into.

And I don't like it.

This is definitely a problem.

Charlie looks suspicious. And amused. Those are not good things for your older brother to look.

"Why are you so interested in Mia? "he asks.

"Just tell me if *you're* interested in Mia."

My older brother is not just smart, he also knows me very well. All three of my brothers do. It's very annoying. His gaze takes in the canvas bag I'm carrying. "I'll tell you what I do with Mia, if you tell me what's in the bag," Charlie says.

"So you *do* something with Mia?" I hate the way my gut clenches. Though this would solve the problem of my attraction to Scott Hansen's daughter. If my brother has something going on with her, I am definitely out.

"I do," Charlie says. He tucks his hands into the pockets of his khaki slacks. "We do it about three nights a week."

Charlie knew her first. He knows her better. He has more in common with her.

I tell myself all of these things, and my rational brain says they make sense.

The knot in my gut doesn't care.

"How long has it been going on?" I ask.

My brothers and I don't sit around and talk about our feelings all the time, but we do share a lot about our lives with one another. Losing our parents so young and everything we've been through has made us very close.

Our youngest brother, Jack, just lost his wife and has moved back to Sapphire Falls with his two young kids. It fucking sucks to watch him go through more loss, and we've all rallied around him.

So, it's hard to believe that Charlie might be serious about a woman and not tell us, but possibly he's keeping it to himself for now with everything Jack's going through.

"Oh geez," Charlie says, thinking about my question. "Over a year."

I frown and step closer to him. "You've been seeing Mia for over a year, and you haven't said anything to any of us?"

Charlie gets an *aha* look on his face. "I'm not dating Mia, David. Don't worry. You're free to ask her out."

Thank fuck.

But I quickly shake my head. "I'm not going to ask her out."

"Don't you think you should? Considering how much you hate the idea of anyone else doing that?"

I sigh. Dammit. This will not be the last time Charlie brings this up. And I'm certain the next time—or the next three times—one or more of our brothers will be there. "I can't date Mia. You know how I feel about Scott."

"Then why are you here and feeling the urge to punch me thinking I'm dating her?"

That is a very good question. I blow out a breath. "I ran into her the other night. She was out at the river, trying to find animal tracks. I found some for her and brought the molds in. It will keep her from going out there alone again."

"Ah, just helping her out. Like the good, noble conservation officer you are."

I narrow my eyes at his sarcastic tone. "Exactly."

"And do you think that scaring off other men from asking her out is helpful to her too?"

"That's not what I'm doing."

Charlie chuckles. "Okay." He claps me on the shoulder. "I'll see you later."

I slap my hand over his, holding him in place. "Charlie."

"Yeah?"

"You haven't told me what you and Mia do together three nights a week."

Charlie grins. "Does it matter? You don't want to ask her out."

I do *want* to ask her out. I'm just not going to.

But I *really* wish the answer to Charlie's question was no. I nod. "Yeah. It does."

Charlie gives me a knowing look, then says, "We write fanfiction."

That was *not* what I was expecting. I blink at him. That wasn't even on the list of top five things I expected. "You what?"

Charlie shrugs my hand off and steps back. "We write fanfiction for a series we both read and liked. Well, she read it first and then challenged me to read it. I did, and it was pretty good. But then she told me about the fanfiction for it. I started reading that for the entertainment but then actually got into it. I write on the mystery side, but I definitely read the sex club side."

I'm staring at him. Is he fucking with me? It's possible. "The *what* club?"

"The sex club. That's the side Mia writes on."

I don't even really know what he's talking about, but I still snort. "Bullshit."

"I'm serious. And she's amazing."

I scowl at him. "What's that mean? Are you having online sex with her? Like in an online chat or something?"

I might kill my brother.

It is not okay that I feel this way about Mia Hansen. But the idea that my *brother* might be saying things to her like... nope, I can't even go there.

"Jesus, no." Charlie laughs.

Laughs.

"Why not? You don't think she's sexy?" I demand.

Charlie looks around, and I realize I've raised my voice.

I also realize that I shouldn't be jealous about him potentially having online sex—or real sex—with Mia and then be upset that he doesn't want to.

I'm losing my mind.

Charlie grabs my arm and pulls me into the alcove just inside the door. "Okay, you need to relax. She's an amazing *writer*. Fanfiction is when fans of something—a book series, a movie franchise, a TV series—write additional scenes or stories for the characters or set in the established world. It's...like an homage. The series is Hot Cakes by Erin Nicholas. It's a small-town rom-com series."

"Rom com? It's a movie?"

"A book series. Romantic comedies. Set in a fictional town in Iowa. The fanfiction takes off where the series ends. But with twists not in the books. There are a couple of mystery fanfic series set in the town. One is cozy mystery that's a little lighter. Most of the mysteries happen in or around the bakery in the town, and the bakery owners, Zoe and Josie, help solve them. Then there are some really gritty ones. Murders and kidnappings. Those are the ones I write in."

I'm not surprised. Charlie has always loved mysteries and police procedurals.

"Tell me more about the ones Mia writes."

Charlie grins. "The series about the sex club."

"Shut up. Yeah."

"Fun, erotic stuff. They're funny, but also *very* hot. Mia's little series does the best. The one millionaire from the series, the uptight grumpy one, Grant, actually started the club in her version. He was apparently her favorite guy in the original series, so she wanted to write more about him and thought it would be funny for the buttoned-up millionaire to own a sex club. Of course, he's not buttoned up once he falls for the heroine in his book..."

Charlie's gaze goes to something behind me, and I look over.

Mia is near the front desk, about forty feet from where

we're standing. She's squatting next to a little girl in short, stubby pigtails, looking at a book the girl is showing her.

She's smiling, and my gut clenches.

But worse....her hair is in a bun. And she's wearing glasses.

And a pale pink cardigan sweater.

Fuck. Me.

CHAPTER 5

MIA

DAVID BENNETT CAME into my library.

Not only that, but I almost had to go over and shush him. He and Charlie were talking by the door and got really loud at one point. I'm dying to know what they were talking about. It looked like Charlie was telling David something important and interesting.

In my library.

I'm used to seeing Charlie Bennett, but when I saw the two brothers together today, I was struck by how very different they are.

Charlie is a bookworm. Quiet. Thoughtful. He has a sarcastic sense of humor, has eclectic reading taste, and is incredibly creative.

David is rugged, much broader, and more muscular than Charlie. He's also quiet, but where Charlie gives you the impression he's in his own head mulling things over, imagining or creating something, David seems to be watching, observing, and taking in all the details around him.

It seems to me that Charlie's world is very internal, while David is all about the external world.

Charlie is all about words, thoughts, and ideas.

David wants to *do* things—get his hands dirty and be out experiencing the world instead of just reading about it.

Of course, I could be wrong. They're brothers, and I'm sure Charlie has been out hunting and camping with David. And I'm sure David reads. At least the sports section, weather reports, and...other things.

God, that sounds so judgmental.

And I'm projecting. I'm sure of it.

Charlie and I have a lot in common. We've gotten to know each other well, not just through his regular patronage of the library but also our love of fanfiction. Especially the one we both write. I'm a lot like Charlie, but sometimes I think I need to be more like David. I love to curl up with a book and forget about the real world. Fictional worlds are safe. I can know the ending of the story before I even start—and can avoid the sad, scary, or painful ones.

I like hiding away. I love when things are predictable. I *really* love when I feel in control of outcomes.

Of course, that all comes from my childhood. I've had enough therapy to know that.

But what am I missing in the real world?

I wonder that a lot.

There's surely a whole bunch of amazing, wonderful things out there.

People like David sure love it out there.

Of course, when I try to get out there, I end up with flat tires, wild animals, and tornadoes...

But then very handsome men with big trucks and shiny badges come along and save me.

Just like in the stories.

I smile as I think about that.

Yeah, last night actually did nothing to quash my thoughts of 'maybe you should venture outside your comfort zone a little'.

It had turned out pretty great, actually.

And while I should probably be interested in *Charlie* Bennett—with his clean-shaven face and his glasses, khaki pants, and extensive TBR—I couldn't stop staring at David in his uniform, with his hair just a touch too long, scruffy jaw, and his big, calloused hands.

And then I found out that he'd brought me plaster molds of six different animal tracks.

That's why he'd shown up at the library.

He'd gone out and gotten the animal track molds I'd wanted.

Six of them. I never would have gotten six myself.

And one mold is of a mountain lion print.

But he left the molds—and a note telling me that he'd towed my car to the garage and that they'd call me when it was ready —on the desk rather than talking to me.

He'd waited until I was helping someone else, then he'd ducked out.

He'd completely avoided me.

I've been telling myself all day that I do *not* have a thing for David Bennett.

But he came to my library. Looking even better in broad daylight than he had last night. And he brought me animal track molds.

So, I definitely do have a crush on him, and I'm not sure what to do about it.

Last night, when he'd driven me home and come around to open the truck door for me, his parting words to me had not been, "This was fun," or "Can I call you?" or "Would you like to go out sometime?"

Nope.

They'd been, "You probably shouldn't tell your dad I found you and that we hung out for a couple of hours."

Right.

David doesn't want me to tell my dad we spent time together.

That makes having a crush on him rather inconvenient.

I just need to get over it. Probably. That would be the best idea.

Instead, I'm driving home from dropping food off at his house.

Just to say thank you for the molds, and the tow, and saving me from the tornado.

Sure. That's why I'm so disappointed that he wasn't home.

I've just turned onto my street when I get a text. I press the button for it to read aloud.

Hey, I'm at your house. Where are you?

It's from my sister.

I can't decide if I'm excited to see her or not.

I am never going to be able to lie to her about where I was. And if I tell her, she'll know that I am not feeling just grateful and friendly toward David.

But maybe that's a good thing. Harlow will make me talk about it.

Harlow is so much like our dad. I know she'll feel protective. She has lots of opinions about my life. But she doesn't have any bad blood with David that I know of.

And she's the only other person who knows what it's like to be Scott Hansen's daughter. Our experiences with that are a little different, but she'll be able to give me advice about our dad.

I hit the button to call her. The call connects, and she picks up immediately.

"Hey! Jefferson has something going on with the football team. Are you free to hang out?"

"Definitely. I need to talk to you about something."

There's a long beat of silence on Harlow's end. My sister isn't great with surprises, particularly ones that have to do with the family and especially ones that have to do with me. I quickly add, "A good thing, I think." Then I say the words she loves more than any other. "I need your advice."

"Oh my God, where are you?"

"Just pulling in."

She's at my front door and turns as I pull into my driveway.

She holds up a bag and grins. It's clearly a to-go bag from the bar downtown, the Come Again. I'm not sure what's inside the bag, but it doesn't matter. All the food is good, and I know Harlow will have ordered curly fries.

Since I was hoping to eat frozen pizza and tater tots with David, and I left all the food there for him, I haven't eaten yet, and my stomach rumbles happily at the idea of seasoned curly fries dipped in the Come Again's secret sauce.

I meet my sister on the porch. "You have perfect timing. I'm starving."

"Awesome. Is everything okay?" she asks as she pulls me in for a hug.

I smile and let her squeeze me. The most important thing in life to Harlow is that all of us are okay all the time. We're not, of course. But we try our best to only let her know when things are *really* bad. At which time she gets upset because we didn't tell her sooner. Then we promise to do better, she promises to stop worrying so much, and we all go back to doing things the way we always have and never really change.

My family isn't perfect, but our intentions are good.

"Yeah. I just have an interesting story for you," I say as she releases me, and I can unlock the door and let us in.

She actually gives a little squeal. "I love interesting stories."

Yes, yes, she does.

I decide to give her another little bit. "And...it's about a guy."

I turn as Harlow freezes in the doorway to my house.

"Shut up," she says, her eyes wide.

I laugh. "Seriously."

"A guy and *you?*"

I nod and smile, kicking my shoes off and padding into the kitchen to grab plates.

"Mia!" Harlow is hot on my heels. "Spill!"

I hand her two plates, and she dumps out grilled chicken sandwiches and curly fries.

"Let's sit down," I say. "It's a long story."

"Oh my god." She's actually bouncing a little as we reheat the food in the microwave, then settle around my little kitchen table with our plates and sodas.

And I proceed to tell her everything about the previous night.

Even the parts she won't like. Like the fact that I was out by myself, where there were wild animals, where I got a flat tire, and there was a tornado.

She lets me just talk. She doesn't eat even one fry.

When I'm done, I dip a fry, pop it in my mouth, and chew, waiting for her reaction.

She takes a deep, dramatic breath, and says, "Okay, you're sitting in front of me, completely fine, and David was the one who showed up to help you, so I am going to skip over all of the dangerous shit and not lecture you about any of that."

I nod and pop another fry in my mouth. "And not tell Mom and Dad."

She narrows her eyes. "I promise not to tell Mom and Dad if you *swear* you won't go anywhere else alone, outside of town anyway, until you have a new phone."

"Fine." I eat another fry. "I did drive out to David's tonight, though."

"Wait, what? Did you just come home from there?" Her eyes scan my hair, my face, and my clothes, then come back to my eyes. "You look totally normal. *Please* tell me this is *not* how you look after sex with David Bennett."

I nearly choke on a curly fry. "Harlow! What?"

"If you went out there and had hot sex with David and came back looking like this—not a hair out of place, not a wrinkle, not a centimeter of whisker burn, I will be *very* disappointed."

I'm staring at her. "He...he wasn't home. I didn't go out there for sex. I took him pizza and tater tots."

She opens her mouth. Then stops and smiles. "Aw, because you didn't get to have that last night together. That's cute."

"Shut up. Why did you assume I'd gone out there for sex? And why do you assume I'd look all..." I wave my hand, not sure what word to use.

She sits back in her chair. "Because that guy has amazing-in-bed written all over him, and that means you would not only be *very* rumpled after, you should not be able to find your panties or even string coherent sentences together. In fact, you shouldn't be sitting here with me right now, eating curly fries. You should *not* leave that man's bed until late tomorrow morning."

I'm just staring at her. All of that sounds...awesome.

"What if he didn't want me to stay over?"

She grins. "He brought you animal track molds this morning. He'd want you to stay over."

My heart does a little flip in my chest. "Maybe he just

doesn't want to have to come tow my car again. Or do the paperwork required when I'm mauled by a mountain lion. Getting the molds himself keeps me away from danger."

She nods. "Okay, maybe. You should probably test that theory."

"What do you mean?"

"I think you need to find a way to be in David Bennett's company, just the two of you, for another two hours—or more. The tornado was kind of a cock-blocker."

"Harlow!" But I'm laughing now, feeling lighter. Harlow isn't acting like this is a horrible idea.

"I'm just saying, see what happens when he's not worried about the weather, and you aren't squatting in someone else's house."

I reach for a fry. This is intriguing. It sounds like fun, actually. Who says I have to wait for David to call me or ask me out? I'm a grown woman. If I want something, I need to find a way to get it. Like spending time with David Bennett.

The only problem is...

"What about Dad?" I ask.

"What about Dad?"

"He and David don't get along."

"So don't invite Dad on your date," she says.

I roll my eyes. "Harlow, you know what I'm saying. And David has already brought it up. He doesn't want Dad to even know he rescued me last night."

My phone lights up at that very moment with a text. My heart kicks. I don't know why. There are a dozen people who could be texting me.

But for some reason, I know it's David.

In the note I left with the pizza and tater tots, I told him to give me a call.

A text is not a call. And I'm not surprised he's not calling.

"Hang on," I tell Harlow.

She leans in, propping her chin on her hand, and watches me read my text.

Thanks for the food, but no need to thank me. Happy to help.

Another text comes in right after that one.

But you know I can't call you. You know we can't see each other. We really can't be friends. I'm really sorry.

My stomach drops.

Another text comes in.

You're great. But we can't be more than that either.

Ugh. I feel a little sick now.

Which is stupid. This is what I expected. But I'm shocked at how disappointed I am.

I show Harlow my phone. "This is worse than a tornado."

She scans the text. Then grimaces. "He's talking about Dad there?"

I nod. "And doing something that would disappoint Dad would be really hard for me."

"I know." She dips another fry, then says, "You know that Dad really only wants you to be happy, right?"

I do know that. "Yes, but I also know he thinks he knows how to make that happen better than anyone."

She nods. "So...maybe there are *two* men you need to prove something to. One needs to realize that you're perfectly capable of figuring out what and who makes you happy for yourself. And another needs to figure out that there is absolutely no use in trying to resist you." A little smile teases the corner of my sister's mouth.

I let her words sink in. As they do, my smile grows bigger and bigger. "I think you might be onto something there."

"God, falling in love myself has made me a sucker for this shit," she says with a little sigh.

I laugh. "Well, perfect timing. You can help me with my idea."

"Ooh, yes. What are you going to do?"

"Well, I'm going to have to work out the details," I tell her, feeling a rush of excitement and, if I'm not mistaken, empowerment. "But if I had to summarize it, I would say I'm going to seduce David Bennett."

CHAPTER 6

DAVID

PINK CARDIGANS ARE a new turn-on for me.

Short sundresses with cowboy boots are not.

They're not new, I mean. They're definitely a turn-on for me.

Mia Hansen dressed in *anything* is, apparently, a turn-on for me. That's new too. And I'm not happy about it. But it's undeniable as she steps into the Come Again with three friends on Friday night.

She's wearing a cream-colored dress and turquoise-colored cowboy boots, with her hair down, her makeup done, and a huge smile.

The dress isn't tight, but it's cinched at the waist. It's got sleeves. Kind-of. The loose sleeves cover her arms from the elbows down, but her shoulders are bare, like someone cut holes in the tops of the sleeves. Holes to tease and tempt the men around her with even more skin. As if all the skin shown off from the hem of the dress down to the tops of her boots wasn't enough to have every male in the room turning to look.

Her hair is most definitely *not* pulled back and up into a

prim little bun. It's falling past her shoulder blades in waves, and not wind-blown-frizzy-and-tangled waves like the other night. Tonight, it's sleek and smooth, and I want to run my fingers through it.

Of course, I wanted to run my fingers through it when it was frizzy and tangled, too, so that's not really a shock.

I am definitely not the only one in the bar who notices the new arrivals.

I'm not even the only one at my table who notices.

Carver Riley gets up with a grin and crosses the room to kiss his wife.

Kaelyn is with Mia, Sloan Bennett, and Whitney Bennett—cousins, not sisters. They're obviously out for a Friday night Girls' Night Out. All of the women are dressed up and look beautiful. Sloan is wearing a short, fitted sundress too. But I can't keep my eyes from returning to Mia over and over.

Her lips are a dusky pink that looks less like lipstick and more like she was just thoroughly kissed. Which makes me think about kissing her and seeing how that makes her lips look. Do they get even darker pink? More plump? Would her cheeks turn pink like that, too? Does her neck flush when she's turned on?

I want to know all of that.

And I definitely can't stop cataloging every detail of that dress. The skirt doesn't hit any lower on her thighs than a pair of shorts would, which leaves a lot of her long, tanned legs bare. How's she going to sit in that skirt without flashing anyone? And come to think of it, I don't notice any panty lines when she turns and waves at someone sitting near the windows.

Yes, I checked out her ass.

I'm not happy about that either, but it just happened.

I check Sloan and Whitney out, too, just to try to even things up, but my eyes bounce back to Mia like she's a bright, beautiful flower and I'm a helpless honeybee functioning on instinct only.

I scrub a hand over my face. Jesus, what is wrong with me?

I know what it is and I know I need to ignore it.

But if that sweet-looking, shy-seeming, cardigan-wearing woman is showing up to this bar on a Friday night in a short skirt and no panties…

I shift on my seat. What am I going to do? Storm over there and demand she go home and put some underwear and blue jeans on? Sure.

Or maybe storm over there, throw her over my shoulder, take her out to my pickup, and show her how much I love that dress and her not wearing panties.

Fuck.

A week ago, that would not have *ever* crossed my mind. I might have noticed that all of the women look gorgeous tonight and might have thought "lucky bastards" about anyone who gets to flirt, dance, or even go home with one of them.

But I wouldn't have been zeroed in on Mia.

I wouldn't have checked out her ass.

I wouldn't have been thinking about her panties.

I wouldn't have already had three nights of hot as fuck dreams about her.

But no, I had to rescue her, almost eat frozen pizza with her —we didn't even do that, and I still can't look at one of my favorite foods without thinking of her—and actually fall into like with her.

Then I had to go to the fucking library.

I shouldn't have done that. That was the second biggest mistake I made.

The biggest one was reading her fanfiction.

Mia Hansen has a very dirty mind.

And I did *not* need to know that.

I blame Charlie. He never should have told me about the fanfiction. He could have kept that information to himself. He could have been a normal guy who doesn't want his asshole little brother to know things like that he writes mystery fanfiction for a contemporary romance series.

But no, Charlie told me all about it. Probably because he's a damned good writer. I read all of his stuff, too.

I watch Carver greet the women, and all of their smiles. He takes Kaelyn's hand and starts to pull her toward our table, but they laugh, and Whitney pulls her friend back toward the all-female pack, shaking her head.

Carver shrugs, kisses Kaelyn again, leans in to whisper something in her ear that makes her nod enthusiastically and him laugh, then he comes back to our table as the women move toward one of the high-top tables closer to the stage where the band is setting up.

The Come Again only has live bands on Friday nights, so we usually do our 'let's grab a beer' thing on Wednesdays or Thursdays to avoid the crowds and so we can actually talk and catch up with each other. But Charlie said Jack needed a night out. An actual fun night with more people and music and not just talking to his brothers.

Fair enough. I said yes without hesitation. Our grandma is watching Jack's kids, and I'm happy to help my recently widowed brother have some fun. A few beers, some good food, and some live music sounded like a great time. Harmless, even.

Until now. Now it looks like I'm going to have another night where it takes me forever to fall asleep, and when I do, I'm going to toss and turn with very inappropriate dreams about a woman who is completely off-limits.

This time I'm probably not going to dream about fucking her against a bookcase at her charming little library, though. I'm probably going to fuck her bent over the tailgate of my truck, with her still wearing those fucking boots.

Dammit.

"What's with you?"

I look up at Jack and realize I cursed out loud. I clear my throat. "Nothing." I look at Carver. "Made your wife come down here so you could keep an eye on her, huh?"

Carver chuckles, not in the least bit insulted. Carver and Kaelyn have been a couple since they were about four years old, and there isn't a soul who knows them who doesn't know that Carver adores the very air his wife breathes. Or who doesn't know that they are very confident in their relationship and often go their separate ways. They are the least clingy couple I know.

"Why are you so grumpy suddenly?" Jack asks. "You're not really worried Carver is going to ditch us for the girl gang, are you?"

"I'm not grumpy."

"You have a problem with one of the girls?" Carver asks with a frown.

Yes, yes, I do Carver. I'm sleep-deprived and having some trouble with a constant semi-erection because of one of those girls. Thanks for asking.

"Of course not," I say.

I can't say yes. Kaelyn Spencer, now Riley, is one of the nicest people I know. And hell, Sloan and Whitney are my cousins.

Not *technically*. Their dads, Ty and Travis, are our dad's brothers, but our dad, Tucker, adopted us. And we didn't grow up like cousins. We don't have childhood memories with them. The girls are a lot younger than all of us. Whit is the oldest of the Bennett grandkids, and she's seven years younger than Jack, the baby of our family.

We were all in high school when they were just little kids, and we were out of the house before they were old enough to be interesting enough to pay any attention to. I remember a big group of younger kids running around at big family gatherings or when I came home from college for Christmas, but I couldn't have even told you which was which.

Now I only know the ones who live and work around here, and I've still gotten Sloan and Melody mixed up before.

"Oh, David's just realizing that our sweet town librarian can look like *that*," Charlie says with a chuckle.

Jack frowns and glances toward the table. "Which one is the librarian?"

"The brunette in the cream-colored dress," Charlie says.

"Ah." Jack nods. "Nice."

I lift a brow. "What?"

"She's really pretty," Jack says with a shrug. "You like her?"

"No."

Charlie and Carver both laugh.

I scowl at them. "What? I don't."

"You do, too," Charlie says. "Mia is *very* nice. You have zero reason not to like her."

"Okay, I *like* her. She's fine. But I don't *like* her." I sigh. We sound like idiots. "Jesus Christ, you guys. We're not in eighth grade."

"You're right," Jack says. "I should ask what I really mean. Do you want to date her?"

"No," I say quickly.

Probably too quickly.

"Do you want to sleep with her?" Jack asks.

"No."

I *definitely* say that too quickly.

Carver and Charlie exchange a look.

"I *can't*," I say instead. Because...yeah, fine. Saying I don't want to do either of those things is going to be a hard sell with these guys.

"Why?" Jack asks.

My brother has been away from Sapphire Falls for about ten years. He was off at college, getting married, having kids. Losing his wife. He's had a few other things on his mind than keeping up with the who's who in Sapphire Falls.

"She's Scott Hansen's daughter," I say simply.

Jack lets that sink in.

My brother has been seemingly moving in slow motion since his wife's death. He's moved in with our mom and dad, which is great because he has help with the kids and doesn't have to worry about things like bills, shopping, yard work, and keeping up with housework. It seems like Jack's having a hard time even doing the basics, like going to work and being present for his kids.

So, I give him a minute to think over what I just said.

Finally, he nods. "That could be complicated."

"Right."

I've been thinking about it ever since Mia and I left Tim's basement the other night. I just don't see a way to date Mia without it being awkward. Scott and I would have to see each other eventually. We would have to address *our* past. I'd have to be willing to forgive him for keeping me off the police force, for not caring about me—a kid who really needed help from an authority figure—back when he could have made a difference.

Should I be over it by now? Should I realize that even Scott Hansen is human and just move on? Maybe. But I've pushed Scott and my feelings about him to the side and ignored them so that I can live and work in this town. I don't know if I want to dig around in there again.

My brothers don't know every nuance of every feeling I

have toward Scott. My therapist is the only one who's really heard it all.

And Mia.

But they know that I don't like Scott and vice versa.

"So, I should probably go," I say, setting my beer down and getting up.

It's stupid, but it feels too hard to be here tonight with her here, looking amazing, and tempting, and already on my mind far too much.

I don't come to the bar every night or even three times a week, but I'm a regular. Mia isn't. I can only hope that she and her friends are here tonight because of the band and that I won't run into her a lot in the future.

"No, come on," Charlie protests. "The band is going on soon. Just stay. This is a night out for us. It's not about them."

He casts a glance in that direction. Whitney is looking over. I see her arch her eyebrows. My brother quickly turns back to our table.

I might not be a "real" cop, but I've got training. And I'm still out making sure people are following the rules and doing things right.

Often, they're not.

I'm lied to a lot.

I have a very good sense for when people are trying to pull something over on me.

"Charlie," I say.

He looks at Carver. Carver shakes his head.

"*Charlie*," I repeat.

He sighs and meets my eyes. "Yes, I knew the ladies would be here tonight," he says, already knowing what I'm going to ask.

"You conspired with Carver and Kaelyn to get me here?"

"Conspired is kind of an ugly word," Charlie says. "We just

agreed to all come to the same place at the same time on the same day."

"You're trying to set me and Mia up," I say.

"Not exactly. We're helping a friend set you and Mia up," Carver says.

I narrow my eyes at my brother. "You're helping Kaelyn set me and Mia up?"

Carver and Charlie exchange a look again. "Well…"

"You guys." I sigh.

"Does it matter?" Carver asks.

"Yes. I don't want people to be disappointed when this doesn't work out. I'll talk to whoever it is."

Carver and Charlie look at each other again. I sigh.

"You should definitely talk to this person," Charlie says. "But, somewhere quiet. Private. So you don't, you know, involve everyone in it. You know how this town can be."

"Fine. Is it Kaelyn or Whitney?"

"It's Mia."

I look at my brother. His grin is huge.

"What?"

"It was Mia's idea," Charlie clarifies. "She wanted us all to meet down here so she had a chance to see you."

I look over at the woman I've been unable to stop thinking about.

She is not looking at me. In fact, her back is to me.

Are these guys fucking with me?

Possible.

But then Sloan catches me looking and nudges Mia. Mia sits up straighter but doesn't look over at me.

What is she doing? Why did she think this was a good idea? I told her we can't see each other. She's an intelligent, nice, respectable woman. How is she not taking 'no' for an answer?

Who would have thought Mia Hansen would be persistent and stubborn? And so hot about it?

Well...me.

She wasn't exactly cooperative the night of the tornado. At least at first.

But I suppose this is a loophole. We're both just out at the Come Again. We're hanging out with our friends. Scott can't be upset if we run into each other in public places. He's not unreasonable.

And if we talk or dance while here, that's just something that happens at bars with live bands.

And if she has a few too many drinks and needs a ride home, I'm just doing a good thing. Something an officer of the law *should* do. And walking her to her door is just nice. And kissing her...

I blow out a breath. Yes, fuck, it's kind of hot that she's pursuing this. That she's pursuing *me*. I'm not sure I've ever had a woman chase me.

She actually wants to see me again and is willing to come up with ways to make that happen.

The band launches into their first song of the night, and they're smart—it's "Don't Stop Believin'" by Journey, the perfect sing-along song. Everyone cheers and Mia and her friends lift their drinks, clink them together over the table, then start singing and swaying.

Her definitely-not-in-a-bun hair sways against her back, her sweet ass wiggles on the stool, and I realize that just watching Mia in this environment could be a lot of fun. Maybe they'll all get up and dance eventually.

I'm going to have a hot as fuck sex dream about her tonight anyway, I'm sure. Why not give my dirty subconscious some hair-swaying and ass-wiggling to work with too?

Plus, I now need to make sure she has a sober ride home.

And that the four guys at the table on the other side of the bar who are watching Mia's group don't get too friendly.

"Fine," I say, re-claiming my seat. "Maybe I'll stay for a little bit."

I can't take Mia somewhere and talk with her privately. God knows what would happen in that private space.

But I can stick around and see what she does now that she's got me here.

Scott can't blame me for this. I'm just a guy, sitting in a bar, having a beer with his brothers.

Whatever comes next is all his daughter's fault.

That's my story and I'm sticking to it.

CHAPTER 7

MIA

NOW THAT I'VE got him here, what do I do with him?

David Bennett is not a flirt. He's not chatty. He's not outgoing.

And he's not going to come over here.

I know that.

He doesn't think we should even be friends. He's not going to approach me in here in front of everyone.

What was I thinking?

I was thinking that maybe he would think this was safe. We just ran into one another here, it's a social setting, it's harmless if we spend time together here.

But he's barely looked at me.

He's sitting at the table with his brothers and friends. There are no women around. Carver has interacted with Kaelyn, of course, but for the most part they seem to be just enjoying a guys' night.

I almost feel like I'm interrupting.

But he's here because of my machinations. So I feel like I need to do something.

I lean in, grateful for the live music to cover my voice. "Now what?"

Whitney, Sloan, and Kaelyn all lean in too.

"Go ask him to dance," Kaelyn says.

I shake my head. "I can't."

"Everyone at that table knows that you wanted him here and why," Whitney says. "They're probably wondering why you haven't yet."

"But that puts him on the spot," I say. "He's made it clear that he thinks this...us...is a bad idea."

"You wanted him here tonight," Whitney points out. "What did you think would happen?"

"I..." I sigh. "I don't know. It's not like I know what I'm doing. I told my sister I was going to seduce him. What the hell do I know about seducing anyone? Especially someone like David?"

Kaelyn grins. "Why is David a special case?"

"Because I'm pretty sure he's used to women knowing what they're doing," I say with an eye roll.

"A confident woman who wanted to seduce a man would probably go ask him to dance," Sloan points out.

"But if he says yes, it's only because he's nice and doesn't want to turn me down in front of everyone," I say.

"So you want him to say no?" Sloan asks.

"That would be so embarrassing." I cover my face with my hands. "See? I did *not* think this through."

"I'll go ask him to dance," Whitney says, sliding off her stool and adjusting her blue dress over her slim hips.

"And then what?" I ask.

"We'll see what he says."

"But then what?"

"Then we'll dance," Whitney says. "Or not, I guess." She

flips her long dark hair over her shoulder. "Though I have a pretty good track record."

I grab her arm as she turns. "No."

"No?"

"Don't ask him to dance." I can *not* be jealous of Whitney. My God, how stupid.

Yes, she's beautiful and confident and sweet and funny and...David would be stupid to not want to dance with her.

But I can't be jealous.

I still feel a little niggle of something that feels suspiciously like jealousy.

This night is starting to seem like a bad idea.

I got David here, and now I have no idea what to do. All of my options seem bad.

Maybe I should just go home. I'm reading a great romance right now. Or I could work on my fanfiction. For some reason, when I'm writing, I always know what to have the characters do.

Whitney gives me a little knowing smile. "Why not? I can ask him if he likes you."

I roll my eyes. "We're not in eighth grade."

Whitney laughs. "Let's just see if he's even interested in dancing. Then we can see *who* he's interested in dancing with."

I sigh. I can't keep David from dancing, just like I can't make him dance.

"Fine, go ask him," I say, letting go of her. "But *don't* ask him about me."

She nods. "Okay. Promise."

I turn back to the table. Since David and his brothers are sitting behind me, I can't watch what happens. I sip my drink, watch the dance floor where everyone else seems to be having a good time, and try to pretend I don't care if David says yes to dancing with Whitney.

But he does not. She does head to the dance floor, but it's with Jack, not David.

"Oh, that's nice," Kaelyn says. "They've all been so worried about Jack."

With good reason. The poor guy. I'm surprised he's dancing even now, but Whitney is basically his cousin, so it's not like there's any thought of romance there. I get the impression from what everyone in town is saying that Jack is heartbroken and dating and romance are the furthest things from his mind. But I'm glad he's out and socializing at least.

I almost laugh at that thought and bring my glass to my lips. I'm not one to be judging anyone else's social life, or lack thereof.

"I'm going to grab Charlie," Sloan says.

"Yeah, I want to dance too," Kaelyn adds, obviously eyeing her husband.

They both slide off their stools and head toward David's table.

I pause with my glass halfway to my mouth.

What just happened?

Now I'm sitting here alone.

As is, I presume, David.

I don't turn to look.

Did our friends just set us up to dance by process of elimination? Or did they all just really decide they couldn't sit still a moment longer?

I wait, still not sure what to do. Will David come over here now?

But, nothing.

The song ends, and another starts, and everyone stays on the dance floor.

Still nothing.

I blow out a breath and pick up my phone.

And text him.

> I was going to ask you to dance but wasn't
> sure if I should.

He answers almost immediately.

> > You know you shouldn't.

> It's just dancing.

> > If it was just dancing, you wouldn't wonder if
> > you should.

For some reason, that makes my stomach flip.

> > Whitney and Jack and Sloan and Charlie are
> > just dancing.

> > But that's different than if you and I danced,
> > right?

Well…yes. Whitney and Jack are not going to date. Sloan and Charlie are definitely just friends.

Now my stomach flips twice.

I want to look over my shoulder at him, but there's something strangely thrilling about texting him, knowing he's probably looking at me, but not being able to see him.

> I got your brother to invite you out tonight.

> > So I hear.

> I thought it would be a casual way to see
> each other.

Sitting across a bar from one another, not
interacting at all, is pretty casual.

I smile.

But that also isn't leaving this alone, is
it, Mia?

My smile dies. But that stomach flip is still there for some
reason.

No. It isn't.

So you're just going to keep this up?

This?

Pursuing this?

I read those words. Then, think about the question. Does
he want me to say no? Does he want me to say yes? I decide to
be honest.

I'd like to. But consent is important. If you
really don't want it, I'll stop.

I mean that. I can't keep insisting David spend time around me
or ask our friends to help get us together if he *really* doesn't want it.

"Mia? "

I look up from my phone, realizing that I have no idea
what's going on around me.

Hunter Graves is standing next to my table with a smile.

"Hi, Hunter."

"Would you like to dance?"

It takes a second for his question to sink in.

He just asked me to dance.

I look from him to the dance floor.

Would I like to dance? Yes. With Hunter? Not as much as with David, but David doesn't think we should dance. Or anything else.

I nod. "Yes. I would."

Hunter's smile widens. He's a good-looking guy. Just a couple of years older than me. Nice, as far as I know. He never comes to the library, but I guess that's okay.

I slide my phone into my purse and leave it on the table. It's Sapphire Falls, we don't have to worry about purses being stolen here.

I feel Hunter's hand on my lower back as we walk to the dance floor and then he puts his hands on my waist as we face each other and the song starts.

We chat about nothing important and nothing I'll remember a single detail about. Every time we turn so that I can see David's table, I intentionally avoid looking. I don't want to see him watching me. I also don't want to see him *not* watching me.

I enjoy the dance and tell myself that if David doesn't like dancing, then I probably don't want to date him anyway.

I say yes to a second dance with Hunter when the band starts a Jason Young song I love. Hunter seems genuinely pleased and pulls me a little closer.

Sure, why not? He's cute. And he dances. And he doesn't hate my dad.

But after only a minute, his hands slide from my waist to my hips. Then lower.

His hands are on my ass. And he's bringing me even closer to his body. I tense up, my hands sliding from his shoulders to his chest. I start to push.

"You know, Mia, I've always thought—"

But I'm always going to have to wonder what Hunter thought because he's yanked away from me at that second.

"Hey!" he protests.

"My turn."

And just like that, I'm staring up at David Bennett.

He's got a foot planted between me and Hunter and his body wedged so that Hunter could reach out and touch me, but he'd have to go past David to do it. David isn't touching me, but he's got a hand on Hunter's arm. David's body is definitely in my personal space, though, and I can smell the laundry detergent from his shirt.

But he's not looking at me. He's watching Hunter with an unwavering glare.

"What the hell?" Hunter asks. "You're kind of interrupting."

"Exactly," David says. He shifts, putting more of his body between us and moving Hunter further back.

Easily, I might add.

Hunter doesn't try to push David away. In fact, he takes a step back, and David lets go of him.

"We weren't done," Hunter says.

"Yes, you were," David tells him.

Then David turns to me. And holds out his hands, palms up. Giving me the choice.

I don't get the impression my choice is to continue dancing with Hunter—which is fine because I didn't like the feel of his hands on my ass at all—but I could actually turn on my heel and walk away from David right now.

He's giving me that chance.

His hands would feel great on my ass, I bet.

Okay, that thought is not helpful.

Hunter has already stomped away and there are only a few people paying any attention to us.

All of the people who came to the bar with us.

No one else seems to care at all.

"See?" I say. "Totally casual."

He quirks one eyebrow, then reaches out and takes my hand, pulling me close and settling his other hand on my hip.

I grin. I'm suddenly feeling a bit triumphant.

We start moving to the music.

"So, you *do* dance," I say.

"Sometimes."

"You turned Whitney down, though," I point out. "I figured you weren't in the mood tonight."

"I wasn't."

"And now you are?"

He turns us, and the light hits his face differently. I can see his eyes more clearly now.

"No."

"No? You're still not in the mood to dance?"

"I'm still not in the mood to dance with Whitney."

"Oh." I smile. "But you're in the mood to dance with *me?*"

"Well, I'm certainly not in the mood to watch you dance with anyone else. Especially to watch anyone else put his hands on your ass."

My smile grows.

He shakes his head. "You're getting ideas."

"No," I lie.

He sighs.

I laugh lightly. "Okay, one idea. The idea that you would rather dance with me than watch someone else dance with me might mean that you like me."

"I never said I didn't like you."

He's right.

"I like you," I say honestly. It's not flirty, just straightforward. "And I think... there's maybe something here. Between us. Maybe." I pause and wet my lips. "Am I wrong?

He watches me for several seconds without speaking.

"David?"

"Fuck..." Then he says, "No, you're not wrong."

My stomach flips again. And I smile.

"But it's not a good idea," he says.

I lean in. "But what if it is?"

His gaze bounces back and forth between my eyes. "You were the good girl, right? Never wanted to rebel or disappoint Scott? Took seriously following all the rules and making sure he was proud of you?"

I feel my grin fade a bit. But I like this straightforward thing and I think it's the right way to go. So I say, "Yes."

"What about now?"

"I...don't know." But I do. I still want my dad to be proud of me. I still hate disappointing him.

But I know where David is going with this. He's going to say this is it. We're done. No more. Stop all of this.

"The idea of disappointing him still bugs you, right?" he asks.

"Yes."

"But at the same time, you want a taste of being bad with me?"

Whoa. I wasn't expecting *that*. My eyes widen. I study David. "You think I'm interested in you because you have a bad boy reputation?"

"I think that might be part of it," he says. His gaze is intense. "But I get it. I stepped over a lot of lines, pushed a lot of boundaries. The people who took me in and saved me were completely aware of it, because I did it to test them." He pauses a beat. "Your rebellion is happening later than mine and for a different reason, but it's still because you had parents who stepped in when they didn't have to."

I swallow hard. "Why..." I clear my throat. "What's my reason?"

One corner of his mouth tips up, and I have the insane urge to press my mouth there.

"You're doing it now because you're wondering what you've missed being grateful and scared."

Wow.

Not only is David *very* straightforward, but he's pretty damned insightful.

I couldn't have this conversation with anyone else. There are other people, unfortunately, who've had a traumatic childhood and have complicated relationships with their parents, of course. But none that I'm attracted to and want to know better the way I do with David.

"What if that's right?" I ask him.

"Well, then you need to figure some things out."

"Some things like what?"

"Well, how do you think that works? We sneak around?" He shrugs. "That could give you a little thrill and let you have some fun, but you'll stay safe, and Scott won't have to know."

I don't know what to say to that.

David Bennett is saying...

"What are you saying? That you *would* like to see me? Get to know me?" I pause. "Date me?" Then I frown. "Is it dating if no one knows we're doing it?"

He gives me that almost-grin again. And I like it. Again.

"I would definitely like to see you. And get to know you. I don't care what we call it." He pulls me a little closer. "I just don't want it to cause problems. I don't want you to regret it."

Oh. That makes my stomach flip but in a new way.

That's sweet.

And kind of sad.

"Scott just wants me to be happy," I tell him.

He nods. "I'm sure that's true."

"So, I can talk to him. Tell him that you and I are…"

David's smile is a real smile this time. "How about *you and I* see what you and I are first?"

That makes sense. I guess. Being this close to him and those little smiles and him no longer saying *no we absolutely can not do this*, realizing that he does actually want this, is making me just want to say yes to whatever.

"Okay," I finally agree.

"Okay," he says with a nod. "But—"

Well, dammit, there's a but.

"You're in charge. You want this? *You* have to figure out ways for us to see each other that won't bother Scott. Tonight, just dancing in a bar, is no big deal, right? We're both here. So what?"

"Right. Casual."

He smiles. "Right. You think you can come up with more things like this?"

I have no idea. But I want to try. "Yes."

His smile is full and real and completely directed at me now, and wow, the stomach flip is also full and real.

"We could do this again," I say quickly. "This works."

He nods. "Sure." Then he leans down a little and says, "But there are a lot of things we *can't* do here."

I suck in a quick breath. Right. I want to do those things. "Okay. I'll come up with some things."

His grin is very real, and almost flirtatious. I like it. A lot.

"Okay. You've got my number. Let's see what you've got, Wild Child."

Then he squeezes my hand and my hip.

And turns and walks away.

CHAPTER 8

DAVID

I REALLY HAD NO CHOICE.

She wasn't going to stop.

She was going to keep being gorgeous and sweet and interesting.

And tempting.

Letting her set up ways for us to spend time together, giving her the rush of sneaking around, was really the best and only solution.

This way, she can see for herself that we're a bad idea.

At least that's what I've been telling myself all week.

While wondering why Mia hasn't texted or called me.

It's been a *week* since I put it all in her hands. And I haven't seen or heard from her once.

I've seen her car. When I've driven by the library. Coincidentally.

No, I don't usually drive by the library during my regular daily activities, but this week I just happened to. At least that's what I'm prepared to tell anyone who asks.

And yes, her car has been there all week.

I also know she's been writing because she's uploaded two new chapters of her fanfiction this week. Two.

From what I can tell looking back and checking dates, her usual pace is once a week at the most. Often she goes two weeks between postings. Once there was even a seventeen day stretch between chapters.

But this is the first time she's posted two chapters in a week.

And they were fucking spicy as hell.

But she hasn't called or texted me.

It's now eight-thirty on Friday night and I'm done for the weekend. I didn't make any plans because I kept thinking that Mia would text and I...

I sigh. I wanted to be available to show up whenever and wherever.

Fuck. Am I already twisted up over this woman?

Apparently. Because I've been waiting around all fucking week for her call or text. And now I'm wondering if I'll cause any heart attacks if I call my brothers and ask them if they want to get together because sitting at home wondering what Mia is doing seems pathetic.

I can at least call Jack. He won't have plans that I don't know about, and if nothing else, I can head over there and hang with him and the kids.

My phone rings just as I get into my truck.

It's my work phone, not my personal though. I frown and answer. "This is David."

"Hey, David, it's Jake Turner."

"Hey, Jake, what's up?" Jake is in his fifties and a regular outdoorsman. Jake, his brothers, and sons all own land around Sapphire Falls and I run into them periodically when they're fishing and hunting in the area.

"My mom just called and said that she saw someone spotlighting out in her north field where we have that big deer stand."

I frown. "Spotlighting? Is she sure?"

"She was coming back from town. I'm not exactly sure what she saw but she certainly knows spotlighting. I'm in Lincoln for another hour and one of my sons offered to go out, but I figured I might as well just call you. Can you go check it out?"

"Yeah. Of course. I'll take care of it. Tell your mom not to worry."

"I appreciate it."

"Anytime."

We disconnect and I start my truck, heading in the direction of Judy Turner's property.

Not only is spotlighting deer illegal, but it's not even deer season. Whoever is out there messing around is in trouble for a number of reasons. I'm glad Judy didn't try to handle it. God knows what's going on out there. I certainly don't want the sweet widowed seventy-something woman out in her backfield dealing with someone who is possibly armed.

I make the short drive and pull off into the field. I know exactly where the deer stand is. I've never hunted out here, but Jake and his brothers were proud of the stand after they built it themselves from scratch and showed it off to anyone who wanted to see it. It's humongous. Ten-by-ten, fully insulated, with a great view of a rolling field of wild grass and flowers to one side, the river on the other.

I've never needed a deer stand this big, but they've definitely brought in some impressive animals from here.

I see the stand and a pickup as I bump along over the uneven ground, but no spotlights. I don't see any people either and as I pull in behind the pickup, I frown. I know this truck. This is my brother Charlie's truck.

What the hell is going on?

I shut off my truck and get out.

"Charlie?" I call.

Not only does Charlie definitely know hunting seasons, and that spotlighting is illegal and unsportsmanlike, Charlie is not much of a hunter anyway. There's no way he's out here spotlighting deer.

I turn a three-sixty, not hearing anything. "Charlie?" I call again.

The truck is parked near the hunting blind, so I decided to check it out. I climb the wooden steps and push the door open.

What I see inside is absolutely dead last on my list of things I expected.

Mia Hansen is lying on the floor of the deer blind.

She's on her back with her knees bent. Her head is toward me, making it impossible for her to see me in the doorway behind her.

It would also make it impossible for her to see a serial killer with a chainsaw in the doorway behind her.

She's illuminated only by the tiniest bit of light coming through the windows of the blind and the phone she's holding up in front of her face, her thumbs flying over the screen as she types.

Her dark hair is spread around her head and shoulders, spilling out from under the camouflage cap she's wearing, and I can now see earbuds nestled in her ears. That explains why she hasn't heard me.

And why she wouldn't hear a serial killer approach.

She's dressed in a camouflaged long-sleeved T-shirt, and camo pants. She's got brown boots on her feet too. She looks decked out to hunt, but I don't see any weapons. And if she *is* here for the hunting, she needs some lessons.

Like, to bring a gun.

To not do it in someone else's blind without permission.

To only do it during hunting season.

And what kind of snacks to bring.

The cheese, crackers, fruit, and wine she has spread on the floor beside her aren't it.

But I can't help but smile and shake my head.

No, she's not here to hunt. But I think I know why she's here. And fuck, it's kind of adorable. If ridiculous.

As I watch, she pauses her typing and reaches for the plate next to her hip. She grabs a cracker, slides it through the hunk of cheese on the plate next to it, then pops it into her mouth.

She chews, the soft crunching noise the only sound filling the blind, as she goes back to moving her thumbs rapidly over the screen of her phone.

I don't know what she's doing exactly, but I instantly wonder if she's writing chapter eleven.

"Mia," I say.

She doesn't respond. What the hell is she listening to, and why does she have it so loud?

I raise my voice. "*Mia.*" I nudge her shoulder with the toe of my boot.

The next thing I know, she has popped up, and a hunk of cheese has hit me in the face.

"Oh my God! "Her hand goes to her chest. "David, you scared me!"

"You're in a hunting blind and your weapon of choice is cheese?" I ask.

She takes a deep breath, then blows it out as if trying to settle her heart rate. "I didn't think I would need a weapon tonight."

"Well, the serial killer stalking through the woods looking for unsuspecting women to murder will be happy to hear that."

Her eyes widen, then she smiles. "You think there's a serial killer just hanging out in these woods on the off chance that someone like me might come to this deer blind?"

"Might be his lucky day."

She tips her head to the side, regarding me. "I don't feel like that's a compliment."

"What the hell are you doing out here?"

She looks around, then back up at me. "Getting in trouble with Game and Parks."

And just like that, I have my confirmation.

She set this up. She knew I would come.

I relax. She's out here for me.

I like that far more than I should.

I lean my shoulder against the door jamb. "You're not out here hunting? Spotlighting deer? "

She gives me a mock surprised look. "Spotlighting deer is illegal. And it's not even deer season anyway."

"That's true. Which is why I was called when someone thought that's what the pickup with the bright lights that isn't supposed to be here was doing."

"I needed the brights to see my way across the field."

"The field that belongs to the person who called to turn you in."

"Hmmm. How interesting."

"This isn't a treehouse in your backyard. You can't just come out here and hang out."

She smiles and looks around again. "It's kind of a treehouse though. And the view out that window is amazing." She points to the window that faces the river.

It is. "It's also on someone else's land."

"Oh. That seems like a waste. It's beautiful out here. Whoever it is should share this."

"I'll give Judy Turner the message."

"Oh, it's Judy Turner's?"

She clearly knows this land and deer blind are Judy's. Mia Hansen is a terrible liar. I find that...also adorable. "So, what are you doing out here, in the woods, at night, in *camo*—I'm shocked you have camo, by the way—with cheese, crackers, fruit, and wine, Mia?"

"Can you keep a secret?"

"Very well, actually."

"This guy that I'm interested in told me that we have to sneak around and that I have to come up with ways for us to see each other without anyone else knowing. He's this big, rugged, outdoorsy guy who works for Game and Parks. So I looked up ways to get him to come to me." She grins. "Turns out hunting off-season and spotlighting deer are two ways."

I don't know if it's her description of me being 'big and rugged', or that she got me out here on purpose this way, or that little grin, but my heart kicks hard in my chest.

I can picture her at the library on one of the computers looking up *ways to get turned into Game and Parks*. Of course, in my imagined scenario she's in a cardigan and her hair is in a bun.

And of course, she didn't just say 'meet me two towns over for coffee'. No, it *had* to be more interesting than that. My little librarian found a way for us to see each other that no one will know about exactly the way I challenged her to.

I think I *really* like this woman.

I clear my throat. I can't say that. So I ask, "You had camo?"

"Nope. I had to order it. Which is why it took a week for me to set something up."

That explains that. "I was wondering."

She smiles at that. "Were you?"

I probably shouldn't have admitted that.

This wasn't at all what I was expecting when I told her she

was in charge of ways for us to see one another without her dad finding out, but it's a little brilliant.

"And why are you driving Charlie's truck?"

She wraps her arms around her knees. "So no one would recognize my car. Because a car out in a field by a deer blind isn't quite as convincing as a truck."

"So you were trying to convince someone you were out here hunting off season so they would call me and I would come out?"

She nods. "And specifically while you're still on the clock, so they don't send someone else, but also at the end of your shift, so you can stay."

I take a beat and really take in all the details. Yes, she's dressed in hunting camo and sitting in a deer blind, but the food she has, and the fact that she drove out here as the sun was setting, and no one else is around...

"So this is a date?"

She smiles. "Not just a date. The perfect date for a guy who loves to hunt and be outdoors, right?"

I'm actually suddenly not sure what to say. I had expected her to suggest we meet in Lincoln for dinner, or that I come to her house, but park my truck four blocks away.

This all took some set up. She did this because she thought I would like it.

And because she has a mischievous streak. I can't forget that part. She looked up ways to get turned in for breaking the rules and get me sent out as an officer. There's an undeniable sparkle in her eyes when she talks about that.

I push off the doorway and step further into the blind. "So now what? No gun, so you don't want me to take you out hunting. It's off-season and too dark anyway."

She sets her phone to the side with the flashlight on, shining upward. It hits the ceiling and lends a soft glow to the enclosure. She criss-crosses her legs and leans in to grab a grape.

"I don't need you to teach me to hunt. My dad taught me, and I don't really like it. I wasn't going to confess that so early into our relationship though."

I wonder if she has any idea how hearing her call this a relationship actually shakes me. This is dangerous. But she can call it whatever she wants, I remind myself. That doesn't change the trajectory. She'll figure out that this is a bad idea, then she'll end it. No matter what she calls it.

So, fuck it. I sink down onto the floor in front of her, also criss-crossing my legs.

"I'm surprised they don't have chairs out here," she says.

"I'm sure they do *during hunting season*."

She grins and pops the grape into her mouth, chewing for a moment.

"So you know how to hunt?" I ask.

"Well, I know how to shoot a gun. And I know the general idea of hunting. But I've never gone. I do *not* want to kill animals." She shrugs. "He taught us to shoot and then invited us along. Austin and Harlow went, and I stayed home. Harlow went the one time and that was it for her. Austin hunted with him though."

"You know how to shoot though?" I press. I had no idea.

And I need to stop assuming I know anything about this woman, clearly.

"Line up some targets or some old beer cans and I don't do too bad."

It shouldn't surprise me that Scott taught his kids to shoot and offered them a chance to hunt.

"I'm better with a handgun though."

I freeze in reaching for a strawberry. "You can shoot a handgun?"

"Yep. I even own one."

"Your dad, right?"

She nods. "For self-defense. He makes us do regular target practice. Otherwise, it is locked away safely at my house. I don't like it, but I'm comfortable enough with it."

"You're a good shot though?"

"If I wanted to hit somebody, I could," she says, tipping her chin up slightly.

"Good," I say simply.

She gives me a faint smile. I don't probe into what that means.

"How about a bow and arrow?" I ask.

"I've only shot one once. My dad's not as into bow hunting. Do you want to teach me that?"

I want to teach her a bunch of things. None of which have anything to do with hunting or weapons.

I shift on the floor. "We can talk about that. How about fishing?"

"I've fished," she says. Then shakes her head. "Also risking admitting to you that I don't love fishing. I do like sitting on the dock or in a boat on the water. Not so crazy about the fishing part."

"Okay. So boating would be more something you'd be into."

She's quiet for a moment and I look up from scraping a cracker through the cheese. "What?" I ask her when I find her watching me.

"I think I'd be up for trying anything with you."

Her words slam into me. I have no idea if *she* has any idea how they sound.

Then, directly on the heels of that thought, I think maybe she knows exactly how it sounds. I have read her fanfiction.

"Okay, well then I'm going to admit something to you," I say.

It's on the tip of my tongue to admit that I know about her fanfiction and have read it, but instead I say, "I'm not that into hunting and fishing either."

She gasps, then lowers her voice. "Can you get fired from your job for that?"

I chuckle. "I *like* it. I've done a lot of it. I completely understand the appeal. And I love helping other people do all of those things safely. But they aren't my choices of weekend outdoor activities."

She rests her elbows on her knees. "What's your choice for a fun weekend activity?"

Again, I have to bite back my initial answer. *Naked in bed, getting up only for food and water* is not the right answer here.

"Four wheelers and dirt bikes," I tell her.

"Of course. You guys have all been into that from the time you were little, right?"

Everyone knows that my brothers and I have always been regulars at the dirt bike track.

"We have. We learned to ride dirt bikes when we spent summers here in Sapphire Falls before our dad died." God, those summers seem like a lifetime ago. I clear my throat and smile. "I've always liked to go fast and hard and get dirty."

And that's true whether we're talking about dirt bikes...or something else.

She smiles slowly. "Now *that* I would love to have you teach me."

I'd fucking love to. "To ride?"

I freeze for a second. Every fucking thing sounds sexual to me tonight and I *have* to knock it off.

But she nods. "I definitely don't go fast or hard enough, and I hardly ever get dirty."

I groan inwardly. But then, screw it—yes, even my internal thoughts are full of innuendo—and I say, "Well, it's definitely better when you have someone who knows what they're doing showing you."

And honestly, that's also true if we're talking about dirt bikes...or something else.

"I would really like to be the one that shows you," I add. "In fact, I think it would bother me a lot if anyone else did."

She swallows. "I don't want anyone else to teach me, David."

Good. That's very good.

Because no one else is showing this woman anything that's going to make her smile, and laugh, and gasp, and make her cheeks pink, make her breathe faster, mess up her hair, or get her dirty.

Whether we're talking about dirt bikes...

Or something else.

CHAPTER 9

DAVID

MIA HANSEN CAN SHOOT A GUN. She knows how to scare off a mountain lion if she runs across one. She writes really fucking filthy fanfiction. I figured she'd find a way for us to see one another secretly, but that it would involve a few white lies to our friends and family and getting outside of the Sapphire Falls zip code.

Instead, I'm eating cheese and grapes in a deer blind five miles from my house. And she's wearing hunting camo.

All of that surprised me because I made assumptions about her.

So I will not assume she's a sweet little virgin who doesn't know what she likes or wants in bed.

I also won't assume that she's thinking about sex the way I am when I offer to teach her things.

But if she'd like to try some of the things her imagination comes up with that she hasn't had a chance to before...I would really like to be the one that helps her out.

I'm not going to lie to myself about that.

Or her, if it comes up.

But, while she's smiling and meeting my gaze directly, there's a pink tint to her cheeks now that makes me think that her dirty little mind is thinking exactly what I'm thinking.

She reaches for an apple slice and dips it in the cheese, then takes a bite. After she's crunched for a few seconds, she asks, "What do you like about the dirt bikes?"

"They're super cool and go fast."

She smiles but shakes her head. "There's more to it than that."

There doesn't need to be more to it than that, but I think I like the fact that she realizes there is. I nod. "Yeah."

I glance toward the window. Like the night of the tornado, I could blame this on the fact that we're alone in the dark and it's conducive to me spilling my guts.

But I know that's not it. This is all about Mia and that she's easy to talk to. I get the impression that she will understand what I'm about to say very well.

"It's controlled chaos," I tell her. "If you aren't paying attention, if you haven't developed your skills, if you don't work on control, the bike can easily take over and become dangerous. But you can master it. You can take this machine, this thing that can't be reasoned with, that has no emotion, that's moving at these incredible speeds and has this power to hurt you, and then completely control it. You can turn that power into an adrenaline rush and fun instead of danger."

She's not smiling now but she's watching me with fascination. "It's the same reason you like your job," she says.

I feel my eyes widen.

But she nods as if she's certain, and I don't have to confirm it.

"You're working with potentially dangerous situations all the time. Weather, wildlife, other humans who are armed or inebriated or just feel rules don't apply to them. You're facing all of that and exerting control over it. Using your influence to make it safe and even fun in the end for everyone who is counting on you."

I knew she'd get it.

She continues, "And you like that because you felt a loss of control and felt like you didn't have any ability to influence the chaos around your parents dying and what happened to you and your brothers after that."

I nod.

Having her understand that, having her understand *me*, is now a problem. Because I like her even more.

"Pretty clear psych case study, right? "I ask.

"Wanting to exert influence over situations that seem out of control and not only control them, but turn them positive?" She laughs lightly. "Yeah, I think it's pretty obvious where that comes from, David." She pauses. "It's the same place that drives me into fictional worlds. In a story, all the motivations are explained to me. I get to literally see inside people's minds. I get to see the journey all laid out, and I can know the ending before I even begin." She takes a breath. "That all, of course, comes from all the uncertainty in my early childhood. All the times I wondered *why* my parents made the choices they did. And not knowing how things were going to turn out."

"Do you read the last chapter first in books?" I ask, already knowing the answer.

"Every time," she confesses. She smiles self-deprecatingly. "Chaos was the theme of your childhood. Uncertainty was mine. You now need control. I love knowing what to expect. Books give me that. And I've discovered that writing..."

I lift my brow. She almost confessed to me. I love that she feels as comfortable with me as I do with her spilling secrets, and deep thoughts.

"Writing what?"

She lifts a shoulder. "I just write sometimes."

I take an apple slice and swirl it through the cheese, then lift it to my mouth. I lick the cheese off before biting into the apple.

She watches my mouth the entire time.

Her eyes on my mouth heat my blood.

"What do you write?" I should confess that I know this. I should tell her that I've read it.

But I want her to tell me.

"Romance," she says.

Hmm, okay, far be it from me to tell the woman how to describe her own writing. Her characters definitely care about each other. "Are you a romantic, Mia?"

"For sure," she says without hesitation. "How could I grow up with Scott and Peyton Hansen and not be?"

I smile. "I feel the same way about Tucker and Delaney."

"There are actually a lot of great examples around here."

"Is that why you write it?" I would *love* to know why she writes what she does. I'm fucking dying to know, in fact.

"Probably in part," she admits. "Also...some wish fulfillment, I suppose."

I almost swallow my tongue.

I'm not saying that her fanfiction has no romance in it. It also has humor and some pretty great heartfelt moments. Maybe that's what she's talking about too. She wants a relationship that has all of that.

But there's no way she hasn't put some real thought into those other scenes.

"Wish fulfillment," I say, after I'm sure my voice will sound at least somewhat normal. "The things you write about are things you want for yourself?"

"Of course."

Of course.

Of. Fucking. Course.

Well, I'm never going to get *that* out of my head.

And I'm probably not going to sleep very well tonight. At least not with any dreams of sweet candlelight dinners with Mia.

But that doesn't mean Mia won't be in them.

"Is your stuff available for reading?" I ask. Fuck. What happens when she finds out I've already read it?

"Yes." She dips her head, looking down at her hands. "It's posted online. It's fanfiction. Though, really, I just borrow the setting and a few characters from the main fiction. The primary characters I write about, I made up. They don't show up in the original series."

"So you started writing it because you were a fan of something else?" I have to play a little dumb here, don't I? I've had Charlie explain it, but I'd love to hear about this from Mia's perspective.

"Right. But then I wanted more from the world. I was sad when it was over and wanted to stay there longer. I wanted to keep going back. Since there were no more books, I started coming up with additional stories on my own. And then I found this great community of other fans and writers and it just kind of grew from there. It's really fun. I feel like I have a chance to explore new ideas and..." She shrugs. "Yes, some wish fulfillment."

"So why not just write your own original stuff?" I ask.

"I've asked myself that," she says. "Maybe I will someday. For now, I love the community and feel at home in that world. It makes exploring new ideas and themes and having these... adventures...feel safer?" She phrases it as a question and her brow furrows slightly when she says it. "I never thought about it, but I think that's it. Since the things my characters are doing and the feelings they're exploring are new and different for me, it's nice that the setting and people around them are familiar. It's as if whatever happens to them, it's still safe, because in this world everyone is good and things end up happy."

She seems to be thinking that over.

"That makes sense," I offer. It does. Completely. "You love books and stories because you can know the ending. You can choose the stories that make you feel a certain way. That gives you a sense of control that you didn't have growing up. I get that."

She meets my eyes, and I feel that getting-familiar jolt of connection.

"If you're writing the stories, you want to be sure they end up good and happy and that you get those same feelings," I say, thinking out loud. "But maybe your mind is telling you that the stories are bound to a set of rules then. Maybe that makes you feel restricted. Like you can't actually tell *all* of the story you want to for fear it won't turn out happy. If you set it in a world you already know and that makes you feel good, that you can trust to give you a happily ever after, maybe your imagination is more free to let the adventure go where you need it to."

She's staring at me now.

I shift uncomfortably. "Or fuck, I don't know. Maybe you're just really enamored with this other world."

She reaches out and puts her hand on my arm. "No. David. You're totally right. I think that's it." She swallows. "My stories are...the heroine is...she isn't very experienced sexually." She swallows again. "And the heroes—there are two—"

Yes. I'm aware of that as well. It's clear to me the heroine is in love with one of them and just very attracted to the other, but yes, there are two men helping this woman explore her sexuality.

"—and that's all new and different and the things she's learning about herself are exciting but a little scary, and she's going through emotions about both men and…" Mia takes a breath. "I think you're right that at least setting it somewhere familiar, that makes me happy, makes it easier to write some of that more difficult stuff."

Charlie would fall off his damned chair if he knew I was just *that* insightful and I impressed Mia Freaking Hansen.

I can't wait to tell him.

"Thanks for helping me figure that out," she says, giving me a bright smile. "That's a really great realization for me to have."

"You're welcome." Now I want to know why Charlie feels the need to kill people in this town in this series he supposedly loves. "So," I hear myself say. "What would happen in your romance story if the heroine and hero—*one* of them," I add.

She smiles.

"—were out in a deer blind together?"

And she blushes.

A dark pink that makes me want to know every single dirty thought that just went through her pretty head.

She sits back, pulling her hand from my arm.

I did not want her to stop touching me. Which is the sure sign that it's good she did.

"Oh, well, if it was at the beginning of the story, they'd talk and get to know each other better," she says.

I nod. "Makes sense."

"But he'd definitely kiss her."

Heat hits me low and hard. My gaze on her mouth, I ask, "*He* would kiss her? She wouldn't kiss *him*?"

She wets her bottom lip with her tongue. "Well, not this heroine," she says, her voice a little softer. "She's not confident enough."

"Ah." How much of Mia is in that woman? Then I do what I *have* to do and say, "We should probably get out of here."

Because we are at the beginning of our story.

But I very much want to do middle-of-the-story things with her.

She takes a long, deep breath. "We should?"

"I told Jake Turner I'd get rid of whoever was out here. There's a pretty good chance he's going to send one of his boys out here to check that no one came back."

"Oh."

"That's the thing about trespassing," I say with a small grin. "The whole point is you can't *stay*."

"Right."

I help her gather everything up and slip the food back into the thermal bag she brought along. I stretch to my feet and extend a hand to her.

She takes it, letting me pull her to stand.

We both pause, only inches apart.

If I were going to kiss her, this would be a really good time.

The position is perfect. The moment is perfect.

But I step back and motion for her to head out the door first. "I'll carry the food. Watch your footing on the steps."

She gives me a tiny eye roll and I swear, if she were my girl-friend, I'd swat her ass for it.

My palm itches with the urge.

But she passes by and I make a fist instead of putting my hand on that perfect ass.

The scent of her shampoo drifts up to me, though, and I'm pretty sure the dirty dream I'm *certain* to have tonight is going to involve spanking.

At the trucks, we both round to the passenger side of Charlie's truck. Mia takes her cap off, tossing it onto the seat and running her fingers through her long hair.

"Ugh, it's so humid out here." Then she strips the long-sleeved camo tee over her head.

My heart stops for a moment, but she's wearing a white tank underneath. She tosses the camo tee onto the seat as well.

Working on breathing evenly, I step around her to set the food on the floor, make a note to call Charlie immediately and ask what he thought was going to happen when I came out here and saw Mia with his truck, tell him that I gave Mia *insight* about her writing, and bribe him with an unlimited supply of tropical Skittles if he promises to let me in on future Mia plans to get me alone that he is privy to.

I'm so caught up in making my list that when I turn, it takes me a second to realize Mia is *right* behind me. Which puts her *right* in front of me.

I should kiss her.

I want to kiss her.

I think we're to the point where kissing makes sense. We're not going to be just friends. This might not last, but I don't think I can live without ever kissing this woman.

I think she'd like it if I kissed her.

"Mia, I—" I have no idea what I was going to say.

Because Mia mutters, "Oh, for God's sake," grabs the front of my shirt, pulls me down, and kisses me.

CHAPTER 10

MIA

THIS WAS ALL *SUCH* a great idea.

From the deer blind to having Judy have Jake call David to just freaking kissing him, I am feeling so damned *smart* right now.

Then David lifts his hands, slides them into my hair, turns me and presses me against the side of the truck, and...brilliant.

All of this is *brilliant*.

I am simply brilliant.

It's not like I'm some kind of kissing expert, but I've written a lot of great kisses. Hot kisses. Sexy kisses. Kisses that lead to a lot more.

But when I kiss David Bennett, I'm still shocked that I actually feel tingles explode in my belly and shoot down through my pelvis and then all the way to my toes.

And that's with me ambushing him.

Imagine if *he* kissed *me* with all the intention of turning me on and taking it further.

Then I start to pull back and his big hand cups the back of

my head, draws me in, and he says against my mouth, "You started this," then he tips his head slightly to the side and meets my lips again with his.

This time the tingles turn into full-blown fireworks.

His stubble abrades my skin, his lips demand mine open, his tongue runs over my lower lip before stroking into my mouth. He doesn't lean into me, but I have the definite feel of being caged in, held exactly where he wants me. Claimed.

There's no mistaking that he has taken over and answered my challenge.

If my kiss is tentative and let's-see-what-happens, his is very definitive and oh-girl-I'm-not-sure-you're-ready.

I'm not sure I'm ready either.

But I know that I don't care.

Just kissing him has the edge of excitement to it that I am craving.

I don't care if I'm out of my depth, it feels like falling without a parachute combined with the assuredness that the landing will still be soft.

That is what David does for me. Even if what we're embarking on feels new and a little scary, I know that he'll make sure I'm safe.

It's exhilarating.

And I definitely want more.

With that in mind, my hands go to his waist, and I thread my fingers through his belt loops, pulling him closer. He closes the inches between us with a groan, now pressing into me.

He moves his hands, so they are braced on the truck on either side of my head, holding himself back slightly, but not letting my mouth go. His lips press, then retreat, press, then retreat. His tongue strokes as if he needs to taste every single inch of my mouth.

I arch closer, willing to let him have whatever he wants.

His hands stay firmly on the truck though, and finally he straightens his elbows, breaking the kiss and staring down at me.

His gaze is hot, his breathing ragged.

"Well?" he asks.

"Well, what?" I ask.

"How did I do? On the book boyfriend scale?"

One of my brows lifts. Book boyfriend? How does he know that term? I laugh lightly. "Very well. Ten out of ten."

He grins. "Oh damn. Well, I guess we don't need to keep working on it then."

My grin grows, but I shake my head. "Three out of ten. Definitely lots of room to work on improving. We should practice a lot."

He chuckles, the sound low and sexy, rumbling through me and making my pussy flutter.

"No, that was an excellent first kiss," I tell him.

"Agree."

I grab the front of his shirt as he tries to step back. "But just first, right? I mean, there will be more, right?"

He lifts his hand and drags his thumb over my bottom lip. I swear my nipples tighten.

"It was nice hunting with you. I'm just sending you home with a warning this time."

"A warning? To not hunt out of season? Or trespass?"

"To not wear a lipstick the next time you and I are alone together. It makes it very obvious that I kissed you."

Then he pulls me away as he opens the door to the truck, lifts me up onto the seat, and says, "Drive back to town safely. I wouldn't want the cop to pick you up for erratic driving or speeding."

Then he shuts the door and steps back. I'm not sure what else to do, so I start the truck and shift into drive.

As I start to pull out, I see him get into his truck. He follows me all the way out onto the highway and then into Sapphire Falls. He does turn off, however, when I make the turn to go to Charlie's house to return the truck.

Charlie answers the door only seconds after I knock, obviously having seen me pull into his driveway.

He props his shoulder against the door jamb. "So how did it go?"

I hand over the keys. "He came out. We talked for a long time."

Charlie motions with his hand for me to go on. "That's it?"

"And I kissed him."

Charlie grins. "Good job."

I nod. "Then *he* kissed *me*."

Charlie nods. "Okay. That's awesome."

I tip my head. "Have you ever told him the term 'book boyfriend'?"

Charlie looks surprised for a moment then says, "I might've mentioned it. Why?"

"He just said it tonight and it seems like a strange term for him to know."

Charlie looks puzzled. "I agree. I don't know where else he would've heard it though. Maybe I said it in passing? I'm not sure."

"Well, anyway, the next date needs to involve dirt bikes or four wheelers. He says that's what he likes to do most outside. And he wants to teach me how to ride. How can we set that up?"

Charlie chuckles. "That's the easiest thing ever. We'll just have a bonfire. Invite some people out. We can ride ahead of time. That's very casual. If a bunch of people show up, it's not like your dad can think it's a date with just you and David."

"That's true." Though I have to admit that I am disappointed by the idea that we won't be alone.

"And then you guys can always linger after the bonfire," Charlie says, practically reading my mind.

I perk up at that. "That's true. Oh. Maybe I could camp out there. I have no idea how to do that. He'd have to stick around and help me right?"

Charlie laughs. "I don't think David is gonna let you camp out there."

I give him a sly smile. "David won't let me camp out there *alone*."

"There you go."

"I really do want to learn about four wheelers and dirt bikes though. Could you give me some lessons?"

"I thought you said David wanted to teach you."

"Yeah, but if I just ask him, he might say no. That kind of feels like a date. I think he's into this, but I almost feel like it's a challenge. Like he really wants me to come up with ideas and like he wants to see how far I'll go to work this out."

"I've got you," Charlie says, pulling his phone out of his back pocket.

"You can't just call him and tell him to take me dirt-bike riding," I say.

"Come on, I won't be that direct. But this is easy." He starts typing into his phone then hits send.

"What did you do?"

"I told him that I'm gonna teach you how to ride."

"What? If you teach me that he won't need to."

"Wait for it," Charlie says.

A couple seconds later his phone dings with a text. Charlie reads it, then grins. He holds his phone up to me.

The fuck you will.

Charlie laughs. "David's *not* going to let anyone else teach you to ride. So the best way to get him out to this bonfire is to tell him someone else is going to."

I feel light and warm in my chest. And lower.

David wants to see me. He wants to keep this up. And it is fun. Sure, I could probably ask him to meet me in the next town for coffee or a drink. But this is fun. I get to come up with interesting ways to steal time with him and prove to him that I really want this.

David is worth it. I want him to know that this is worth some effort.

And I have never been a pursuer before.

Who says the girl can't go after the guy?

This is good for me too. It's making me come out of my shell, it's giving me some confidence, I get to be creative, and then get the endorphins when my plan works and he's thrilled.

Not to mention the way he kisses me.

I definitely want more of all of this.

"Okay, let's do it. Thanks, Charlie. It's fun conspiring with you."

"My brother is a lucky guy." Charlie grins at me. "And you're lucky too. He's a great guy. I'm really grateful that you're showing him that."

"My pleasure." I turn to leave, but then think to say, "Oh by the way. Maybe don't read the most recent chapters of my Hot Cakes fanfic."

"Yeah? Why is that?"

"They are especially spicy. And I've had a recent surge of inspiration. Knowing what you know, you might be a little uncomfortable."

He groans as I descend his front steps. "You could've just not said that and I might not have thought of it."

I laugh. "Just don't read the most recent two chapters. Or the next several."

"I just realized that this is going to be a problem for me."

"Not sorry," I call back.

Not sorry at all.

I HAVEN'T SEEN David in four days, but we've texted every day since Friday night. And I'm having a really good time.

Like yesterday when I sent him a video of people launching dirt bikes off high ramps and flipping them in the air. I added the message, *I want to learn to do this.*

His response had been a simple, *absolutely not.*

I've been expecting that. His protective streak is wide and deep.

But then he'd followed it up with, *I like you in one piece.*

I have a feeling for David Bennett that's pretty flirtatious. Especially considering he doesn't really want to be flirting with me in the first place. Or at least he is still telling himself it's a bad idea.

It's just after lunch on Wednesday, and I'm sitting at the front desk of the library, grinning as I text him a photo of a gorgeous woman in very short denim shorts and a crop top leaning against a dirt bike. I follow it with the message, *this is what I'll be wearing Friday.*

His response is almost immediate. There are no words. He

just sends me a photo of all the protective gear I need to have for dirt bike riding and links to where to buy.

I laugh. That is far more gear than I could possibly need.

I text back. *I have no time to get all of that before Friday.*

Don't worry, I have you covered. Literally. Covered head to toe.

I am giggling but note the front door of the library opening. Dang, I have to get back to work. I tuck my phone in my back pocket and look up. Then straighten. Jack Bennett is striding toward the front desk. He has a serious look on his face.

"Hey, Jack."

"Hi, Mia."

"Can I help you with anything?"

"I hope so. I need some...resources."

I smile. "Well, you came to the right place."

He sighs. "Is there anything like librarian and client confidentiality?"

My brows arch. "There can be. What do you need help with exactly?"

"Chelsea's birthday is coming up. I want to throw her a really great party. But I have no idea where to start."

Chelsea is Jack's oldest daughter.

I smile. "You need ideas for a little girl's birthday party?"

"Well, I have an idea for it. I just don't know how to pull the idea off."

"Okay. How old is she going to be?"

I have only a general idea of how old Jack's girls are. Chelsea, named after Jack and David's mom, is middle-school-age-ish.

The second girl—her name is Rafaela, after Jack and David's dad, but everyone calls her Ray—is a couple of years younger.

The baby, Del—named after their aunt-turned-mom,

Delaney, but 'Del' so things don't get confusing—is in kindergarten. I only know that because she came into the library with her class for a school visit.

The girls have also been to the library a couple of times with Delaney, but they were pretty quiet and knew what they were looking for, so I didn't have a lot of time to talk with them. They seemed sweet and were very well-behaved, and they were talking and laughing with Delaney. I can't help but feel my heart ache when I see them, though. Losing their mom had to have been so hard. I know how it feels to have a mom one day, and then just not have her the next.

"Eleven." Jack runs a hand through his hair. "Every year they get older, they're going to get even further into things I don't understand."

I keep my expression stoic. But I feel for this guy. He was raised with all brothers. Even Delaney and Tucker's two kids that came after they adopted these four are boys. Now, he's raising three little girls on his own. It doesn't surprise me that he's feeling a little out of his depth.

"So what ideas do you have?" I ask. "What is she into?"

"That's the thing," he says. "She wants to do manicures with her friends. And face masks. It was something she used to do with her mom. I was kind of surprised. I thought maybe she wouldn't want to because it would bring back memories. But it's something she's missed doing. My mom isn't really into that stuff. So Chelsea hasn't done it since…"

He doesn't say since her mom died but he doesn't have to. My heart squeezes. I understand what he means about his mom. Delaney does home renovations and interior contracting work. She's great with a sledgehammer and can restore any piece of furniture. But manicures are definitely not her thing. Even if she was into them, it would be a waste of time and money. No way would polish last through a single workday, and I'm sure she routinely breaks nails.

"Does she want you to take her and her friends somewhere for the manicures?" I ask.

He shakes his head. "She hasn't actually asked me for it at all. I heard her talking to her sisters. They are trying to not make me feel bad." He gives me a self-deprecating smile that seems very, very weary. "Since we moved here, they spend a lot of time outside with me. We take care of the animals, go on walks, ride horses, we've even been fishing. And they like all of that. But they've definitely not played beauty salon, or done as much with their dolls, or played dress up." He shakes his head. "I know it sounds very gender specific, but those were things they did with their mom. She was a cosmetologist. She did hair and makeup and nails. The girls loved to go to work with her and they've been having their hair done and nails painted since they were little." He takes a deep breath. "The girls don't want to make me sad by asking for things their mom used to do. They try to just do things I like. It's sweet and messed up. I know that."

Oh man. I want to give this guy a hug so badly.

"So, I guess I thought if I could surprise Chelsea with this, it would show them that I'm fine with them doing those things and it doesn't make me sad. That I want them to do the things they love too."

Ugh. He's such a good dad. Because I suspect some of this *does*, in fact, make him sad.

"I can definitely help you find some things, Jack. Books and probably some videos. But do you think that the girls would like to have someone come and help them learn to do their nails with hands-on lessons?" I ask. I pause, then add, "Would *you* like to have someone come help with it?"

He blows out a breath. "I would definitely like that. But I

don't want the girls to feel like I'm making a big deal of the fact that they don't know what to do. Or that I don't."

I shake my head. "No, we could definitely make it seem casual." I pause, thinking about how David and I have used that term, too. "Do you know who's really great at that stuff?"

Jack looks at me with interest. And hope that makes my heart squeeze again. "Please say you."

I laugh and hold my hand up, wiggling my fingers and my short nails that are painted with clear polish. "Not so much. Though I do love a good manicure and face mask. But Sloan is really great at it."

"Sloan?"

"Sloan Bennett." I almost smile at his confused expression. "Your cousin. Ty's daughter."

He nods. "Right. That Sloan. I guess she is kind of my cousin. It's hard for me to keep track of all those younger kids."

And Jack and his brothers were adopted, so technically, they're not cousins. But his stepdad is Sloan's dad's brother. Whatever. Their family dynamic isn't important. "Anyway, Sloan is definitely into hair, makeup, and nails. And I think she'd love to help your girls out."

"I wouldn't want to be a bother."

"We'll just have to come up with a reason for us to be out there and for the subject to come up," I say with a shrug. "If you have some books and videos on the subject open on the table, then Sloan could say, 'Oh my gosh, I love doing that stuff' or something."

"Okay. Why would Sloan be at my mom and dad's?"

Right. Well, surely we can come up with a reason. Then, a thought occurs to me. "How about I get some books about manicures and some supplies? Then, I can deliver them. The girls will just see their friendly neighborhood librarian bringing resources. And her friend. That's really good for my branding with kids." I smile. I'm not kidding about that. The more kids like libraries and librarians and understand our superpowers, the better.

He studies me for a moment. "You would do that?"

"Sure. Why not?"

"There's no reason that you should feel like you have to help me with my girls."

"Except that I'm a nice person, and this is a really nice thing you're trying to do for your daughter, and you need some help. You came to the library for resources. I'm getting you resources."

He chuckles softly, and I'm relieved to see this clearly stressed-out single dad looking a little happier. "I feel like this is going above and beyond your librarian job duties."

I smile. "I have actually gone over to someone's house and helped them plant a garden in their backyard. I have shown up at the senior center and taught them all how to line dance. I once fostered two stray cats that someone found injured but couldn't keep themselves. I learn things and love to apply them in real life. Especially if it means that other people get to learn them too."

He shakes his head. "That is kind of amazing. And I am desperate. If you can help my daughter's birthday be amazing, I will be forever in your debt."

I grin widely. "And I also have a town full of people who owe me favors. That's never a bad thing."

Now he outright laughs, and I feel extremely proud of myself.

"That is a good point," Jack says. "Okay, you can add me to that list. When are you available?"

"How is tomorrow?" I ask.

"Really?" he asks, his eyes hopeful. "That's not too soon?"

"It's never too soon to do a good deed."

"And it's never too soon for me to start practicing painting nails," he agrees. "If I'm going to do ten manicures, I'm going to have to get good fast."

"You're going to do *ten* manicures at her party by yourself?"

"I'm sure Delaney and my grandma will help," he says.

"And Sloan and me. And I'm going to recruit some more friends. Kaelyn and Harlow for sure."

Jack's shoulders actually sag with relief. "I'm not even going to ask you if you're sure, in case you have second thoughts."

I laugh. "Why would I have second thoughts? Do you know my mom? She's a *huge* party planner. She would be ashamed of me if I *didn't* jump in and make this party over the top."

"Now I feel great about it," he says. "If it gets you proud mom points, this is definitely a win-win."

I grin. "Exactly. I'll see you tomorrow."

"You're my hero, Mia."

Jack leaves with a smile, a straighter spine, and a more confident stride.

Exactly the way I want everyone to walk out of my library.

And I can't help but think that I really like *all* of the Bennett boys.

CHAPTER 12

DAVID

ON THURSDAY EVENING, I mount the steps to my mother's front porch. As I hit the top step, her front door swings open and she steps out to greet me.

"Well, hi," she says, smiling.

I lean in and kiss her cheek. "You don't seem surprised to see me."

"Why would I be?"

I start to answer but I don't have a good response. We all stop by without notice all the time. I shake my head. "I guess you wouldn't be *surprised*. But you seem to have been expecting me."

She gives me another smile, this one slyer. "I was."

I nod. "Because Jack told you I would be stopping by."

She laughs. "Actually, Jack just told me that Mia was stopping by. *Charlie* said that meant you'd be here too."

I sigh. I shouldn't be here. It is my mother's house and I do stop by routinely, but tonight, I'm here because Mia is here. I won't lie to myself about that. Or to my mother. But I shouldn't be here because of her.

"You don't seem surprised by that either," I say to my mom.

"That you came out here because Mia Hansen is here? Should I be *surprised* by that?"

"Maybe?" Mia and I have never really spent time together before. Why does everyone seem to think this is so obvious?

"You're an incredibly intelligent person. Mia is wonderful. I'm not at all surprised that you realize that."

I shake my head. "I shouldn't be...seeing her."

My mom studies my face for a moment. "Well, you can't really help it if she's at your mother's house when you stop by," my mom says, tucking her hands into the back pockets of her jeans.

I narrow my eyes. "I mean, I shouldn't be *dating* her."

My mom gives a light chuckle. "If just running into her at your parents' house, hanging out with your brother, riding four-wheelers, and painting nails with your nieces is your idea of a date, I'm not really surprised you're still single."

I open my mouth, then shut it as her words, tone, and expression sink in.

Charlie filled her in completely. Not just that I might be interested in the fact that Mia would be here and might be stopping by, but the entire plan. That Mia is making up reasons for us to run into each other. That it's supposed to seem casual. That we're essentially sneaking around behind her father's back.

My mom is now in on it.

"I guess it's not completely out of the realm of possibility that I would run into her here," I say.

My mom lifts her shoulder. "She is the librarian helping your brother with what he needs to put together a birthday party for his daughter. And you're a good uncle. Who would care about that birthday party. Seems to me you're both just very nice people. And I like to invite very nice people to stay for dinner at my house."

Yep, she knows all about it. And evidently, approves. Of course she does. There is absolutely nothing about Mia Hansen that any parent would disapprove of.

Me on the other hand...

Then the rest of what my mother said sinks in.

"Wait, riding four-wheelers?" Surely Mia didn't tell them all about our conversation about four-wheelers and dirt bikes.

"The girls took her and Sloan out. They couldn't wait to show them how to ride when Sloan told them that Mia has never driven a four-wheeler before."

Wow, I don't have to worry about other men horning in. It's my own adorable nieces getting in the way of me getting Mia dirty in new-to-her ways.

Just then, as if on cue, I hear the sound of four-wheeler engines in the distance.

"Those girls are always on time for dinner," my mom says.

I chuckle despite myself. "Who's cooking?"

She sticks her tongue out at me. "Jack."

My mother is good at a number of things. Cooking is not one of them.

My brother isn't *awesome*, but he's okay and he's really trying. It's one of his goals to start making meals that his daughters remember and enjoy. He did help with cooking before his wife died, though he did not do the bulk of it. He handled things like pasta night and taco night. And apparently, he's great at putting chicken nuggets and fish sticks in the oven. Anything dealing with sautéing, roasting, or baking fell to Kaitlyn though.

My mom turns and heads back inside, probably to lend her help to Jack—and she's not a bad sous chef—but more likely to give me a chance to take in the sight that drives into her front yard.

It's very possible that my mom knows exactly how the sight of Mia riding a four-wheeler, her grin huge, her cheeks flushed, her hair tousled and falling around her shoulders as she pulls the helmet off her head, will hit me low and hard in the gut.

My mom and dad are madly in love. They are romantic, there's no question. And my mom has always found my dad sexy on a dirt bike.

Not that I'm thrilled to know that, and I certainly don't encourage her talking about it, but she has shared that information with us, like it or not, on more than one occasion.

Almost worse, my dad has explained how much he loved teaching my mom to ride dirt bikes, and how sexy it was to have her get interested in something he loved so much.

Now I totally get it.

I would've loved to have been there when Mia first climbed on, but it doesn't take away from how fucking gorgeous she looks now climbing off of a four-wheeler after her first ride.

The huge smiles and giggles from my nieces add to the emotion of the moment.

How can I feel so incredibly turned on by Mia and so warm and happy looking at Chelsea, Ray, and Del at the same time?

These girls have been through so much sadness and heartbreak over the past few months, and seeing them happy right now, with this woman who has been making me so happy over these past few days, sends a jolt of endorphins to my system that I can't deny.

"Uncle David!" Del calls when she spots me.

Mia's head snaps around and our gazes collide.

"Hey, kid," I say as Del runs up the steps to me. I catch her and hoist her up for a hug.

"Are you here for dinner?"

"I am."

"We're going to paint our fingernails!" she exclaims.

"No way."

"Yeah! Mia and Sloan are going to help!" She shoots a grin over her shoulder at the two women who are approaching the porch now. Del lowers her voice. "Grandma isn't good at nails, but Sloan is super good so we're going to practice with her."

I nod, unable to look away from Mia. Sloan Bennett is a gorgeous, confident, sweet woman. But she could have been approaching bare naked, or wearing a giant clown head, and I wouldn't have noticed.

"That sounds great," I tell Del, eyes locked on Mia.

"I *know*," Del gushes. "We get to do manicures for Chelsea's birthday but we need to practice! Daddy says we're going to *do all of it!*"

Charlie's text had said, *Mia and Sloan are going to Mom's tonight to do manicures with the girls to practice for C's bday. In case you find that interesting.*

I hadn't responded. But I had found it very interesting.

Obviously.

I know pretty much nothing about manicures.

I have no idea what 'all of it' means.

But I do know that Jack probably doesn't know much more than I do and I know he will want to do whatever he can to make his daughter's first birthday without her mom as good as he possibly can.

If Sloan and Mia are willing and able to help, I will be so fucking grateful.

I might just have to kiss one of them for it.

Del starts squirming and I let her down.

"Hi, David!" Chelsea, or maybe it's Ray, says running past me into the house.

"Hey," I greet.

"Hi, David," Sloan says.

"Hi," I return.

At least, I think it was Sloan. Fuck it could have been literally any other female on the planet. I don't even look. I barely register her voice.

I'm staring at Mia.

She's stopped in front of me on the porch.

My nieces have run past her. Sloan—or whoever—has walked past and into the house.

Now we're just standing here, on the porch, the two of us, staring at each other.

"Hi," Mia says.

"You let someone else take you for your first ride."

Her cheeks get even pinker than they were from the adrenaline and wind. She tucks a strand of tousled hair behind her ear. "Your nieces are irresistible."

They are. I can't really blame her.

Fuck, I want to kiss her so badly.

I've been replaying our kiss from Friday night over and over. It was, hands down, the best kiss of my life and that is a big problem.

But I want another.

"I guess I don't need to show up at the party tomorrow night now," I say.

Instead of looking disappointed or saying anything—or *begging* me to come tomorrow night—she gives me a half smile and says, "I guess I'll have to find someone else to help me set up my tent."

Then she turns on her heel and sashays into my mother's house.

I stare after her.

Tent?

There's going to be a tent?

Is that a euphemism for something else?

But I don't think it is. I think Mia Hansen is going to camp out at the river. Probably for the first time. She probably bought a tent just for this.

And probably has no clue how to set it up.

There is no fucking way anyone else is going near her tent.

Even if it is a euphemism.

And as I follow her into the house, I realize that she knew I was going to show up here tonight.

Just like she knows I'm going to show up tomorrow night.

I sigh.

Should I just accept that I'm wrapped around her little finger now or should I put up *a little* more resistance?

Like thwart her tent plan tomorrow night?

I grin as I hear her laughing with my nieces as they set the table, and feel the sound and moment reach into my chest and wrap around my heart.

Oh yes, I'm going to thwart her tent plan.

But...I'm also very much wrapped around her little finger.

CHAPTER 13

MIA

I COMPLETELY GET the attraction to single dads, or even just men being wonderful with babies and kids. I see it all the time at the library.

But I have never found a man interacting with kids as attractive as I find David with his nieces.

Of course, I already find David attractive, so that's part of it.

And his nieces really are irresistible.

Chelsea is so sweet and protective of her sisters. She had Del, the youngest, drive with her on the four-wheeler and went faster and over bigger rises and dips just to make Del laugh. She is completely tuned in to her sisters.

Ray is the wild one. I rode with her. And there wasn't a curve or ramp-like hill that she missed, and it wasn't for me. It was all for her.

Del, the baby, thinks her sisters are amazing. Only slightly less amazing than their grandma and grandpa, who are only slightly less amazing than their dad. She looks at Jack with stars in her eyes. She's the talkative one. The outgoing one. The one who asks a million questions. Questions that Chelsea patiently answers correctly, and Ray answers with outrageously wrong answers. But answers that are so wrong that Del even knows it, and laughs as if every single one is the funniest thing she's ever heard.

My two hours with them have flown by, and I wish I could come up with a reason to see them again.

But now that David is here too, I never want to leave Delaney and Tucker's house.

Unless David wants to take me to *his* house.

And it's getting worse—better?—by the minute.

Right now, the rugged, broody, over-protective game and parks officer, who looks so good in work boots, and his uniform, stomping around outdoors, is sitting at his mother's dining room table with his big, calloused hands spread on top of paper placemats, letting his youngest niece paint his thumbnail a bright fluorescent blue.

I'm painting his other thumbnail a pretty pale pink.

Which means I get to touch that big, warm, calloused hand. A lot.

I'm touching it—and his thick wrist and his muscular forearm—more than I really need to. Though I'm sure he doesn't know that. There is no way David Bennett has ever had a manicure before. But he actually needed this. His cuticles were a mess before we made him soak his fingers, then pushed back his cuticles, and trimmed them.

I did that part.

Not because I got to hold his hand and touch him even more. Okay, not *just* because of that, but because there is no way five-year-old Del could handle the cuticle cutters.

Sure, Sloan could have done it right after she did Jack's and Chelsea's. She is quick and efficient. But I wanted to do it.

Even though I'm no manicure aficionado. And even though I made two of his cuticles bleed.

He swore he didn't even feel it.

I actually believe him. Especially after he used the opportunity to tell the girls about all the different animals and bugs that have bitten him over the years.

There have been a lot.

The wide eyes and "wows" from his nieces are worth a little blood.

Okay, easy for me to say. But the girls are *very* impressed.

As am I, actually.

He might be making it all up, but I don't think so.

The guy is tough and, dammit, that's sexy. I'm a bookworm who really likes the indoors, but this guy who spends more than fifty percent of his time outside in the elements, with wildlife, really gets me going.

So, I promised him I would massage oil into his cuticles *extra* carefully after he's all painted. He gave me a lazy smile when he said, "I'm holding you to that," which made heat swirl through my stomach.

And panties.

"My mommy used to paint every one of my nails a different color."

I lift my head quickly to look at Del.

David is looking at her too. I think he's holding his breath.

I know I am.

"I couldn't pick a favorite color, and she said I didn't have to, that all colors are great and I could have all the colors," Del says, her face scrunched up as she concentrates on David's thumbnail.

I swallow and look over at Jack. He's seated across from us with Chelsea on one side, painting his right hand, and Sloan on the other, painting his left hand. The idea is that the adult woman will demonstrate painting the nails on one hand while the little girl does the other hand.

Of course, Chelsea and Sloan are now staring at Del. And Jack looks like his daughter just slapped him.

I assume they talk about Kaitlyn, but maybe he just wasn't expecting Del to bring her up so casually.

Chelsea's expression is impossible to read. I lost my mom at the same age. I know how hard it is to process that loss at an age where you're old enough to understand she's not coming back, but you're too young to really know how that's going to impact everything for the rest of your life, and you discover it over and over again.

Then I look over at the middle girl, Ray. She's on Tucker's lap with Delaney beside them. Ray already has three of her grandpa's fingers painted.

She's staring at his hand but not painting. And not saying anything.

All of the adults are staring at Del, though.

I share a look with Sloan. Her expression clearly says, "Oh my God, help, what do we do?"

I have no idea. We're the guests here.

"That sounds *very* cool, can you do that to mine?"

My eyes go to David's face. He's concentrating on his niece. He's looking at her with wide, excited eyes and a big smile.

If I weren't this close to him, I wouldn't have noticed the stiff way he's holding his shoulders or how fast the pulse at the base of his throat is pounding.

Del talking about her mom is killing him a little, but she won't see anything but happiness.

"I guess so." Del looks at me. "Can we do that many colors?"

I nod quickly. "Of course. Part of the fun of manicures is getting to do whatever you want to *your* nails. You look at them the most so they should make you smile whenever you look down."

I'm smiling widely too and praying that the little girl can't yet tell when adults are faking it 'til they make it.

Del looks up at David. "Would it make you smile?"

Oh, my god. I swallow hard.

"Are you kidding?" David asks. "Your mom was *so* cool. I want to do anything she did."

Del sits up straighter. "She was cool?"

"*Very* cool," David tells her.

"You were her friend?" Ray asks.

David looks at his other niece. "Definitely."

His neck is straining with keeping his smile in place. I can't resist—I squeeze his hand. His fingers wrap around mine immediately. Tightly.

"Your mom was so cool and so sweet," David goes on. "She always made everyone feel good and..." He hesitates.

I don't know what he's about to say, but I squeeze his hand again. He should say it. I don't know how I know that, but I do.

He takes a little breath, then says, "I miss her a lot."

Oh...

My heart flips, and I feel tears prick the backs of my eyes.

But I look at Del, and I know that yes, he definitely should have said that. These girls need to know that their mom was loved and that she's missed.

Del gives him a little smile that's sad around the edges. "I do too."

"I know you do, baby," David says roughly. He leans over and kisses the top of her head. "So I definitely want you to paint my nails with The Kaitlyn. Then I can look down and smile and think of you and her doing this together. That will make me *so* happy."

Del's smile grows.

"The Kaitlyn?" Ray asks. "What's that?"

"This nail paint," David says as if it's obvious. "You know how they sometimes name motocross tricks after certain riders who do it first or do it really well?"

I have no idea what he's talking about, but Ray nods. And I make a mental note to look up motocross and motocross tricks later.

"So this is The Kaitlyn after your mom."

Ray's smile is wide now, too.

I hear Chelsea sniff, and I have to swallow hard again as I see Jack pull her up against his side in a hug.

"That's so cool," Ray says.

"It is. Can I have that too?" Tucker asks.

"Only on one hand," Delaney says. "We've already got that hand almost done." She looks at Ray. "But you can paint mine too, if you want to."

"You're going to get your nails done?" Tucker asks, his tone teasing.

"I don't do my nails because of the manual *work* I do with my hands every day," Delaney informs him. "But the girls can practice on me."

Tucker acts offended. "I *farm*. You don't think that's manual work with my hands?"

"Sure, it is," Delaney says, patting his arm. "It's just not...*as* manual."

"What?" Tucker demands with an over-exaggerated gasp.

Delaney nods, but she's grinning now. "You have tractors and combines and all kinds of tools. You don't really get your hands in it the way I do my work."

Tucker draws himself straighter. "I'll bet your manicure lasts longer than mine does."

"I'll take that bet," Delaney says, nodding.

"But you can't smudge it or chip it or take it off on purpose," Tucker warns.

"Tucker Bennett, are you saying you think I might *cheat*?" Delaney demands.

Tucker leans in. "That's exactly what I'm saying."

Everyone is grinning now. Delaney laughs. "How are we going to keep each other honest?"

"Ray goes with you to work, and Del comes with me," Tucker says.

"Yay!" Both girls cheer.

"But you have to tell on Grandpa if he messes with his manicure," Delaney tells Del. She leans over. "And you can't let him buy you off with ice cream."

Del giggles. "I won't."

"Yes, you will," Ray says. "I should go with Grandpa, and Del should go with Grandma."

"Okay!" Del agrees.

"But you have to tell on *Grandma* then, and you can't let her buy you off with cookies," Tucker says.

Del is laughing so hard now David has to take the polish bottle from her.

And just like that, the melancholy memories of Kaitlyn pass.

We settle back in to paint nails, and everyone around the table ends up with a manicure, including at least one hand that is a rainbow of colors.

We also have an entire birthday party planned, and Sloan and I are invited and accept happily.

Chelsea also wants cupcakes in a variety of colors to go with the nail polish colors, and Delaney texts my mom to place the order from the bakery as we're all sitting together.

It occurs to me to worry that she'll say something about me being here. But then I realize that I'm here helping with manicures. It's completely innocent. David just happened to be here too. But this is hardly a date.

It still feels like a date in a strange way.

I feel closer to him than we were yesterday.

I know him better.

I definitely like him even more.

I want him more.

So when Sloan and I head out to my car and David says he needs to get going at the same time, I'm thrilled.

Sloan goes to the car, leaving me on the porch with David.

"I saw the books you brought out," he says before I can say anything.

I brought Jack an adult-focused book about nail care and manicures—we surprisingly only had one—but the other two are for kids. One is a story about an alligator getting a manicure on her day off, and the other is about how nail art, hair color, tattoos, and other personal expressions can help people enhance their self-confidence. It's more age-appropriate for Chelsea than for the other two, so I told Jack to be sure to read it first.

"Jack stopped in asking about manicures."

"I didn't realize the librarian delivered."

I smile up at him. "Now you know."

"I'll keep that in mind."

I would really love for David to 'place an order' at the library and ask me to bring it out to his house.

What books would he ask for?

I feel a curl of heat and anticipation in my belly.

That could be *really* sexy. Especially if he wants to read together. Or read out loud to me...

"Thanks for doing this," he says. "It was *really* great of you. And Sloan."

"I enjoyed it," I tell him honestly. I add, "You're a really good uncle. And brother."

"It's easy with them."

"You would do it even if it was difficult."

He shrugs. "Of course."

I know David would do anything for his brothers and, by extension, their kids.

I smile. "Can I do something I *really* wanted to do inside, but I resisted even though it was really difficult?"

He lifts a brow. "Is it a bad idea?"

"Not *bad*," I say. "But you're going to think I shouldn't do it."

He just looks at me for a long moment. Then he shocks me by saying, "Yes."

I don't give him a second to re-think it. I step forward, slip my arms around his waist, press my cheek to his chest, and hug him tightly.

I feel his surprise in the way he stiffens for a moment, but then his arms come around me and he brings me against him more fully.

I close my eyes and just absorb the moment.

"I thought you were going to kiss me," he says against my head after a few seconds of holding me.

I smile. Then realize that he said yes to that.

I tip my head back. "I'm afraid to ruin how great the kiss last Friday was."

Surprise flickers through his eyes. Then they narrow. "Excuse me?"

I fight my smile. "It was a really good kiss. I don't want to do it again and ruin it."

"You don't want to do it again?" he repeats. "Ever?"

I shake my head. "Nope."

I know he knows I'm lying.

This could go either way.

He's either going to kiss my pants off—maybe not literally on his mom's porch but *very* metaphorically—or he's going to call me on my crap.

His gaze roams over my face, almost as if he's trying to memorize my features.

Then he says, "You've got a point."

And he lets me go.

Calling me on my crap.

Got it.

I can't hide my smile.

"So I'll see you…Oh, I guess not tomorrow night. Since I don't need four-wheeler lessons." I shrug. "So, see you around sometime?" I move toward the steps.

"Yes," he says.

I look back at him.

"You *will* see me around, Mia."

And that promise sends tingles skittering down my spine and adds a bounce to my step that I can't deny even when I slide behind the steering wheel and Sloan looks over and simply laughs at my enormous grin.

The grin that doesn't leave my face on the entire drive back to town, or after dropping Sloan off, or after getting home, showering, and slipping into bed.

And definitely not after my phone pings with a text from David that reads *book delivery request from the Sapphire Falls Community Library for the following titles: Caleb's Camping Catastrophe. The Most Horrifying Camping Trips Ever.*

Then he includes *my* address as the delivery destination.

I laugh out loud as I look up both. Caleb's Camping Catastrophe is a children's book about a boy named Caleb who goes camping with his parents and hates the entire trip. The other is non-fiction and actually chronicles about fifty truly horrifying stories of real camping trips that went terribly wrong. There are four actual murders and the discovery of three dead bodies among the stories.

And I can't help it... I download both to my e-reader app on my phone because that's funny.

I wonder if David's intended outcome was for me to like him even more.

If not, he's screwing this all up.

Because I think I'm actually falling for him.

CHAPTER 14

DAVID

No bonfire or four-wheeling tonight.

I ACTUALLY HESITATE over the send button.

I look out over the bonfire site down by the river.

The bonfires have been happening in this same spot for years. Two generations of Sapphire Falls people have been cranking up the music, cracking open the jars of Booze and other drinks, and gathering around bonfires right here.

But not on nights after huge thunderstorms have pummeled the area for twelve hours straight.

The rain has stopped now, but the river is rushing only a few yards away, and the packed dirt area that was long ago cleared of grass, had an enormous fire pit dug into the center and then surrounded with cut logs, is basically a mud pit.

I knew it would be, but I drove out to confirm it before I disappointed Mia.

Yes, that's why I'm hesitating to send the message cancelling the party tonight. Because Mia is going to be disappointed.

I sigh. I don't worry about people's emotions when it comes to telling them no, they can't do something they think will be fun. I ruin people's plans all the time. I tell them they need permits to do things like hunt, fish, and boat. I make them move their campsites to safer spots or off private land to public. I cite them for drinking too much, or for making a mess, or for disturbing other people. I make them put out fires, I take fireworks away, I confiscate alcohol from minors, I write tickets for all kinds of things.

I'm a total killjoy a lot of the time.

Of course, it's all for their own good and for the good and safety of the people and environment around them.

I also spend a lot of time encouraging people to get out and enjoy nature and outdoor activities as well. And I educate them about how to do that safely and respectfully.

But yeah, often people hate to see me coming.

And I don't care.

Except when it's Mia.

I hit send and wait for her reply.

Two minutes later, the sad-faced emoji she sends me actually makes my heart squeeze.

I roll my eyes at myself and type in,

> it's a fucking mess out here. Maybe next
> weekend.

> *crying emoji*

Dammit. I know she's being dramatic on purpose. She probably had already guessed that the party would have to be postponed, but I don't like the idea that she's even a little sad.

Which is why I already have an alternate plan for tonight. For her.

Just her.

No one else is invited.

And I want it to be a surprise.

> It's not safe. You can't light a fire in that
> muddy mess anyway. And the four-wheelers
> would get stuck.

> But that's GREAT.

I frown.

> What?

> There's this hot game and parks guy who
> would have to come to my rescue and pull
> me out if I got stuck. *fire emoji*

I feel my smile even as I shake my head.

I do plan to come to her rescue by saving this night from being a total let-down. But I don't want to pull her out of the mud.

> Game and parks guys can be kind of
> hardasses about people doing unsafe things.

> Right? That protectiveness is so hot. *sweaty
> face emoji*

I study the message even as I grin. I like flirty Mia. But does she mean that? A little? Does she like my protective side?

That could be a very good thing, considering how big that side is.

> Plus, all that growliness is just covering up a
> soft side.

My brows arch. Is that what she thinks?

Well...she's right. Where she's concerned, anyway.

I don't feel soft for most of the people I'm reprimanding about their conduct, but judging by the setup in my backyard at this very moment, Mia is an exception to that rule.

> Maybe he's being soft on you hoping that will
> make you more likely to listen to him and
> follow the rules.

I know that is not at all the case. For one thing, I did not intentionally set out to be soft on her. It just happened. Despite knowing that being soft on Mia and being involved with Mia, getting closer to Mia, *liking* Mia is complicated.

For another, I don't think there's any tricking or even convincing Mia Hansen to do anything. She knows what she's doing and why at any point. I know that no matter what she's doing, she's fully researched everything about it and has resources for the various possible outcomes. My protective instincts toward her have nothing to do with her or how capable she is and have everything to do with *me*.

> Hmm...maybe that's what it is. I have to
> admit that I do like listening to him. I hope to
> have lots more chances.

And that's not flirty. That's just sweet.

She's getting to me.

> How about tonight?

I start to type a second message, trying to hint that I want to see her but not give it all away.

Her response comes before I can even type in *I was thinking...*

Yes.

I smile.

I didn't even tell you my idea.

Doesn't matter.

Fuck. I'm done for.

You're up for anything?

Yes.

That makes my thoughts automatically start down a path that is a lot dirtier and less romantic than what I've actually got planned.

Did I plan something romantic for Mia tonight?

Yes. I'll admit it. To myself only.

In fact, I'm planning for no one but Mia to know anything about it.

But yes, fuck, it's romantic. I know that. The only other way to spin it would be to insist that it's just about helping her salvage some of what she wanted from tonight.

She said she wanted to camp. I can make that happen despite the storm that tore through the area.

But the twinkle lights and movie screen I set up probably push it into 'romantic' territory.

What if there's not enough room for anyone
else?

Just you and me?

Yeah.

I'm completely fine with that.

My heart kicks. And I'm suddenly thinking about the non-kiss from last night.

I should have kissed her.

I should have kissed the hell out of her.

She's afraid to ruin the kiss from the deer stand? That's not going to happen. It's only going to get better from there.

But our next kiss *is* going to ruin something.

Like my ability to keep telling myself that this is just casual.

Like my ability to want to kiss anyone else.

So I'm going to make sure it also does that for *her*.

And I couldn't kiss her the way I really wanted to on my mother's porch with my nieces right inside and potentially running out the door at any moment and with Sloan sitting in the car.

Our next kiss will be amazing. And it will need to be in *private*.

I focus on the texts instead of jumping ahead to later tonight. When we will be together, in private.

What will we tell people if they find out we
spent time alone tonight?

I'm starting to care a lot less about that and that should be a huge red flag. But it's part of this fun little flirtatious game we're playing.

That you pulled me out of the mud.

I lift a brow.

So we'll lie?

I didn't say that.

It only takes me a second to catch on.

She is *not* going to go get stuck somewhere on purpose.

Mia, stay away from four-wheelers today.

Okay.

My eyes narrow. That answer came too quickly and it's too simple.

I don't feel reassured. I should have been more specific. Or maybe *less* specific. I should tell her not to get *anything* stuck in the mud. But I'm torn between wanting to keep her out of the mud and wanting to see what she comes up with to see me tonight.

My plans are for once I have her with me. Having this sweet, funny, smart librarian "trick me" into showing up is fun, and I've got to admit, good for my ego.

I just need to get the rest of my surprise for her set up so I can take her straight to my place after...well, whatever she comes up with.

I'm only two miles down the county road leading back to the highway when I realize that my plan is going to take even longer to implement, though.

With a sigh, I turn onto the access road into the pasture to the east and follow the three four-wheelers I glimpsed from the road.

Did I manifest them?

No. The storm brought them out.

More specifically, the storm brought the rain that made the mud that brought them out.

I know exactly what they're doing. And it's not cool.

I watch as they disappear over a rise and press the accelerator.

Yep. I know *exactly* what they're doing.

Besides trespassing on Brett Elwin's property.

I stop at the top of the small hill and throw my truck into park, getting out immediately. I'm glad I'm still in uniform. I opted for my tall boots today because of all the rain, and I'm glad I've got them on as I sink into the soft earth heading down the hill.

The kids on the four-wheelers are gunning their engines, then slamming on their brakes, spinning and sliding through the mud, throwing up water, chunks of grass, and mud every-where. Their four-wheelers sink into the mud further in some spots, and they press harder on the accelerators to climb out. They fly up out of the stickier spots, then land hard, spraying more mud, coating themselves and the riders next to them.

They're laughing and yelling over the sounds of their engines.

And I get it. It's fun. Driving fast and getting dirty. What could be better?

My brothers and I went mudding a number of times.

But then a kid in the next town was thrown off his ATV when the front tires hit a hidden rock while he was going about twenty miles per hour. He landed on his head, broke his neck, and ended up in a wheelchair. For the rest of his life.

Our parents forbade any further four-wheeler use on land we didn't know well and where we couldn't see the path.

And then we were caught mudding again. By Scott Hansen.

I thought he was going to kill us. I really did. I'd never seen him so angry.

Three days after he hauled us home for our mom and dad

to deal with—they called our grandma and grandpa too, which was even worse—Scott came to talk to me one-on-one.

He brought me out to the field we'd torn up with our four-wheelers and explained to me all the negative effects we'd had on the area.

He'd shown me how our tires had torn up the vegetation and left bare dirt that would wash into the river and impact the fish, birds, and animals that needed the river to be clean.

He explained how we'd destroyed native grasses and plants that the birds and animals needed for food and habitat, and told me that weeds and noxious plants would move in instead. He'd also shown me how we'd wrecked areas where animals built burrows and nests. He said it was possible we'd smashed eggs or demolished tunnels. He said that meant the animals would move to other areas, possibly places where they'd be less safe.

Scott had written us up, and we had to do community service. Our parents and grandparents had agreed. I remember our grandfather pushing for a stricter punishment, in fact.

Scott had assigned my community service that day: to research all the animals and birds that could possibly live in a field like the one we'd torn up and write a report on each of them. Then, I was to return to the field and see if I could find any of them.

I had done all of it. I'd found several of the animals, too.

And I'd loved every second of it.

Not that I'd ever admitted that to him.

I don't know what he said when he talked to each of my brothers, and I don't remember what their community service had been, but mine had definitely stuck with me.

I'd never suggested mudding again, and the next time my brothers brought it up—on our own land, incidentally—I talked them out of it using the information I'd learned.

I'd felt bad about the kid over in Coralville but, honestly, knowing the effect we'd had on the animals had really hit me hard.

Now I stand on the rise, hands on my hips, watching the three kids tearing up a field. I reach into my truck and lean on the horn.

One of them looks up and notices me. He pulls his vehicle over and motions to the other two. They also look up at me and stop.

"Get up here!" I bark.

They look at one another, and I brace, wondering if they're dumb enough to take off.

I've seen their ATVs now. Their helmets. I will find them.

Finally, one pulls his helmet off and says something to the other two. Then they start toward me.

When they pull up, I say, "Kill the engines."

They do.

"What are your names?"

The one without the helmet tells me. "I'm Kyle. This is Haden and Colt."

"This land yours?"

It's not. They look to be about twelve or thirteen, and Brett's kids are older than that, but it's possible they're related. It won't matter, though. I'm still giving them the spiel about why mudding is bad.

Kyle looks sheepish. "No."

"Do you know the guy who owns it?'

"No."

"So you don't have permission to be here?"

"No."

"We're just having fun," Colt pipes up. "We're not hurting anything."

"Yeah, Brett doesn't plant anything in this field," Kyle says. "It's just grass and stuff."

Ah, perfect opening.

"Well, that's not true," I say. But instead of launching into my monologue, I point. "See that ridge?"

They all look over at the slight rise about fifty yards away.

"Yeah," Kyle says. The other two nod.

"There's a fox den there. There are five pups in there. They're about four months old."

"Okay." Kyle is looking at me like I'm speaking French.

"You could be scaring them off. If you get closer, or if you drive over it, you could cause their den to cave in."

"We're pretty far from their den," Haden protests. "And we didn't come in from that direction."

"But for sure, you're messing up the nests of mice and rabbits those guys eat," I say. "And you're tearing up the grass they hide in. Grass that will keep the rain from washing down from here to their den and possibly flooding them next time." I point toward the slight valley that runs from where we are to where the den is situated.

Haden glances at Colt and then back to me. "We didn't know all of that."

I nod. "Well, now you do. Fields are never empty, and "just grass and stuff" is still important. Mudding isn't okay. Four-wheelers are great for getting to spots trucks and cars can't. But not for this."

"Fine," Kyle says. "We'll leave."

I nod. "Yeah. And you'll be doing some community service."

Kyle scowls. "What? No way."

"Oh yeah. You're trespassing and causing a disturbance."

"Come on, man," Colt whines. "No way."

"Yes," I say firmly. "I want this to sink in. You're not doing this again."

"Fine! We promise!" Kyle says.

I hear the sound of a car behind us. I turn to look.

And sigh.

It's the sheriff.

Great.

"You called the *cops* on us?" Kyle exclaims.

"No. I don't need to call the cops on you." I was handling it. "Brett probably did."

Kyle groans. "Come *on*, this is not that big of a deal."

Scott pulls up next to my truck and gets out. "Hey, guys." He comes to join us. "What's going on?"

"Nothing!" Kyle says. "Nothing is going on! We were riding around, and this guy stopped us and started chewing us out."

I open my mouth, but I guess that is one interpretation. I look at Scott and shrug. "Mudding." I gesture to the area behind the kids. The tire tracks, along with the boys, coated in mud, make it clear. "And no permission to be here."

Scott nods. "Brett called me."

Kyle throws his hands up. "It's not like we killed someone!"

Scott lifts a brow. I frown.

"I explained to you why this is a problem," I tell him. I look at Scott. "I've got it. Community service." Then I look at the kids. "This time."

Kyle mutters something I can't hear, and Colt and Haden are smart enough to just stand there looking chastised.

"Community service?" Scott asks. "Like what?"

"Park clean-up. Yard work. I don't know. That's not really my department."

He nods. "Right." He looks at the kids. "You guys can't be riding out on just any old field."

They nod. "Yes, sir," Kyle replies.

"How long have you been riding?"

"Since we were little," Colt offers. "Like six or seven years."

"When you're out in unfamiliar fields and pastures, it can be dangerous," Scott goes on. "Logs, rocks, holes, pipes. Stuff you don't know about. When you add in all the mud, it's worse. You need to stick to your own property."

Kyle doesn't like that, but he nods.

I frown. "And you need to just ride, not go tearing things up when it's all wet and muddy. For all the reasons we talked about. There are animals, birds, and plants on your property that are important too."

"Fine," Kyle says. "We get it."

I look at the other boys. They nod.

"Okay, then, I think we can say you learned from today," Scott says. "By the way, I'm really glad to see your helmets and jackets."

Besides good quality helmets, the boys are wearing thick leather jackets that will protect their skin if they fall or ride past branches or through overgrowth.

"So we can go?" Kyle asks.

"I think so," Scott says. "But remember everything Officer Bennett told you, okay? He knows what he's talking about and he's serious."

"Okay," Kyle says.

Scott looks at the other two boys. They both nod and mutter, "Okay," as well.

I stare at him. "That's it?"

"Yeah." Scott nods. "I think that's it."

The boys don't wait around to see if anyone changes their mind. They start up their four-wheelers and take off toward the road.

Which means I can immediately turn to Scott and demand, "What the hell?"

He frowns. "What?"

"*I* wanted to give them consequences. I'd already

decided on community service. Then you show up and change it? That is *not* okay, *Sheriff*. That's not how this works."

He looks seriously confused. "I was called by the property owner. Why are you here?"

"I saw them from the road."

"So you just stepped in."

"Yes. As is my *job* when I see something."

He nods in agreement. "Fine. But...I'm here."

I feel my eyes widen. "Seriously?"

He holds up a hand. "I didn't mean it like that. But Brett called me. He just wanted me to scare them off. He isn't going to want anything else to happen."

"They were *mudding*."

"I know."

I plant my hands on my hips. "That's dangerous."

"Can be," he agrees.

"And bad for...lots of things."

"Yeah. I'm glad you told them about that."

"Scott!" I finally yell. "What the hell?"

"What?"

"You hauled me and Henry and Charlie and Jack home practically by the scruff of our necks! You put it on our records! We had to do community service!"

He shakes his head. "I didn't put it on any records. And you were the only one that did community service." He points a finger at me. "And you *liked* that project."

I stare at him, speechless. What the *fuck*?

He clearly reads my confusion.

"I didn't make your brothers do anything extra. Your mom, dad, and grandparents worked them hard on the farms and we agreed that was enough. But I knew that if *you* understood why it was so harmful, you'd teach your brothers, and I wouldn't have to worry about *any* of you again." He gives me a little smirk. "And I was right."

"Seriously?" He knew that? Even back then? And my parents had been in on it? And...

Dammit, he *had* been right.

I look in the direction the boys disappeared. "And that's not worth trying with those guys?"

"They're not out here tearing things up because they love the outdoors and can't stand to be cooped up. They're just out here fucking around."

"So you don't think they'll really care what they're doing?'

He shrugs. "I think they'll think about what you said. Maybe it will sink in. But..."

"But what?" I press when he trails off.

"They aren't you."

I scowl again. "What's that mean?"

"It means, they might stop because that's the rules. Because we're around, keeping track."

"But not because they actually agree with the reasons like I did? Is that what you mean?"

He nods. "Yeah."

I shift, uncomfortable suddenly. It sounds like Scott knew me back then, saw something in me, and invested in that.

I don't want to talk about that.

Or even think about it too hard.

"You undermined me in front of those kids," I point out. I do *not* appreciate that.

"I showed them two authorities working together and cooperating. We made an important point with them, but we were also fair."

I narrow my eyes. "Don't bullshit me, Scott."

He takes a breath. "Okay. You're right. I did kind of undermine you." He meets my gaze. "But you were overreacting."

"They could have gotten hurt!"

"They still could."

"They're tearing everything up!"

"They're kids. They're going to do that."

"There is a family of foxes over there!" I point at the den.

Scott claps me on the shoulder. "That's why it's so great that you're here."

Then he turns and heads for his car.

I think about stopping him. Then realize I don't want to talk to him anymore.

I watch him drive away, lifting my hand reluctantly when he waves at me.

Fucking Scott Hansen.

I sigh and head for my truck. As I trudge through the wet grass and mud, I can't help but think about how I plan to spend my evening because of this mud.

With Scott Hansen's daughter.

I wonder how he'd feel about that.

For the first time, I *actually* wonder.

I've been hesitant to let everyone know Mia and I are seeing one another because I have beef with Scott. I don't feel like showing up at his house for dinner with the parents or spending time with him and making nice at things like a birthday party for Mia or Christmas Day brunch.

But how would *he* feel about it? Really?

I really don't fucking know.

I'm not sure he'd be thrilled. But I don't actually know how Scott feels about me. And that drives me even crazier than if I knew he hated me.

I head for my farm.

I need to put Scott out of my head, that's for sure.

I have a plan for tonight, and it's about Mia and me.

Just Mia and me.

Is that a good idea? Maybe not.

But I've already essentially told her we're going to see one another, and if her being disappointed about a thunderstorm was enough to move me to hang up twinkle lights, then there's no way I'm going to be able to cancel plans on her.

I'm going over the rest of what I need to set up and trying to figure out a way to get her out to my place, when I notice a car at the end of my mile-long drive.

But not just any car.

A silver Ford Fiesta.

I slow down, shake my head, and grin.

I guess getting her out here won't be a problem. She's just going to come to me.

Okay, then.

But as I pull up next to the car, I realize it's not stuck in the mud. It's just parked along the road.

There's also no one inside.

I pull into the end of the drive and get out.

"Mia?" I call. What the hell is she up to?

"Oh, hey!"

I turn and look down.

She's in the ditch. Knee-deep in the mud.

I shake my head. "What the hell are you doing?"

"I need someone to get me unstuck," she says, lifting a shoulder and giving me a grin.

I want to kiss her so badly.

I want to stomp down into that ditch, haul her sweet ass out of the mud, and kiss her.

But once I start, I don't want to have to stop.

"Okay," I tell her. I start back for my truck.

"Um, David?" she calls after me.

"Yeah?" I stop at the driver's side door.

She's still standing in the ditch. "Where are you going?"

"I have something I need to do up at the house. I'll be back."

"You're going to leave me here?" she asks, her voice rising a bit.

"Yep. For a few minutes."

"I'm actually really kind of stuck," she says, trying to lift one foot. Her foot comes out of the mud, but she's only wearing a sock. "My boot is definitely stuck in there."

I give her a grin. "Good."

"*Good?*"

"Yeah. We're definitely not going to have to lie about me pulling you out of the mud this way." Then I slide behind the steering wheel and head up to my house.

CHAPTER 15

MIA

HE LEFT ME.

Stuck in the mud in the ditch outside his house.

I can't believe he actually left me.

I slide my foot back into my boot. I look around. I pick my other foot up, but the same thing happens. The mud traps the boot, and my stockinged foot slides out.

This mud is *really* sticky.

I eye my car. It's only a few yards away. I could make it if I leave my boots behind.

I look toward the drive that leads to David's house.

He'll come back. He's not going to leave me out here.

I'm pretty sure.

I smile as I remember the look on his face when he turned and saw me down here in the ditch.

He was happy to see me.

Yeah, he'll come back.

I'm just not sure how long it will be.

I decide to start plotting the next scene in my story to kill time. I left my phone in my car, so I'm just standing out here in a short-sleeved sundress and these boots. I can't type or dictate any notes. But I can at least get a few ideas going.

After David *didn't* kiss me last night, I was inspired to write a scene between my two main characters where *they* kissed. I made the scene everything I'd wished the scene with David could have been.

I'd also made it so there were no family members just inside the house or a friend sitting in the car, so it had gotten steamy and inappropriate for a sweet front porch.

It was awesome.

It feels like an hour, but it is probably only ten minutes later when David drives back down his long lane.

On a four-wheeler. Wearing hip waders.

I grin as he pulls up next to my car. I watch as he opens the car door, pulls my bag and my keys out, locks the door, and puts the bag with the keys inside, in the storage compartment of the four-wheeler.

Then he climbs down into the ditch.

"You came back," I say.

"Of course, I did."

"What if I'd left?"

"I wasn't worried. You're basically stalking me," he tells me. But then he lifts his hand and tucks a strand of hair behind my ear. "But I would have come after you."

My heart suddenly flips over and starts beating harder. "You would have?"

"Yeah. I went to a lot of work, and I'm not going to sit out in my backyard by myself."

"You went to a lot of work in your backyard?" I don't know what that means.

"I did. And it's a good thing you can't tell anyone about the time we're spending together, because my brothers would definitely figure this out if they heard what I did."

He's still got his hand against my face even though that piece of hair is secure. I turn my cheek slightly, pressing into his palm, loving the feel of him touching me. "Figure what out?"

His voice drops. "That this isn't so casual after all."

My heart is galloping now.

And I really need to see his backyard, apparently.

"What did you do?" I ask. "That will be so obvious to your brothers?"

"Why don't I just show you?"

"Okay. I guess I—"

But before I finish whatever I was about to say, David's big hands are on my waist and he's pulling me up, out of the mud. And my boots.

Without boots on, I have two choices: step down into the mud in my socks, or wrap my legs around David.

I choose the latter.

And he doesn't seem to mind.

His big hands cup my ass as if that was what he intended for me to do and he grins at me. "Hang on tight."

I wrap my arms around his neck and try to grin back.

But my brain doesn't have enough synapses available to form a smile. It's too busy cataloging everything about being pressed up against, wrapped around, and carried by David Bennett.

The overall summary? It's *very* nice.

He strides up out of the ditch with me in his arms and goes straight to the four-wheeler. He deposits me on the seat.

At least, he bends over to deposit me on the seat.

I make it difficult to actually do the depositing, though, because I don't let go of him.

Why would I? He's big, and hard, and warm, and my entire body wants nothing more than to be as *against* him as I can get.

"Uh, Mia?"

"Yeah?"

"You gotta let go so I can go get your boots."

"What boots?"

He chuckles, and with him so close, the low sound vibrates through me.

"We're just gonna stay here like this all night?" he asks. "I like this, but I had bigger plans."

I like the sound of that. I pull back slightly to look into his eyes. "I'm intrigued."

His gaze drops to my mouth, and I feel heat slide through me.

"And if I stay this close to you, I might kiss you. Wouldn't want to ruin the memory from the deer stand."

I deserve that, considering my sassy remark last night. "I'm starting to think it might be worth the risk," I tell him.

He takes a short breath. "I'm glad to hear that. But maybe we should go up to the house."

That seems like a great idea. I lean back further. "Okay."

He stands staring down at me for a moment, his hands braced on the seat on either side of my hips.

Then he mutters something that sounds like dammit before leaning in and pressing his lips to mine.

And just like that, I'm convinced that stopping this to go up to the house is a terrible idea.

I slip my arms back around his neck and arch closer, tipping my head as one of his hands slides from the seat over my hip, up my side, to the back of my neck. He holds me still as he deepens the kiss, his mouth opening, and his tongue seeking entrance. I readily part my lips, and he groans.

He tastes my mouth fully, and I deeply regret not kissing

him last night. I won't make that mistake again. I now hope that David Bennett will kiss me every single day for the rest of my life.

That realization slams into me, and I jerk back.

I blink up at him, breathing quickly. *Oh crap.* I am falling into this head over heels. I'm thinking things like *the rest of my life* on our *second* kiss.

That is not good.

Yes, he just hinted that this is feeling less casual to him, but that doesn't mean that he's thinking in terms of never kissing anyone else again.

I take a deep breath as I try to calm my heart rate and spinning thoughts.

He seems to be studying my eyes.

"You okay?" he asks.

I nod quickly. I'm not *not* okay. I realized what was happening and I stopped it. I'm aware that I'm going too fast. I'm not blindly falling in love. I'm not broken-hearted.

Yet.

David Bennett probably kisses every woman the way he just kissed me, and as long as I understand that and don't get caught up in thinking this is like my fanfiction, where everything works out the way I want it to, then I'll be fine.

"Yeah. I'm definitely okay," I say, giving him a wobbly smile.

He doesn't look entirely convinced. "You still want to go up to my house?"

So much that I probably should say no, actually. But I nod. "Yes." I want to see this backyard surprise. I want to spend more time with him. I *do* want to kiss him some more. I just need to keep my thoughts and feelings about it all realistic.

The way he smiles at my answer does not help me feel any less oh-crap-I-want-so-much-more-than-I-expected.

He pushes away from me, shoves a hand through his hair as he studies me for another moment, then turns and climbs back down into the ditch to retrieve my muddy boots.

He somehow straps them into the back of the four-wheeler, then comes around to climb on. But not before he eyes my bare legs beneath the skirt of my dress.

"Not really four-wheeler attire," he comments.

"I got a very firm text from Game and Parks saying that tonight wasn't a good night for four-wheeling."

"I see. And you're such a good listener, huh?"

I grin. "Of course. Sweet, introverted, unassuming librarian, remember?"

One of these days, I might shock him and tell him about my fanfiction. He'd see a whole new side of me.

And possibly run for the hills.

He'd realize then that flirting and banter and *kissing* the way he just kissed me is serious stuff in my world.

Your fantasy world. Your imagination. Get a grip.

"Right. Well, Miss Sweet Librarian, you're going to have to be a little less than lady-like for a few minutes and straddle that seat."

That sounded very dirty. I can't help it. I know he means it literally, but my whole body is hot and tingling after that kiss, and David has absolutely been the inspiration for several recent dirty scenes I've written.

Knock it off. You're not falling in love with him and you're not going to mentally fuck him all night. He's being a good guy, and you're having fun, and sure, the kissing is great, but it's just kissing to him, and he's not trying to seduce you.

"Got it," I say, making my voice as normal as I can. I hold my skirt down between my knees and throw one leg over the seat, showing nothing inappropriate.

He looks like he wants to say something but thinks better of it and simply climbs onto the four-wheeler in front of me.

"Hang on tight," he tells me for the second time tonight.

I would love to hear him say that to me in bed.

Knock it off, for fuck's sake! I tell my inner hussy.

But she won't be silenced. As David starts the four-wheeler and the engine rumbles beneath us, I have to wrap my arms around him again, now from behind, pressing up against the hard, bunching muscles of his back. My earlier story plotting takes a sharp turn into another sex scene, this one happening on the back of a four-wheeler.

I wonder if that's possible.

I'll have to look it up.

Or you could just ask David. See how he responds to that question.

I sigh inwardly. I can't shut this voice up.

It's going to be a long night.

It's only a mile up to David's house, which takes us just a couple of minutes, and yet that entire scene is full and vivid in my mind by the time we get there. My imagination doesn't seem to care if it's *possible* to have sex on a four-wheeler. It happens in graphic detail in my head.

It can't be that different from doing it on a chair. He's sitting on the seat, the woman is on his lap. She could face forward or face him. Facing him would be more fun...

I hope David thinks that the pink in my cheeks is simply from the humid August air.

He pulls into the garage attached to his house, and I notice that his truck is missing.

David shuts off the engine, climbs off, and sheds the hip waders—which is far sexier than it should be considering they're green rubber and covered in mud—leaving him in blue jeans and a plain dark gray T-shirt. Then he holds out a hand to me. "Come on."

I take it and he helps me off, then opens the storage compartment and retrieves my bag. "I'll hose your boots off later," he says. "I wanna show you something."

I'd forgotten about my boots. And my bag.

He leads me through the huge garage that houses another truck and an enormous workbench with numerous tools hanging on the wall over it, stacks of wood next to it, and a circular saw attached to one end. He heads for a door that I assume leads into the backyard.

I am so ready to see whatever the surprise is that would immediately tip off his brothers that he's not feeling casual about me.

What does that even mean exactly? Not casual. That's not 'just friends'. That's not 'you're nice but I don't want to kiss you'. He clearly does want to kiss me. But not casual doesn't mean he's going to get down on one knee.

Should I just ask him?

I could just ask him.

We're in our thirties for fuck's sake. I shouldn't be wondering about and analyzing every word he says, and I shouldn't be having arguments with myself about my feelings.

He pushes the door open and ushers me through. I step onto a stone pathway that runs alongside a deck built onto the back of the house.

Yes, I should just ask him what he means. We should talk about what's going on. I should tell him that I'm developing feelings and let him decide if that means this is over or if he wants to keep going and see what happens.

He takes my hand and tugs me along the path, past the deck and into the backyard.

That's a good plan. I'll tell him how I'm feeling. I'll say

something like 'David, we should talk. I really like you, I've been having a lot of fun, and our kissing has made me realize...'

I forget everything I was just thinking when I step past the deck and see his backyard.

Because...yeah, this isn't just casual.

David might just be an amazing kisser, and other women might have been kissed the way he's kissed me, but I do not think he's done *this* for a lot of other women.

I look up at him, unsure how to respond.

He gives me a grin. "You said you wanted to camp. It's way too wet and muddy, but I had to figure out a way to make it happen."

I swallow hard. *Be cool. Do not tell him you're falling in love with him.* I nod. "Not to mention you probably have fewer serial killers and dead bodies here."

Okay, good. That was good. That was *not* a sweet, romantic, clingy thing to say to the man who has his pickup parked in his backyard, tailgate down, an air mattress filling the back, and piled with multiple blankets and pillows.

The truck bed is facing the deck, where he has mounted a white sheet between two poles and has a projector sitting on a small table, pointing at the make-shift movie screen.

There are six more poles surrounding the truck with fairy lights strung between them, forming a soft white light canopy over the truck.

The sun has not fully set, so we're going to be able to see the gorgeous colors of the sunset off to the west, and once darkness falls, I can only imagine how gorgeous the starry sky overhead is going to be.

It looks incredibly cozy and comfortable, and it's thoughtful and definitely romantic.

But despite my talk of dead bodies, David chuckles. "Yes. Camping can be harrowing at times."

I snort. Dealing with a serial killer seems a little beyond harrowing, but I love his sense of humor. Not only did he send me that book, but he also finds it amusing that I read it, and we can joke about it.

"Are you trying to tell me that camping isn't always like this?" I ask him, gesturing toward the truck, fairy lights, and pillows.

I'm still gobsmacked but trying to be cool. And not throw myself at him.

"It is not."

"So after this, I may never want to camp any other way." I meet his eyes. "You might ruin me."

A sentence has never felt truer. In so many ways.

His eyes flare with heat, and his smile has a wicked edge. "Maybe we should just make a rule that you always go camping with me. Whatever you want to try, I'll make it happen."

Okay, come *on*. He had to mean that in a dirty way, right? That can't be entirely my imagination.

I squeeze my thighs together and swallow hard.

Stop. It.

He's being sweet right now. But he doesn't actually mean that if I want to go camping in Yellowstone National Park five years from now, he'll be up for making that trip with me. 'Not casual' and 'forever' are two very different things.

"That's a big promise," I finally say. My voice sounds funny.

He moves a little closer. "You're right. How about we see how this goes and how I do with this first camping attempt? Then you can decide what comes next."

There's a lot of underlying meaning behind his words. He's not talking just about camping. He's saying I get to decide what comes next in general.

But do I? What does *he* want? Does that mean he wants

whatever I do? What if I want something serious and long-term?

He wanted tonight to happen. He could have used the storm as an excuse not to see you.

It really hits me for the first time that he set this night up. And what that means.

He didn't have to. The storm cancelled the bonfire, and that would have been the perfect excuse to not see each other tonight if he didn't want to. If he was just humoring me with all of this 'running into each other casually'. If he wasn't enjoying it as much as I have been.

He did want to.

He not only wanted to, but he also set the whole thing up. He didn't just go along with some plan I came up with, like the bar, the deer stand, or the bonfire tonight. He turned his back-yard into a cozy, romantic 'campground' for just the two of us.

He didn't have to show up to paint fingernails either.

No. No, he didn't.

I let that realization really sink in.

David wanted to see me tonight. He wanted to spend time with me. Just the two of us.

I look toward the pickup.

"Are there going to be s'mores?" I finally ask, hoping my voice doesn't sound too scratchy.

He scoffs. "Please. What kind of camping would it be without s'mores?" He pauses. "I'm almost afraid to tell you..."

"What?" I ask, probably too eagerly.

"I've got *three* kinds."

My eyes widen. "Three kinds of s'mores?"

He nods.

"Oh my god."

His smile turns into a full-on smirk. "Yeah, but maybe we should just stick to the classics. Wouldn't want to *ruin* you."

I want you to ruin me.

I can't say that out loud. But I have to press my lips together to keep it from spilling out. I get myself under control, then say, "Yeah, that might be best."

Then, much to my delight, he shakes his head. "On second thought, I'm pulling out all three. I don't want you to ever eat a s'more again without thinking of me."

And yeah, this isn't casual, there's nothing I can do about my feelings, and I might already be ruined.

"HOW HAVE you never had a s'more made with chocolate chip cookies?" I ask as Mia makes a second one with cookies instead of graham crackers. This time, she also slides a peanut butter cup into the middle instead of the classic milk chocolate square.

There are several other variations I've tried over the years, and now I can't wait to show them all to her. She's like a little kid who just discovered marshmallows.

"I don't know," she says around a bite of chocolate and peanut butter. "We didn't go camping, and the few times I've had s'mores have been at bonfires, and we just do the basics."

I shake my head and turn my attention to the marsh-mallow I'm heating over the small propane stove. I made a table out of a long piece of wood that rests on either side of the truck bed. We're sitting on the air mattress, propped against the pillows resting on the cab of the truck, with the 'table' pulled across our laps. The stove, the s'mores ingredients, and bowls of plain and white cheddar popcorn are spread in front of us along with a thermos of hot chocolate—

yes, despite the eighty-degree August night—and a thermos of lemonade. I've also got water and soda in the cooler on the tailgate.

Is it overkill? Probably. But I don't know what Mia likes. Yet.

I've already figured out that she prefers sweet snacks to salty and that she likes natural disaster movies. She chose *Twisters* over the rom com *Anyone But You,* but she did approve of Glen Powell being the star of both. And she mentioned we could watch them both tonight.

Which means she's all for staying longer.

Which made me happier than I'd expected.

I intend to know *all* her preferences, but knowing everything about her will take time.

That's called dating.

Yep.

It sure fucking is.

Which means we're going to have to talk about what this is going to be and how we're going to let people know.

Because I want to date Mia Hansen.

Publicly.

We're only a third of the way through our first-ever movie together, and I know I want to keep doing this for a very long time.

Forever.

I ignore that word flitting through my brain. That's an over-reaction. There's no reason to think in those terms right now. We don't have to label this.

I just want to watch a lot more movies with her, eat a lot more snacks with her, and kiss her *a lot* more.

"If I'm honest," I tell her. "I would be happy with just the toasted marshmallows."

"It is hard to beat those," she agrees.

I move the perfectly golden marshmallow away from the flame and pull it from the end of the skewer.

Suddenly, Mia's hand is wrapped around my wrist, and she pulls my hand toward her mouth.

I, of course, let her. If she wants any part of my body near her mouth, I'm on board.

With an impish smile, she takes the marshmallow from my fingers with her teeth. But the crispy outer layer pulls off, and she has to close her lips around the gooey melted marshmallow inside to keep it from dripping. That means her lips also close around my fingertips.

That also means heat and lust immediately shoot through me.

My gaze locks on her mouth. And my cock jumps as her tongue drags over my fingers, licking the melted sugar from my skin.

I reach over and push the long board-slash-makeshift table away from us. I turn more fully toward Mia and cup the back of her head. Her big green eyes are locked on mine as she licks the rest of the marshmallow from my fingers. I drag my wet index finger over her bottom lip, and her breath catches.

"The tornadoes rip up a lot of shit, but they survive, the experiment is a success, and they fall in love," I tell her. We're watching *Twisters*.

She swallows. "Okay. Why are you telling me that?"

I give her a slow smile. "Because we're going to miss the rest of the movie."

"Oh."

Then I kiss her.

She immediately opens her sweet mouth.

It's literally sweet now. She tastes like chocolate, sugar, and cookies. I like all of those things. But fuck, this woman is the most delicious thing I've ever tasted.

And I want so much more.

I meant it earlier when I told her that she gets to decide what comes next. In every way. But I'm done saying stupid shit like 'casual' or thinking this is short term or that we're just becoming friends.

I want her.

However she'll let me have her.

For however long.

I taste her mouth fully, loving the way she meets my energy perfectly. She kisses me back with enthusiasm, arching closer, her tongue seeking mine, her fingers gripping my shoulders. Her little hums of pleasure fire my blood, and I need her closer.

As if reading my mind, I feel her shift. She pulls her mouth from mine, reaches over and pushes the board with our snacks even further toward the end of the truck, then slides into my lap, straddling my thighs.

My hands settle on the bare skin of her legs, exposed when her dress hikes up, and she cups the back of my neck with both hands, linking her fingers.

Then she kisses me again.

Our mouths are hotter now, the kiss immediately deeper and more urgent.

I run my hands up and down her smooth, bare thighs. She grinds closer. She's not up against my cock. Fortunately. If she were, she'd not only feel how hard I already am for her, but there would be one of two results. Either I'd flip her to her back and make this first make-out session into something far more intense. Or I'd come in my pants in a way I haven't since I was a teen.

Neither is ideal.

This is our first official date.

And I don't intend for either of those things—

"I have an IUD."

I pull back so I can look up at her.

Did she just say…

She nods. "I have an IUD. So no worries about birth control. I mean, condoms are important for other reasons. If you want to use those, I'm good with that. I got negative results the last time I tested, but it's been a long time. But I also haven't had sex in a long time. Even longer than since I got tested. Obviously. I mean, that's the point of testing, right? Anyway, I'm fine with condoms. But just wanted to let you know the birth control thing is covered."

It would really help if more of my blood flow was going to my brain. I would be much more able to have rational, mature conversations if my entire existence wasn't focused on this woman's body and my cock at the moment.

Of course, this topic *is* related.

I clear my throat. "Okay." I nod. "Yeah. That's good. We should talk about that. I guess."

She nods. "We should. I know it's not romantic, and it kind of kills the hot vibe a little. But we should talk about it before we take our clothes off, because then it will get much more difficult to remember details other than how much I want to lick you all over."

My brain is still a little slow, but my cock reacts to her words.

I don't know why this surprises me. Nothing about Mia has been what I expected from the very first minute.

I run my hands from her calves up to her thighs, squeezing gently. "You go from zero to sixty, huh?"

She gives me a mischievous grin that makes my cock ache. "If you think we were at zero prior to right now, we are definitely not on the same page."

I slide my hands up further under her skirt, and the soft cotton of her dress against the back of my hands is strangely hot. I cup her ass encased in the warm silk of her panties. I squeeze. "Oh, we're on the same page. But maybe not exactly on the same paragraph."

"Which paragraph are you on?" she asks, her fingertips sliding up and down the back of my neck.

I desperately want those hands on the rest of my body.

"I just think you jumped ahead a few paragraphs. I'm still back on the one where we make out heavily, and I get to run my hands and mouth over all of these sweet curves right here in the back of my pickup."

Her smile is playful, pleased, and sexy as hell.

"Well, I wasn't going to just unzip you and climb on."

I tip my head back and groan. I wonder if I'll ever get used to the impulsive things that come from this woman's mouth. I kind of hope not.

"I don't think our sweet little town knows how naughty our quiet, cardigan-wearing librarian is," I tell her, lifting my head to meet her gaze again.

She leans in and presses her lips to mine, then kisses along my jaw until her mouth is against my ear. Then she says, "I don't think you do either."

That's it. Mia Hansen wants to play? We are definitely going to play. With my hands still on her ass I suddenly twist, and tip her onto her back. She gives a little gasp and giggle that I fucking want to bottle so I can replay it fifty times a day.

I reach over and turn off the propane stove, then lift a foot and push the table the rest of the way down to the end of the truck.

I focus on her again. Her lips are parted and she's breathing faster, her cheeks flushed pink. I've never seen a more gorgeous woman in my life.

"There, plenty of room now."

She reaches her arms up over her head so she's fully

stretched out beneath me. "Good. No reason you can't get at every inch then."

I give a growl and lower my mouth to her neck. "Be careful what you wish for," I say, giving her throat a little nip.

I feel the shiver that goes through her body and the way she arches slightly closer. "Oh, David, you have no idea what kind of wishes I wish."

I kiss the spot I nipped before kissing along her collarbone and then down to the top of the bodice of her dress. "I would very much like to hear these wishes. In graphic, dirty detail."

I'm really going to have to tell her that I have read her fanfiction one of these days and have a pretty good idea how her dirty mind works.

But I would love to hear it out loud straight from the source right now.

"Unbutton my dress," she tells me without hesitation.

The dress has sweet little buttons that fasten from between her breasts to about where I suspect her belly button will be. And they're not just buttons, they're little white flower-shaped buttons. Because, of course they are.

I love these innocent touches that cover this mischievous, naughty woman.

I shift so I can lean onto one elbow next to her. "You'll have to help me," I tell her.

Again, without even a pause, she lifts one hand and together we begin undoing the buttons. We quickly reveal the simple white bra underneath, and for some reason, I love the fact that it's white and unadorned, with not even a lacy edge.

She pulls one side of the bodice open, and I spread the other away from her breasts.

I rest my hand on her stomach, my rough, tanned skin a stark contrast to the smooth creaminess of her stomach.

"Now what?" I ask.

"My bra has to go," she says. But of course, she doesn't stop there. "I want your hands and mouth on my breasts. On my nipples."

My erection presses insistently against my zipper hearing her say 'nipples'.

"Unhook it for me," I tell her.

She arches her back and reaches underneath for the tiny hooks. The moment the clasp gives, I reach up and drag it down and away from her perfect breasts.

"Damn, you're so fucking gorgeous," I tell her. I'm unable to come up with pretty or even graphically dirty words. I just tell her the honest truth.

"Touch me, David," she says, her voice breathless.

I slide my hand from her stomach to her right breast. I groan as she gasps.

I knead gently, then run my thumb over the hard tip.

She squeezes her thighs together and sighs. "Yes, like that," she tells me.

"So pretty," I say.

"More."

Gladly. "I like the one-word answers, sweetheart. You don't have to say anything complicated. Here's all I need—kiss, suck, lick, touch, squeeze, pinch."

Her chest is rising and falling with her rapid breathing. "Lick."

God, I like this girl. I lean over and flick my tongue against the breast I'm not holding. She moans, and I give her a longer lick, dragging my tongue against the pert tip.

"Suck." Her voice is needy.

I do as she demands. Happily. As I suck on her nipple making her whimper, her fingers sink into my hair, holding my head closer. "David."

Oh yes, I love hearing my name like that.

I need to see her face. I look up, replacing my mouth with my fingers, rolling and plucking at the nipple.

"Did I say squeeze instead of suck?" she asks.

I smirk. "You did not. I've decided to add to the rules. Besides giving me verbs, you need to give me nouns." I pinch her nipple a little harder, and she gasps. "Tell me where too."

She wets her lips and nods. "Stomach."

Excellent. She knows exactly the direction I want to move.

I drag my mouth along the valley between her breasts, down the center of her torso to her belly button. Then I pause, hovering.

"Kiss," she tells me.

I press a long, open-mouth kiss just above her belly button. But I don't give her any tongue or suction. She didn't say lick or suck after all.

"Lower," she says.

I don't lift my mouth, sliding my lips along her silky, soft skin to just above her panty line. Again, I pause.

"Kiss."

I do, though it is difficult to keep from licking.

Her hand slides out of my hair, and then she's reaching up under her skirt. Her panties move away from my lips as I shift slightly to give her room to remove them. When she pushes them as far as her knees, I decide to be a gentleman and help her out. I reach up under her skirt, grab the top of the scrap of silk, and drag it the rest of the way down her legs.

"Thanks," she says with a smile.

"Always happy to help."

Then she drops her hands to the skirt of her dress and starts bunching it up.

I find myself holding my breath, waiting for her to expose herself to me. She does so unabashedly. Her skirt bunches around her waist, and as her gorgeous lower half comes into view, she bends one knee and lets it fall out to the side.

I can't breathe. It's not how beautiful and sexy she is, though both are certainly true, but it's that she's here with me like this. Not shy, not hesitant, happily baring herself, being vulnerable with me. She's eager, wanting me as much as I want her.

"Fuck." I take in the sight of her lying in the back of my truck, rumpled, her dress unbuttoned, and her skirt hiked up. Her hair is spread around her head, the long tresses wild. Her eyes sparkle in the white fairy lights draped around us. And most of all she looks excited yet content.

She's happy to be here. There is no second-guessing.

I run my hand from her ankle up her leg until it's resting on her outer thigh. My thumb rests in the crease of her hip.

"Kiss," she says softly.

I lean in and kiss her inner thigh.

She sucks her belly in and her hand slides into my hair again.

"Higher," she directs. "Kiss."

I shift, pressing a kiss to her mound, breathing in the scent of her arousal, the summer air around us, the popcorn, the lingering scent of chocolate, and what I can only label as intense, spicy anticipation.

"Lower."

My gaze latches onto hers. I move my mouth lower, hovering just over her clit.

"Lick."

I keep my eyes on hers as I lean in and touch the tip of my tongue to her clit.

"Yes," she says, practically whispering. Her fingers tighten in my hair. "Again."

I shift, one hand sliding beneath her ass, the other moving to spread her open.

"You're a fucking dream," I tell her before I lean in and drag my tongue over her fully exposed clit. Firmly.

She cries out my name and I've never heard anything more beautiful.

She doesn't have to ask me to do it again. I lick again, then again.

Then she says raggedly, "Suck."

Fuck yes.

I suck on her hard and slide a finger into her tight, wet heat.

"David!"

Her hips lift up and I squeeze her ass as I bring her even more firmly against my mouth.

I don't need any further direction. I lick, suck, and pump my finger deeper.

"Yes! Oh yes!" she encourages me.

I did not intend for this to happen tonight. I knew it was a possibility, and I wasn't opposed to it, obviously, but I had no expectations. But now that Mia Hansen is wild and wanton in the back of my truck, nothing could keep me from staying right here as long as she needs me.

It turns out that is only about another minute.

I slide another finger into her, curl my fingers, and suck hard, and suddenly she's coming apart.

She pulls my hair as she cries out, her pussy clenching around my fingers, her body lifting closer to my mouth and then sagging against the air mattress.

I lift my head, focused on her face.

She's breathing hard, and she has thrown an arm over her eyes.

"Mia?" I ask when she doesn't say anything or move for nearly thirty seconds.

"Oh my God," she groans.

That's not a good, happy groan.

I pull my fingers from her sweet pussy and shift, stretching out along her side, running my hand over her hip and squeezing gently.

"Are you okay?" Suddenly, I'm concerned. Is she regretting this? Did I hurt her somehow?

"I have never... I can't believe..." She moves her hand from her face and looks up at me. "I'm sorry."

I stare down at her. "*Sorry?* For what?"

"That I... God, you must think..."

She starts to cover her face again, and I grab her wrist, pulling it away. I lean over her, our gazes locked.

"Talk to me. What's going on?"

"I've never come like that. That fast and easy. I'm so sorry. That should've lasted longer."

I feel my eyes widen. "Are you seriously apologizing to me for coming?"

She squeezes her eyes shut and nods. "Yes. God, how embarrassing."

I reach up and grasp her chin. "Mia, look at me."

Her eyes open, but she pulls her lower lip between her teeth.

"That was amazing," I tell her firmly. "I fucking loved that. If you're telling me that I just made you come more easily than you ever have before, that does nothing but make me happy and, honestly, feel a little cocky."

She frowns but then laughs lightly. "Really?"

"Are you kidding? Making you feel good like that is everything. There is absolutely nothing for you to apologize for."

"It's just been a while," she says. "And honestly, no one has ever done that to me that easily. It always has to be full-on sex for me to orgasm, and then I usually have to…" Her voice gets quieter. "Help things along."

I feel my grin grow, and I couldn't have stopped it if I wanted to. "Not helping the cocky thing at all. I am feeling very good about myself right now."

Now her laugh is louder and more genuine. "Really? Well, I guess gold star then."

"Do you really not know that that makes me feel really good?"

"You didn't get to feel anything," she protests. "I haven't even touched you. You don't even have your shirt off." She says it slightly outraged, as if she's just now realizing it. "As a matter of fact, I think you should take your shirt off right now." Her hands go to the bottom of my T-shirt and start to tug.

I circle her wrists and stretch them back up over her head, pressing them into the mattress. I lean over until our noses are almost touching. "We have plenty of time for all of that. Making you feel good, making you come, that's what that was all about for me. I'm fine. I am good, in fact. Let's just take a minute here."

She pauses, and I hope that my words are sinking in. Finally, she takes a long deep breath and seems to relax against the mattress. I brush her hair back away from her face and then run my hand down her side to her hip, pulling her in against my body. "Just to be very clear," I say. "I'm having a very good time."

She laughs. "Me too. Though I feel like it is very clear."

I chuckle. "Yes. Very clear. And thank you for that."

I lie looking down at her and feel something warm and strange in my chest.

I have been very fond of women before. I've even thought I was in love a couple of times. But everything with Mia feels different. New. Bigger and better.

And I am suddenly hit with the realization that now, as of tonight, now that I've had my hands and mouth on this body, now that I've made her come apart, and now that she's been vulnerable like this, and we have shared this very intimate moment, I'm not getting over this.

I'm not getting over *her*.

If we actually have sex, I will be in very, very deep.

Too deep.

I probably already am.

With Scott Hansen's daughter.

There are some things I need to come to terms with before I go any further and let Mia think this is more serious. Okay, before I let *myself* think this is more serious. It's only fair to both of us that I make sure I can deal with everything that would come with a relationship between us.

Like not liking my would-be future father-in-law.

"So about taking your shirt off..." she says.

I shake my head.

"A lot of the fun of sex is the anticipation. The buildup. The foreplay. How about we take a rain check on me losing my clothes?" I ask.

I don't want to not sleep with her. I just need to be fully honest about what this means. First with myself. Then with her.

But yeah...first with myself.

Do I want to do this?

With her lying here, sweet and amazing and post-orgasmic, yes. But I need to be sure. And maybe not pressed right up next to her near-naked body when I decide.

Her eyebrows arch. "I don't even get to look at you naked?"

I chuckle. Yeah, slowing things down is a good idea for my common sense...and my heart...but it might be fun too. I nod. "Yeah, I think I'm gonna make you wait."

She huffs out a frustrated breath. "This is bullshit."

I laugh. "Well, this way, we're both definitely going to want to see each other again soon, right? Considering how well tonight went?"

She looks up at me thoughtfully. "Does that mean that I don't have to come up with ways of tricking you into being in the same place at the same time I'm there so we can pretend we're just bumping into one another?"

I know what she's asking. She wants to know if I'm done playing games.

It's a fair question.

And the answer is yes.

"I want to see you every day. No matter where you are or what you're doing," I tell her honestly.

She hesitates for a moment, watching my face. Then asks. "No matter who I'm with?"

I take a second to answer, and I know she knows why. "With very few exceptions," I say honestly. "And I'm going to work on that. Okay?"

She smiles, and there's a touch of concern in her expression. She knows where I'm coming from, and I'm glad we shared everything we did from the very beginning.

"Okay." She lifts and presses her lips to mine. "You're a really good guy, David."

I kiss her back, but then say playfully, "Don't be fooled. I'm still the bad boy that you're obsessed with, don't worry."

Her smile grows. "Big talker."

I give her a little growl. "Just wait."

"I will. For a while. But if you don't step up, I might have to take things into my own hands."

My cock reacts to that. He's been there when I've read her fanfiction, after all.

She starts to sit up, reaching for her bra.

"What are you doing?" I ask.

"I guess getting ready to go?" But she puts a question mark at the end of her answer.

Right. We're just on a date, and if we're not going to mess around anymore, I guess that makes sense.

And I really do think I need to hold off on messing around with her more. For now. I need to be sure I can deal with her dad long-term before I make a bigger commitment to her. That's the good guy thing to do. And bad boy in the bedroom or not, I am a good guy.

Dammit.

But I don't want her to leave.

"Camping entails sleeping outside overnight," I tell her. "You can go, of course. But you won't be able to count this as camping."

She seems surprised that I'm trying to prolong our date. But then she smiles. "That's a good point." She looks over my shoulder toward the movie screen. "Oh look, we didn't even miss the end."

I shift, rolling to my back and pulling her with me. She settles against my chest, and we both watch the screen.

It's the end scene, where the hero chases after the heroine as she's leaving.

My hand drifts down to rest on Mia's ass as the thought hits me that I would definitely chase her.

Yeah, I'm in trouble here.

I'm falling for this woman. I'm halfway there. Maybe more. I want to see her every day, I want to know everything about her, and I definitely, definitely want more nights like this.

That's complicated, considering intertwining our lives means intertwining my life with Scott's.

"What!" Mia pushes herself up, staring at the screen. "They don't even kiss?"

I chuckle. "Do they have to kiss? It's pretty clear that they're staying together."

"Of course they have to kiss."

I pull her back down, take her face between both of my hands, and look into her eyes. "I agree. They definitely should've kissed."

The movie credits roll as I kiss her, but eventually I begrudgingly let her button her dress up.

But she settles down against me again, and I start *Anyone But You*.

"Do you think maybe Glen Powell has some clause in his contract where he doesn't kiss in his movies?" I ask.

She laughs. "God, I hope not. If he doesn't kiss the heroine in this movie, a *rom-com*, this is the last Glen movie I'm watching ever."

She wants to stay. Even though I told her I think we should slow down, even though I told her we weren't going to have sex, she wants to stay. That's a good thing.

I want her to stay. That's maybe not such a good thing.

Being involved with Mia will definitely mean seeing Scott regularly. Spending time with him. Talking to him and being nice. Not sarcastic or rude the way I am sometimes now. There will be no walking off when he pisses me off. God, I might even have to do something like cut down a Christmas tree with him or wish him a happy birthday. Fuck, will I have to buy him a gift? For Christmas *and* his damned birthday?

Do I want that? Can I do that?

Those questions spin through my mind as I shift so Mia can be as comfortable as possible snuggled up against me.

With her warm weight against me, the scent of her hair drifting up and surrounding me, the curve of her ass under my palm, I realize that yeah, I can do that. I don't really want it, but I can do it.

At least, I can try.

When she falls asleep, I pull a soft fleece blanket up over both of us, shut the movie off, and happily fall asleep with her.

I wake up early the next morning with a raging erection pressing against Mia's sweet ass, but I ignore it. Mostly. I slip into the house to make breakfast burritos that we eat in the truck bed before I take her back to her car, kiss her goodbye, and tell her I can't wait to see her again.

Which is true.

That truth, and the sweet smile she gives me along with the, "I had an amazing time last night," is what has me pulling my phone out of my pocket before her car is even out of sight.

"I need some advice," I tell Charlie when he answers.

"Just me or Jack too?"

"The more the merrier. Actually, probably really good to bring the guy who actually had a successful relationship with a woman."

"Oh, have you already messed up?"

"Is falling in love with her already messing up?"

Charlie pauses as if surprised and then chuckles. "Maybe."

I sigh. "You see why I need some help?"

"I can be there in thirty minutes. But I need to see what Jack's up to."

"I've got breakfast burritos," I tell him.

"We'll be there as soon as we can."

I drive back up to my house and walk into my backyard. I should definitely pull all of this down and put it away before my brothers see it.

Then again, maybe I need to let them see this, so they know exactly what we're dealing with here.

CHAPTER 17

DAVID

"YEAH, YOU'RE IN LOVE," Jack says two hours later, after we've eaten more breakfast, and they've heard about my night with Mia.

Not all of the details, of course. We are way too old to be kissing and telling, but the twinkle lights and pillows in the truck bed give them all the information they need. Along with my "dopey in-love grin". Or so I'm told.

I sigh and don't even try to argue. "So what do I do? She's Scott Hansen's daughter. That means I'm going to have to hang out with him."

"Okay, you don't like the guy," Jack says. "But I don't get why. I guess I've always just known it was a fact and never really thought about it. But I've run into him several times since I've been back. He seems like a great guy. Everyone likes him. What's your problem with him?"

Two or three weeks ago I would have replied defensively that he's just a jackass and he's always been a dick or something, but now I take a breath and blow it out. "I've been thinking about this a lot," I say. "In fact, something happened yesterday that really got me thinking it over."

I tell them about stopping the kids four-wheeling and how Scott showed up.

"Do you guys remember when he caught us on the four-wheelers and chewed our asses?" I ask.

They both nod. "We had to do a ton of chores after that," Charlie says. He gives me a look. "But I remember you getting out of a lot of them."

I'm mildly surprised. "You remember that?"

"Didn't we all remember every time anyone got a different or lesser discipline than we did?" he asks with a chuckle. "Mom and Dad tried, but it was hard to keep things equal with four of us."

We all laugh in agreement.

"Well, I got disciplined," I say. "I just didn't do chores at home. I ended up doing an entire project and spending a bunch of time with Scott."

Charlie sits back in his chair. "Yeah, I remember that. A bunch of stuff about animals and plants, right?"

"Animals, plants, soil. He was all into what we had done and how it impacted the environment and natural habitats."

Jack shrugs. "That sounds right up your alley."

"Yeah, *now*," I agree. "But not necessarily back then. I did end up loving it, but it's weird that Scott knew that, don't you think?"

Jack seems to consider that.

It's always interesting to talk with my brothers and compare memories of the same incidents. We all have our own perspectives, and the way we each recall things that happened is slightly different, even if we were all there at exactly the same moment.

"So, you think he saw your interest in all of that before anyone else did?" Jack asks. "Even before you knew?"

I nod. "Yeah. Actually, that project and Scott's interest impacted me a lot. It was when I first realized not only my own interest in those things, but that people like Scott can be really influential. People who are in authority positions can really steer people—in good ways or bad—depending on how they react to situations and circumstances." I pause. "It was why I thought he was so great," I admit.

"And then you started giving him a hard time."

I look at Charlie. "I started giving *him* a hard time?"

"Well, okay, so you gave each other a hard time," he says. "I mean, you were a wild child. You were always, if not breaking the rules, certainly bending them. Testing your boundaries, stepping over the lines. You went through a long stretch where you tested every single rule anyone gave you."

I nod and slump down in my chair. "Yeah, and after yesterday with those kids, I realized that how Scott reacted when we were messing around with those four-wheelers must've sunk in even deeper than I thought. He was really mad at us. Because he was really concerned. We could've gotten seriously hurt. He also wanted us to care about what we were doing and how it affected the environment, the animals, and everything else. He helped me see that. So that was all great. I thought he was amazing for doing all of that and taking an interest. But he was worried about us too."

Charlie and Jack both nod. "I agree," Jack says.

I take a breath and confess, "And then I got older and was doing all kinds of stupid shit, but he didn't seem to care and...I think that hurt. It had sunk in for me that this cool guy I looked up to really cared about me and then...I don't know if he just gave up on me, or maybe I just completely hyped up how much he cared in the first place."

Charlie and Jack are both frowning, but Charlie is the one who sits forward in his chair. "What do you mean?"

"I was partying, drinking, fighting, getting other kids into trouble. Scott would come and break the parties up, and haul me home. He held me downtown and had me sober up before he took me home a couple of times. But he never really pushed it hard. He never really disciplined me. Not like he did after that four-wheeler incident. He never did anything that really made my choices and consequences sink in."

Charlie is frowning now. "Come on, David. You knew your choices were bad. Everyone knew you knew they were. Scott knew you were a smart guy."

I shrug. "Yeah. Still. Why didn't he try to stop me?"

"Aren't you glad he didn't actually arrest you or anything?" Jack asks. "Having that on your record would have limited your career choices in law enforcement, I'd think?"

I've actually thought of that before. I was glad when it came time to apply to my programs and jobs.

"Sure," I say. "That did end up good for me." I clear my throat. "But Scott was the one who told me I'd make a terrible cop."

"No way," Charlie says.

"Oh, yes."

Jack frowns. "Did he tell you why he thought that?"

"He knew I was angry about Mom. He said angry cops are bad cops."

Jack thinks about that for a moment. "That makes sense."

"Does it?" But I know it does.

"Cops are there to protect people and make communities safer and better. If you were in it for revenge against random "bad guys" or because part of you blames the cops back then for not saving Mom, that is a very different motivation than serving and protecting," Jack says.

He's right. That's what I've realized since, but at the time, it had hurt. "Scott knew me better even then," I admit. "But it felt like an insult at the time, and I carried that for...a while."

"But you realize now he was right?"

"Yeah. And I'm happy with how things ended up." I run a hand over my face. "I've been fine just existing alongside Scott but not interacting. Just being here but not involved."

"You're here to show him that you turned out great," Charlie says.

I look over at him. "I'm here because this is home."

My brother nods. "That too. But you like being able to show Scott that he was wrong about you."

That hits me like Charlie just threw his drink in my face. "I..." I can't deny it.

"Except he wasn't wrong about you," Jack points out. "He knew you'd be great at Game and Parks. Even back when you were still a kid."

I have to swallow before I say, "Yeah, well, I don't know if he really gives a shit."

And it hits me *that* is my issue. He didn't care when I was a reckless, trouble-making teen, and he doesn't care now that I've straightened up and turned out well.

"My hero fell pretty far off his pedestal, and I guess I've been blaming him for that when really it's my fault for putting him up there in the first place."

"But..." Charlie glances at Jack, then back at me with clear confusion. "What about the intervention?"

I lift both brows. "The intervention you all did for me? Yeah. Exactly. Scott could've stepped in at any point before it came to that, but he didn't."

Charlie looks at Jack. "Do you remember any of that?"

"I just remember Mom and Dad coming in and telling me that I needed to be a part of it. That we were all going to sit down with David and tell him that he had to stop doing dangerous stupid shit."

Charlie nods, then looks back at me. "We intervened because Scott told us we had to." He shakes his head. "I don't mean to make that sound like we didn't want to. But it was Scott's idea."

"What?" I sit up a little straighter.

"Every single time you messed up, he came to Mom and Dad and told them about it. He told him he was worried about you and wanted them to step in. And they did. You were grounded, you got extra chores, all of that. But it never seemed to matter. So when it finally got really bad, Scott came out and told Mom and Dad that if they weren't going to do it, he was. He was going to sit your ass down, and haul you into counseling, lock you up in jail for an extended period, whatever he had to do. He wanted to know if Mom and Dad needed his help. He knew they were struggling, and he wanted to help them, but he was frustrated with them too."

"I..." I'm not sure what to say. My mind starts spinning, replaying memories from that time.

Around the time he's talking about, my mom's parents were going through a lot.

My grandpa, her dad, had had a stroke, and my grandma wasn't handling it well, so my mom had been going out to Colorado to help pretty often.

But she did have six kids at home. The Bennett family always stuck together, and my parents had a lot of help, of course, but that wasn't the same as having our mom here.

Our dad was great, but one of my younger brothers was struggling in school. Shane has dyslexia and has always had a harder time at school than the rest of us.

I frown. "The intervention was Scott's idea?"

"Not just an idea. It was basically do it or else."

"Seriously? Why didn't he just do it if they needed the help?" But my heart is pounding. This is new information. I'm not exactly shocked. But it does change things to know that Scott was prepared to step in, I have to admit.

"I mean, it was our job, wasn't it?" Charlie asks. "We're your family. Scott cared, and he was more than just a town cop to us, but he really had to give Mom and Dad a chance. I know Mom was exhausted, and she felt like she had totally failed you. Scott told her the intervention—giving you firm boundaries and consequences—would make *her* feel better too. They got me, Henry, and Jack involved, too. It had to be a united front. And trust me, Henry and I were just as worried as anybody. Though I have to admit, I felt a little guilty that we hadn't stepped in more forcefully." He sighs. "As your older brothers, we should have."

I quickly shake my head. "By that time, you guys were off at college. Henry was doing an internship. I think he and Emma were pretty serious by then, too."

Charlie shrugs. "Yeah. Trust me, we all gave ourselves all the excuses that we could. And honestly? We may not have known how bad it really was. I think it was bugging Scott to not be able to step in more, to be honest. He was trying to respect Mom and Dad, give our family a chance to come together and rally around you, but I think he very much wanted to throw your ass in jail and shake you until you woke up and realized that you were doing stupid, dangerous shit."

I take a deep breath. I feel like I should be more shocked. That this should be a huge revelation, and I should be reeling from it.

But the truth is...this makes the most sense of anything.

This all feels very true. This sounds like the Scott Hansen I thought I knew. The Scott Hansen I wanted to be real.

"So can you get past all of this for Mia?" Jack asks.

That's the question.

My feelings about Scott still feel muddled, but I do feel better.

"I think Scott and I need a chance to spend time together, maybe get to know each other again," I say. "Without my attitude getting in the way."

Jack smiles as if he's proud of me. "That's a good idea. It won't be hard to show Scott that you're a good guy who will treat his daughter well."

Fuck. I run a hand over my face again. This would be easier if I were just trying to extend an olive branch to Scott for the sake of our jobs or the town or even my own peace of mind.

Involving Mia makes it a really big deal.

But... "Yeah, I need to try for her," I say.

"I think I know the perfect thing," Charlie says. "He and a bunch of other guys in uniform—a couple of cops, firefighters, EMTs—are working down at the park to redo the picnic structure and skate park. They're tearing down the old structure that has all the graffiti and stuff on it. The one no one ever uses."

"That thing's been there since we were kids," Jack says. "I don't think it's ever even been painted."

I know it hasn't. It's at the back of the park, past the baseball fields and swimming pool. There are newer ones toward the entrance to the park that get a lot more use. The structure they're talking about hasn't hosted a picnic in years. But it's hosted lots of drinking, smoking, and fighting. I know firsthand.

"Yeah, it's pretty beat up by now," Charlie says. "They're taking it out and building a new one. They raised the money for it last fall." He looks at me. "You should go help with that. Scott is heading it up. You'd fit right in."

I automatically try to come up with a reason not to. It's my knee-jerk reaction, though, and I catch myself. I nod. "Yep, that sounds perfect. A community service project means we won't be alone and won't have to talk a lot, but we'll spend time together, and I can make that first move toward cooperation."

"There you go," Jack says, looking proud. "Great idea."

"Yeah, get down there and charm the guy," Charlie says with a grin. "He'll be begging you to date his daughter."

I don't grin. Or laugh. Or even nod.

Because this is going to require swallowing my pride and being nice to Scott. Probably even smiling at him.

And there's a good chance he still won't think I'm good enough for Mia.

But then I remember how she felt snuggled against me during the movie. How amazing she was telling me where and how she wanted me to touch her. How funny and sweet she is. How fucking much fun I've had since we've been hanging out.

And yeah...I can swallow my pride and be nice.

I'll even bring the guy coffee.

"Just don't go in there and start telling him how you think he should do things," Charlie says. "Let him lead the project. Let him be in charge."

I frown. "Of course. It's his project. I'm cool."

"It's just that..." Charlie trails off.

"What?" I ask.

"There was just a lot of talk at the city council meetings about it. One side wanted to turn it into a big picnic pavilion with built-in grills and bathrooms and stuff."

How had I missed this?

Oh yeah, I don't go to city council meetings. Or read city council minutes. Or ask about city council meetings.

"That sounds awesome," I say. "What's the problem?"

"Other people wanted to preserve the skate park and..." He grimaces. "There is a feral cat colony back there that some people have been taking care of. Building the bigger structure will take up more area, take out the skate park, and displace the cats."

I frown. "Which side is Scott on?"

"Didn't they find a big beehive, too?" Jack asks.

My frown deepens. "What?"

"Yeah," Charlie confirms. "They tore into the backside of the old building and found a huge-assed hive. They say they can be moved, but that's obviously an ordeal."

"You know about moving bees," Jack says to me.

"Yes, I know I do," I tell him. Why hasn't anyone called me about this? There are other people in the area, but I'm from Sapphire Falls.

But I know the answer without asking. Scott didn't want to call me.

"How do you know about all of this?" I ask Jack. "You just moved back and haven't exactly been city-council-ready."

"Mom and Dad go to the meetings and talk about it all at dinner," he says with a shrug.

"No one's asked me about moving bees," I say. I lean in. "And they could move the cats, but that takes time. They should be working on that now."

Charlie nods. "Yeah. And there's a fox den back there. Which has some families riled up about putting a play area back there."

"Healthy foxes very rarely interact with humans. They tend to flee rather than fight," I say. "It's extremely uncommon for a fox to attack. And there are also ways to move foxes, for fuck's sake. We'd just have to have a plan. And people who know what they're doing."

"It's been...a deal," Charlie says. "All the more reason for you to get involved."

"Why haven't they called me?"

"It's all volunteer," Charlie says. "Maybe that's why?"

But I think I know why. "Which side is Scott on?" I ask again, already knowing the answer.

"He thinks a pavilion will get more use than the skate park, and if they put in a new play area back there, families will use more of the park."

I sigh. "So I'm going to go into this project already concerned about issues on the other side from Scott."

Charlie shrugs. "It's still the perfect way for you to spend time with Scott and show him what you do, know, and care about."

"Yeah." But it is probably not the best way for me to cooperate, let him lead, and keep my mouth shut. I sigh. "Well, now I have to get involved and, I guess, if I'm going to date Mia, Scott will need to get to know the real me. I'm not making trouble with beer and my fists anymore, but that doesn't mean I won't frustrate the hell out of him."

Jack grins. "Wow, you are *definitely* in love."

Fuck. Yeah, I definitely am.

THE FEEL OF HIS HOT, *insistent mouth sucking on my nipple sends shocks of heat and lust through my body. My clit is aching, and as if he can read my mind, his thumb finds the sensitive nub, pressing and circling with the perfect amount of pressure. I whimper against his mouth.*

"Lift up. Use the handlebars."

I do as I'm told. As always.

I use the handlebars behind me to lift my body, and he growls in approval.

"Good girl."

He rewards me by sliding two thick fingers into my pussy.

We've never fucked outside of the sex club and the fact that we are not role-playing tonight makes all of this even hotter.

I had wondered about sex on a four-wheeler, and it turns out that it is just as hot—and possible—as I'd hoped.

The back kitchen door slams, and I jump and look up quickly. Between my headphones and being lost in my writing, I'm mostly oblivious to the sounds around me, including my mother banging pots and pans as she cooks and humming along to whatever music is playing in her head.

But my dad just slammed the door hard enough that I could hear it through my headphones.

I watch as he crosses the kitchen to my mom and pulls her into his arms. She grins up at him and says something I can't hear. He nods, then lowers his mouth, kissing her.

My parents are extremely affectionate people, still clearly madly in love after all of these years, and they never try to hide or curtail the PDA even when their kids are around.

My dad's hands drop to my mom's ass and I can see her say something against his mouth.

He chuckles, then pulls back, looking down at her the way every woman should want and expect the man she spends her life with to look at her.

Then my dad grasps my mom's waist and hoists her up onto the counter, stepping between her knees. She laughs, and then he's in front of her, his back to me, blocking my view of her and what *exactly* they're doing.

Yes, they are clearly in love, and I don't expect them to hide their affection, but I've seen part of this show before. I need to stop it before it goes too far.

I pull my headphones off and say, "Daughter in the room."

Without missing a beat or even looking over at me, my dad says, "You could fix that."

I laugh. "You two are so gross," I tease.

I absolutely do not mean that. My parents' love, affection, and yes, even their passion, have been a great source of comfort for me throughout the years I've lived with them.

Do I want to see my parents making out? Not especially. However, the fact that they are so open and honest about their feelings has always made me feel incredibly secure. They don't hide how they feel about anything—each other, their work, this town, the causes that matter to them, and yes, me. Their ability to love out loud has always extended to me, and so when they get a little frisky in the kitchen, it honestly just makes me smile.

"Well, at least don't make her burn dinner. It's one of my favorites," I say, making absolutely no move to give them any privacy.

"What are we having?" he asks.

"Parmesan spinach pasta," Mom answers.

Dad quickly steps back, holding up his hands. "I definitely don't want you to burn that."

Mom laughs and slides off the counter. "Okay, but rain check on what we just had going here."

He shoots her a grin, then slaps her on the ass. "You know it."

I look down at the screen on my computer. Is it any wonder I feel totally comfortable sitting at the kitchen table writing a sex scene while my mother is in the room cooking dinner?

Dad smiles at me. "I'm glad you're here tonight. I feel like I haven't seen you in a while."

I do close my laptop, though, as he crosses to the table to join me. My dad doesn't need to read this.

"Yeah, I've been kind of busy. Had some stuff going on the last few evenings." I almost grimace. I'm not *lying* to him. And there are no laws that require me to tell my father everything I do, every minute of the day. However, I'm purposefully not giving him details, and I hope he doesn't ask, because it involves David.

I really want my dad and my boyfriend to get along. To even like each other. No, even more than that. I want them to respect each other, admire one another, and even develop a level of affection for each other. My family is very close, and we've been through a lot. I never want our closeness or how easy and comfortable we are together to change.

"What have you been up to?" He drops into the kitchen chair perpendicular to mine.

"Well, I helped Jack Bennett with some birthday party planning for one of his daughters."

"That's nice," Dad says, though he does look a little surprised. "Are you and Jack…"

For a second, I'm confused why he would even ask, but then I realize that maybe that sounds like something a girlfriend would do rather than a librarian's task.

And fair enough, it probably is.

"Jack came into the library looking for ideas and resources for how to do manicures and a spa day theme," I explain.

"Oh, you should've asked Sloan to help," Mom says, leaning against the counter now that she's slid the pasta bake into the oven.

"I did actually. We both went out there."

"That's so nice." Mom smiles. "Jack needs all the friends he can get. I still can't believe everything he's been through."

I nod. "I know. It's heartbreaking. But they seem to be doing okay. They have Tucker and Delaney, of course, and then…" I hesitate and then kick myself mentally. *Don't hesitate. Don't draw extra attention to the discussion about Jack's brothers.* "He's also got his brothers. Charlie and David have been very supportive."

Very good. I didn't even trip over David's name.

"They're a great family," my mom agrees.

"Those boys have always been close," my dad adds. He looks over at my mom. "Speaking of David Bennett."

My heart flips over so fast, I swear I get a little lightheaded. I then hold my breath, which doesn't help.

"Oh no, what happened?" my mom asks, her tone indicating that it isn't entirely uncommon for her to hear about David from my dad.

"He showed up at the site for the new pavilion today," Dad tells her.

I'm aware of the pavilion project because my mom and dad have discussed it frequently. My dad's excited to tear down the old picnic structure where kids like to hang out to drink and smoke. I've seen the plans for the new pavilion, and it's amazing.

But this sounds like David's involvement is new.

"David's really handy," I say, then quickly add, "Right? I assume all the Bennett boys are."

Okay, decent save. But their mom does a ton of renovating and building. No, not huge park pavilion structures, but I'll bet Delaney could if she wanted to.

"And he's a guy who wears a uniform around here like the rest of you," I point out. I know the rest of the men involved in the community service project are cops, firefighters, and EMTs, and there are even a couple of National Guardsmen helping.

"Yeah, it makes sense," my dad says with a heavy sigh. "And I've been thinking I needed to call him anyway. But I've been putting it off because I knew it would be a pain in the ass."

Okay, yes, David hasn't been involved before now.

I fight the urge to frown at my dad's clear exasperation.

My mom chuckles at my dad's evident annoyance, and he shoots her a frown.

She holds up her hands. "Oh, come on, you and David butt heads because you are so much alike."

Dad rolls his eyes.

"Are they?" I ask, risking the conversation about David deepening and having something show in my face or voice.

My mom's eyes widen as if this is the most obvious thing in the world, and she nods. "Not just the uniform thing either. They're both super protective, absolute rule followers, perfectionists, and stubborn as hell."

I think about all of that and realize she's spot on.

"They would do anything for this town and the people in it," my mom continues. "They love Sapphire Falls, and sleep, breathe, and eat ways to make it better every day."

I also think about that. She's right, and I feel a little pang in my heart thinking about how David feels like my dad has kept him from doing more of that.

"So why were you frustrated that David showed up today?" I ask my dad.

Hey, we're just having a conversation here, and the topic of the conversation right now is David. It's not weird or giving anything away that I ask further questions about him.

I hope.

Dad sighs again. "The new pavilion is going to be much larger than the picnic space we're pulling out. It's going to impact the area around it. Some cats, some bees, stuff like that."

Dad doesn't have to say anything more. I already know that David's annoyed. He doesn't like disruption like that.

Or really *any* disruption to his normal life and the way he thinks things should be.

"And David doesn't think you should do it?" I ask anyway.

Dad is quiet for a moment, then says, "It's not that. He just wants us to approach it differently. Take our time. Get everything moved before we start pounding and digging. And I should've called him about a month ago and asked for his help doing that. But I didn't. I mean, I didn't even call him today. He just showed up. I am assuming he found out about the project from Delaney and Tucker."

"So now he can't help? There's not enough time?" I ask.

"He can help. He can move the animals safely and effectively. Or he can just help with the building. He said he'd do it either way and it was my call."

My brows arch. "So, that's good. He's letting you be in charge."

"Right," my dad says wryly. "I'm in charge." He shakes his head. "If we do things David's way, it will lengthen the time-line, which makes it more difficult to get it all done in time for a couple of events people have scheduled. One is a big family reunion, the other is a wedding anniversary party. The families are excited to use the new facility and have paid up front which has helped us fund some of this."

"What happens if you *don't* do it David's way?" Mom asks.

"He'll still be there and help, but remind me constantly that we should have done it his way and annoy the shit out of me every single day," Dad says.

But I swear I see the corner of my dad's mouth twitch, as if he's fighting a smile.

"He said that?" I ask, knowing full well that he did.

Dad nods. "Yep. And..." He blows out a breath. "He's right. His way is the right way to handle it. I should have called him before this, and he's annoyed that I didn't."

My mom frowns at him. "You felt like you *couldn't* call him?"

"No. I just didn't want to," Dad admits. "I kept thinking I'd do it tomorrow. And now it's been a month." Dad shrugs. "He's just kind of a sarcastic little shit. But it's my own fault I put it off too long."

"A sarcastic little shit?" I ask. "He's thirty-eight." Then I realize it may seem strange that I know David's exact age. "Or something like that. He's a grown man."

"Your dad has a hard time seeing you kids as old as you are, too," Mom says. "And he and David had a few...encounters... when David was growing up. I think your dad has a hard time seeing him as a responsible adult."

"I don't," my dad protests. "I know he's responsible. He

does a great job. It's the way he does it. He's almost *too* responsible. He's so rigid about the rules, and his protectiveness is over the top sometimes."

My mom coughs, and it sounds like *pot-kettle.*

My dad frowns at her. "And I always have this feeling he's trying to prove something to me."

Mom nods. "And you're dying to mentor him, and you know that he would tell you to fuck off."

I turned wide eyes on my dad. "Is that true?" I probably sound way too interested for the casual I-barely-know-him I'm supposed to be projecting. But I can't help it.

My dad glares at my mom, but then lifts a shoulder. "Maybe. The kid went through some hard times, but I always knew that he, all of his brothers, were going to be okay. David's great at his job. He's a real asset to the community. But are there some things that I think I could teach him or advise him about? Yeah, I think so. But we have some history, and I don't think David wants to hear that from me."

"What kind of history?" I ask, curious about my dad's side of things.

"I was just always really honest with him. I figured he could handle it. And he usually did. But he was a hardheaded kid with a big rebellious streak. I didn't really mind that. I knew he was going to be okay. He had a lot of people who cared about him. But then he came and asked if I thought he should be a cop, and I said no."

I tried to act surprised. "Why would you say that? Don't you want good men to become cops?"

"I do. But they need to do it for the right reasons. I think everyone should get into a career they can be passionate about. His passion for being a cop was misplaced. And look at him. The passion he has for what he does now is perfect." He looks down at the table. "I've often wondered if I handled that the right way. If maybe I was too blunt. But I..." He trails off, then surprises me by saying, "I thought I was protecting him, too."

I lean in a little. "How?"

"The way he lost his mom was traumatic. Then losing his dad not long after...he—*they*—just went through so much. I guess I didn't want him to get into a job where there was more pain and trauma. I wanted him to find a way to make the world better, healthier, more...beautiful." Dad gives a soft chuckle and shakes his head. "That's cheesy maybe, and yes, law enforcement can do good things, but to get to the good, you have to also see the crime, see people hurting each other...what he does now directly makes the earth better and he can see people doing happy things—camping, fishing, hiking—and teach them how to appreciate animals, plants, nature. He was so happy outside. I wanted him to have that." Dad takes a deep breath. "But maybe I should have said that instead of telling him he'd be a bad cop."

I sit stunned.

That's all...so my dad. *This* is the man I know and love. This is why it's so hard for me to reconcile that David doesn't like him.

My mom walks over and wraps her arms around my dad from behind him. She squeezes him hard. "I love you, Officer Hansen," she says against his cheek.

He covers her hands with his and squeezes back. "Thank God for that."

She kisses him, then straightens and turns back to the stove. "Is the pavilion still a go?"

"Yeah. David's gonna do his thing and I'm sure it's going to all work out. We'll get extra people out to help and make up some time."

My mom glances over her shoulder. "And are you going to apologize for not looping him in sooner? Because I know you didn't do that today."

I meet her gaze, and she winks.

"Stubborn as hell, super protective, great guys," she says. "But they have a really hard time admitting they don't know everything and that sometimes they get it wrong."

Yeah, I can see that about David, too.

My dad stands from his seat. "Yes, probably. Eventually. And now I am going to go take a shower and remove myself from this room where I'm getting no sympathy."

My mom laughs as he leaves the room. "Poor baby." After he's gone, she looks at me. "Stubborn men can be amazing. Because they're stubborn about loving hard, they're stubborn about protecting their families, they're stubborn about doing the right thing. But they can also be stubborn about apologizing and getting over things."

"Okay." I believe all of that. "Why are you telling me that?" I ask suspiciously.

She shrugs and turns back to the stove. "Oh, no reason. Just sharing a little motherly advice."

I narrow my eyes. Does my mother know something she shouldn't? And if she does, how does she know it?

But I'm not going to ask. Because then I might have to confess something.

Instead, I pull my phone out and text David.

Because if my dad is frustrated after spending time together this afternoon, I am sure David is even more so.

And I cannot have my dad scaring David off. I know that this is David's biggest issue with the two of us being together, and I'm going to need to remind him that there are reasons worth putting up with Scott Hansen.

But before I've even typed two words, an idea hits me.

And instead of texting David, I dial Judy Turner's number.

I get up from the table and head for my childhood

bedroom. My mom doesn't need to hear this either. I shut the door just as Judy answers.

"Hello?"

"Hey, Judy, it's Mia Hansen."

"Hi, honey. What's going on?"

"Oh, just that in a couple of hours, someone is going to be riding a four-wheeler around your east pasture, and lighting some fireworks. You're probably gonna want to call someone about that. Specifically, David Bennett. He is the perfect one to go out and check on that for you."

The older woman chuckles. "Just shoot me a text and let me know when the 'perpetrator' is in place."

I grin. "Thanks, Judy. I'll do that."

Then I text my sister.

> Are you coming to dinner at Mom and Dad's tonight?

> Yep, on our way.

> You wouldn't happen to have or know where I can get some fireworks?

> I do. Do I want to know why?

> How about you just read it in my fanfiction chapter in a couple of days?

> *heart eye emoji* *heart eye emoji* *heart eye emoji* *fire emoji* *fire emoji* *fire emoji*

CHAPTER 19

DAVID

> I think sex on a four-wheeler is very possible,
> but would like you to confirm.

I GRIN AT THE MESSAGE. Mia and I are openly talking about sex now and I fucking like that.

Before I can reply, I get a second message.

> But don't tell me you've actually done it. Just
> say you think it's probably possible

Oh, and a touch of jealousy. I like that a *lot*.

> I think it would definitely be possible.

I haven't actually had sex on a four-wheeler. Why would I? There are much more comfortable places to have sex. And typically when I'm on a four-wheeler, I'm riding with my brothers.

If I were to have sex on a four-wheeler it would purely be for fun, for the adventure, and because the woman wanted to do something daring and unusual.

Or because she texted me about it and got me thinking about it, and then when I was four-wheeling with her, I wasn't able to wait until we were back to a more comfortable place.

> The woman would just straddle the man, right? It'd be like having sex sitting down almost anywhere, wouldn't it?

This. Woman.

One day I'm going to spontaneously combust or forget to breathe or read a text while eating something and choke and die.

But what a way to go.

> Probably something like that. But his legs will be spread wider to straddle the four-wheeler.

> Would that be better or worse?

> Depends on how in shape he is. It'll take more strength to thrust from there.

> Well, she would just have to do a lot of the work then.

Fuck.

I'm definitely going to have sex on a four-wheeler now.

Like right now. Or in less than an hour anyway. I'm just leaving work and it won't take me more than thirty minutes to get home, shower, and change, then get on my four-wheeler and get to Mia's.

I start to type in a response, but my phone rings before I can finish telling her it would be really great if the woman in question was wearing a skirt or dress in this scenario for easier access.

"This is Officer Bennett."

"David. It's Judy Turner. There are fireworks going off in my west pasture."

I stop on the top step of the Game and Parks office. I frown. "*Fireworks?*"

Stupidly I look up at the sky. It's not dark yet. How does she know? Of course, fireworks also make noise. But her west pasture is miles from her house.

"Yes. Fireworks." She sounds like she's rolling her eyes.

"Do you have any idea who it is?" I continue down the steps and head for my truck. I'm off duty, but Judy's is on my way home.

"I'm seventy-eight years old. I'm not going out there to do an interview. That's your job. All I know is it isn't me, and I'm the one who owns that pasture, so that means someone is trespassing."

Yes, it does. And lighting fireworks without permission.

My eyes narrow as I slide behind the wheel of my truck.

Just like someone was trespassing on her property in the deer stand.

That's a lot of trespassing on land that is out in the middle of nowhere.

"You're sure it's not your grandkids?" I ask, starting the truck and pulling out onto the road.

"If they did, they didn't tell me about it. Call me back if it's them and I'll just chew them out."

I open my mouth to suggest she call her grandkids and ask them, but shut it and shake my head. It's not her grandkids. I'm ninety percent sure I know who it is, though.

And yes, I definitely need to go check this out.

"I'll swing by and see what's going on," I tell her.

"Okay. 'Bye." She hangs up on me.

Ten minutes later, I turn into Judy's west pasture and rattle my teeth as I bump along the tiny dirt service road that leads through the pasture and down to the river.

Even though I was expecting to see her, my heart still trips as I pull up and see Mia sitting on my brother's four-wheeler holding a sparkler.

She's so fucking gorgeous. And it's not the way her hair is pulled back into a French braid, or that she's wearing a pretty little pink sundress, or the ankle-high boots that are at least kind of appropriate for walking around in a field of grass.

It's not even the four-wheeler.

It's the smile she gives me when our eyes lock.

And just the fact that she's here.

One word goes through my mind as I shut off the truck, open the door, and my feet hit the ground.

Mine.

She's mine. She's here for me, and we're going to make this work. And anything and everything I have to put up with to be with this woman is worth it.

I stalk toward her.

"Hi," she greets as I stop next to the four-wheeler.

Her sparkler reaches the end and splutters out.

I take it from her fingers and toss it into the bucket on the ground where there are three other burnt-out sparklers along with the remnants of other fireworks.

I look from the fireworks to her. "You really lit fireworks off?"

"A few."

"I thought you'd just gotten Judy in on this whole ploy to get me out here."

She grins. "Oh, I did. But I had these fireworks. I thought I might as well actually light them."

It's one thing to be attracted to someone, to feel want and desire, to have lusty thoughts. But to look into the big green eyes of a woman who is equal parts sweet and naughty and to have a nearly overpowering urge to see the rainbow nails on your hand that your nieces painted *because of* her, curved into her hip while fucking her from behind is a shocking thought.

I look down at my hand, though. My nail polish is still intact.

Sloan assured us that the clear protective topcoat she applied would withstand all of our jobs for at least a couple of days. She was right and yeah, I want to see my fucking rainbow nails against Mia Hansen's creamy skin.

I take a deep breath. "Trespassing. Burning without permission. Riding without a helmet. And you shouldn't fucking be out here by yourself. What if you get hurt? What if you burn yourself? What if you start a grass fire? What if the four-wheeler breaks down? What if you get stuck?"

She gives me a smile and reaches into the pocket of the bag she has hanging from one of the handlebars. She withdraws a phone and wiggles it at me.

"I got a new phone. And there's good reception out here."

Fuck, I want her so much.

I reach up and slide my hand along her bare shoulder, under her hair, to the back of her neck. "What if you hit a rock and the four-wheeler tosses you off and you break your pretty neck?"

She lifts a brow. "Is having someone out here riding with me going to prevent that from happening? How? They'll catch me before I hit the ground?"

I blow out a breath. That scenario hadn't actually occurred to me until just now when I saw that she actually has a damned four-wheeler here. And no helmet that I can see.

But now that I am picturing her lying crumpled on the ground, seriously injured, my heart is pounding.

"This is not safe. You at least need a helmet."

She gives me a smile. "Wow. I was looking forward to four-wheeler sex before, but knowing I'll need to wear a *helmet* for it makes me *really* curious about what it's like."

I growl. We'll discuss lighting fireworks in grassy fields without permits later.

Instead, I pull her forward and lean in at the same time.

Just before I kiss her, I say against her mouth, "Your dad isn't going to scare me off, Mia."

CHAPTER 20

MIA

THAT MIGHT BE the hottest thing he could've said in this moment.

At least combined with the gruff tone in his voice and the way he's looking at me.

I turn on the four-wheeler to face him. "I'm very—"

Then he's cupping my face and says, his voice even huskier, "You up for doing a little extra work?"

My pussy clenches, and if he is not referring to us having sex on this four-wheeler, we are not as on the same page as I've been assuming.

"Definitely."

He kisses me, hot and deep, his mouth opening immediately, so his tongue can stroke along my lips and then against my tongue as soon as I grant him access.

He gives a little growl as I moan into his mouth.

Sliding to the ground accomplishes two things. One, it gets my body up against his more fully. Two, it allows him to take a seat on the four-wheeler. That's the only thing that pulls our mouths apart, and not for long.

He climbs on the four-wheeler and then reaches out, lifting me onto the machine with him. I'm facing him, straddling his thighs, my skirt hiking up high on my legs.

His big hand rests on the back of my neck, and he kisses me deeply with his other hand against my lower back, grinding me against his hard cock.

Shudders of heat and lust go through me, and I happily help with the grinding.

"Can't get totally naked on a four-wheeler," he says against my mouth. "Someone could drive up. And lots of potential bug bites."

"This will have to do," I say, reaching for the tie behind my neck that's holding my dress up. I pull on the end of the bow and the bodice of my dress gapes and falls away from my breasts.

My bra-less breasts.

David growls his approval. "This will more than do."

One hand drops to cup my left breast, his rough thumb rubbing over the tip, causing my pussy to clench and heat to build in my gut.

I'm about to say something about him getting his clothes out of the way, but then he says something that makes me freeze.

"Lift up. Use the handlebars."

My gaze flies to his. Those are the exact words I wrote in the latest chapter of my fanfiction. I've only published half of the scene, and it *just* published about an hour ago. That has to be a coincidence. My mind spins. There are probably only a few ways, maybe one, to give that instruction. That has to be it.

"Mia? Put your hands on the handlebars and lift yourself up."

I know. Right. I need to do that.

I reach back and grip the handlebars, lifting myself slightly. Okay, that totally works the way I imagined, though it's going to take more muscle stamina to hold myself here than I really thought through. It also leaves me unable to use my hands for anything else.

That doesn't seem to be a problem for David. Both of his hands slide to my outer thighs, then slip up under my skirt to rest on my hips, his thumbs in the creases of my hips.

His gaze is hot as he studies me, my breasts fully on display, my back arched slightly by the position of my hands. His gaze goes from my breasts to my eyes, then back to my breasts.

"Holy shit, you are a fantasy come true," he says. He leans in and puts his mouth on my nipple, sucking hard as his hands strip my panties down my legs. Without any encouragement needed, I lift so that he can slide them all the way off my legs and toss them somewhere. I don't care where at all.

I settle back down onto the seat. I'm shifted back enough that he's able to undo his buckle, then the snap and zipper of his fly. His eyes are still glued on me. He lifts his hips and pulls denim and cotton out of my way.

"One disadvantage to this is I can't see you as well as I want to," I tell him.

He gives a little chuckle and reaches for one of my hands, bringing it forward to his cock. I happily wrap my hand around him. He's thick and hot and steely hard.

"I guess you're gonna have to go by touch," he tells me, his voice tight.

"Guess so," I say, my voice breathless.

I stroke up and down his length twice before he says, "The other disadvantage is I don't think it's going to work to sit you up on those handlebars and bury my face between your legs."

Now I suck in a breath, my eyes wide. Not because of the

thing he said...okay, yes, because of the thing he said. But not because David said it to me. Because my *hero said it to my heroine* in my latest scene.

Since it's not something I could just type into a search bar, I'd actually looked up the measurements to a four-wheeler, then got a tape measure out, trying to figure out if there was a way for the hero to comfortably eat the heroine while she was balanced on the handlebars.

I decided that while it might be *possible* and perhaps people would suspend their disbelief for a hot scene like that, it made more sense for them to just get right to the sex and leave him going down on her for another time.

"You okay?" he asks me.

There's something in his voice. Almost like he's teasing me.

"Why did you say that?" I ask.

"Because after last night, I'm addicted to your pussy. I'm probably always going to be thinking about if I can get into position to get my tongue on you."

I flush with heat and my clit aches a little, wanting his tongue.

"Think about that," he says. "If we're going to keep seeing each other, know that wherever we are—The Come Again, Dottie's, a bonfire, my mom's kitchen table, your parents' back-yard—I'm always going to be thinking, at least a little, about when I can next see, touch, and taste this gorgeous body."

The heat and ache intensify. "I'm..." I swallow. "I'm okay with that."

He gives me a grin. "Good. 'Cuz I'd probably be thinking it even if we weren't together, but if we're dating, at least that means it's foreplay instead of pure torture."

God, I want to kiss him so badly. I want that mouth and those hands all over me.

But I shake my head and make myself ask, "Did it just occur to you to maybe sit me up on the handlebars?"

I can see a smirk tugging at his mouth. "I read something like that. But the guy didn't think it would work." He runs his hands up my thighs and squeezes my hips. "I think he's right, but for the wrong reason."

I'm staring at him. He *read it* somewhere? "Why do you think it won't work?" I ask, that question overriding my curiosity about how he knows about it.

"It's not so much the height—I would happily bend myself into a pretzel to get another taste of you. It's that you don't have anything to lean against or really hang onto. I don't want to risk you falling off when you're coming nice and hard."

He's got a point. That's actually my first thought.

My pussy can't get over the idea of having his mouth on her again.

But the immediate second thought is *where* did he read about this?

It's possible that I'm not the first and only author to think about sex on a four-wheeler, or oral sex with the woman on the handlebars, but this all just seems a little too convenient.

"You read about it? Where? Sounds like my kind of literature."

"Oh, it sure is. I was delighted to find out you're the author."

My heart thumps hard as surprise hits me directly in the chest.

He knows about my fanfiction. *Oh my God.*

"How?" I ask simply.

"Charlie," he answers, just as simply.

Of course.

"When?"

"The day I came into the library with the print molds for you."

My eyes widen. "You've known all this time?"

He grins. "I'm your biggest fan. I've even helped with a couple questions you've asked."

I shake my head. "What? You and I have *chatted online?*"

He nods. "Hi, TUFFGUY1."

My mouth drops open. TUFFGUY1 is a newer user but he has, in fact, been commenting on all of my stuff lately. He's been so encouraging, so enthusiastic, and has given me a couple of really great prompts. Like how taking the couple out of the sex club would mean their relationship was progressing.

I can't believe that's David.

"You've...I've...I just..."

He squeezes me. "Are you mad? I love your stuff. I love your sweet and your naughty side, Mia. I want to make every fantasy come true for you."

"I..." But I realize I'm not mad. I publish fanfiction. I put my stuff up on a public page. It's a page I never would have expected David to find, of course, but I can't be upset that people actually read the stuff I publicly publish.

"I've read the books too. I did that first. And I think it's hilarious and fun you made Grant the owner of a sex club. It's a great series and your stuff is definitely hot, but it's also got substance. And you clearly love the source material." He rubs small circles on my hips. "It's made me feel closer to you."

I wet my lips. "It's been fun talking to you online. I've appreciated your encouragement to make the relationship more than just a sexual one inside the club."

He nods. "It felt really natural the way you've written them."

I swallow. "Thanks. I've liked the challenge of expanding beyond the dirty stuff."

He grins. "Good. But your dirty stuff is *really* good."

I feel a surge of what I can only describe as empowerment. I've affected him with my writing. I love that. "I haven't finished the scene."

"I noticed." He leans in, bringing his mouth closer to mine again. "Are you using me tonight just to get ideas?"

"Research is very important," I tell him.

He laughs. "Indeed. And if you hadn't been absolutely obsessed with me, I'd wonder if I'm nothing but an experiment for you."

I laugh. "But you *will* help finish the scene?"

His smile goes from purely happy to a little roguish. "Oh, yes, my sweet, naughty, surprising librarian writer. I will happily help you finish. At least twice."

My entire body gets hot and I wiggle against him. "Thank you, David."

He chuckles. "So our boy is going to tell her to ride his cock like the sweet dirty girl she is...but only for him."

Oh, I like that. "Okay," I say breathlessly.

"She can go crazy," he says. "Say and do anything with him." He squeezes my ass. "Isn't that right, Mia?"

I nod. I, of course, understand that, right now, *I'm* the sweet, dirty girl in this scene.

"And then what is she going to say?" he asks, pressing me down against his cock.

"Oh God," I moan as he hits my clit.

"Yes, that's good. But I know our girl can be more specific."

I take a deep, shaky breath. I know I can say anything to him. Not only because he's been obviously reading my dirty thoughts right there on his computer screen and knows some of the filthy stuff that comes out of my imagination—I'm going to have to think about that later, but my first instinct is to love it— but also because David makes me feel free.

There's no judgment here. He seems to get a huge amount of enjoyment out of seeing me try new things and express things that I truly like and want. Thinking about how he has read my stories bolsters my courage. Not to mention the heat rushing through my body at the memories of what he did to my body last night. And the absolute pleasure he seemed to take in doing those things.

"I need you to fill me up. I'm aching for you," I tell him.

There's a rumble from his chest, and his fingers tighten on my ass. "Good. But I think she could be even dirtier."

Oh, he's going to push me. Okay. "Fuck me, David. *Please.*"

Again, his fingers flex against me. "Better. More. Tell me what you want. Be as graphic as you need to be."

It's the way he puts that that really frees me. This isn't about him. He's turned on. He's right here with me. He's ready to go. This isn't about getting him in the mood. He truly wants me to say whatever is on my mind.

I reach up and grip the back of his neck with both my hands, squeezing, so he understands the intensity I'm feeling. I lower my face, so our noses are nearly touching. I look into his eyes and say, "I want you to fill me up with your huge, hard cock. I want you to fuck me so deep and so hard that every time I sit down tomorrow, I'll think of you. I want you to make me come so hard that all I can think about is your name. I want you to ruin me, David. Please."

He's quiet for a moment, then his mouth stretches up in a wicked grin. "Thatta girl."

He brings my mouth down and kisses me, hotly, possessively. I feel the strokes of his tongue along my entire body. I am tingling and aching. I need him more than I ever imagined possible.

Instinctively, I start to reach between my thighs, needing pressure and friction against my clit. But he feels or senses what I'm doing and his big hand encircles my wrist, stopping me.

"No, no. That's all mine."

"Then do something," I say, my voice thick. He knows what I want. He's gotten me to open up and talk dirty. I'm not going to hold back now. "Please, David. Right here. Now."

"Oh, it's absolutely going to be right here and now." He presses against my ass. "Lift up."

I reach back for the handlebars and I lift myself off the seat. He gathers the skirt of my dress, lifting it up to my waist. I shiver, the combination of his eyes on me and the humid summer breeze rushing across parts of me that are never exposed outside in grassy fields.

He runs a big hand up the inside of my thigh, brushing over my folds.

"So wet," he comments.

"Do. Something," I say, my voice tight.

He runs his finger over me, masterfully finding my clit, brushing lightly as I gasp. Then he presses harder and circles faster, and I whimper.

"Can you hold yourself up there while I make you come?" he asks.

I have no idea. My arms are shaking a little, but I want this orgasm. "I'll try."

"You have no idea how fucking gorgeous you are right now," he tells me. "My wild outdoorsy girl."

Despite where his finger is and what it's doing, I giggle. "If I'd known what kind of activities I was missing out on, I would've become an outdoorsy girl a long time ago."

His finger slips inside me, stretching me slightly, the friction of his rough skin on me eliciting amazing sensations.

"I'm so fucking glad I'm the one who gets to make you wild," he says. He adds a second finger, teasing in and out twice, slow and deep, before spreading his fingers apart and giving me a sweet, delicious stretch.

I gasp. "Me too," I tell him. "I can't imagine it being anyone else."

"Remember that," he says, as he curls his fingers and rubs on that spot that makes my eyes cross.

"David!"

"Coat my fingers," he commands, gruff and firm. "Come for me so I can fuck this sweet pussy without hurting you."

That sends me over the edge. It's just that easy for him. I cry out as my orgasm slams into me. And no, I'm not able to hold myself up. But that's okay. David's there. As always. Fingers still deep, his other arm wraps around me and he pulls me into his lap, holding me against his chest as the ripples of my climax continue. His fingers slowly stroke in and out, his thumb lazily circling my clit, keeping me on edge.

"You're amazing," he murmurs against my temple. "I don't think you're the one who's ruined."

I like that way too much. I know I am, in fact, ruined. I can't imagine sex being this fun and dirty, but comfortable at the same time with anyone else. But I love the idea that somehow this is special to him.

"I need more of you," I tell him. It's only been his fingers. We haven't even actually had sex. But I want it. All of it. So much.

"Right front pocket. Get the condom."

I shift slightly not wanting to move too much and yet wanting to move like crazy. I just had an orgasm, and yet I need more friction, more thrusting, more stretching. I need him inside me. Right now.

I find the condom and rip it open.

"Put it on me."

I shift back and his fingers slide out of my pussy. I want

them back, but I know that I'm about to have something even better. I start to roll the condom on and then gasp as he puts his two fingers against my lower lip.

"God, the things I want to do to you," he says almost as if he's talking to himself. His fingers trace along my bottom lip, coating it with my own juices. Then he slides his fingers into his mouth and sucks on them.

My lips are still parted in surprise. He gives me a grin, then leans in and drags his tongue over my bottom lip, licking the same path his fingers just took. "Best thing I've ever tasted." He kisses me deeply, his tongue sliding along mine. I don't know if I actually taste myself or if I'm just imagining it, but it's all dirty and filthy and definitely stuff I've written.

I roll the condom the rest of the way down his length. "Now," I say simply.

"What would our beautiful dirty girl do or say now?" he asks.

"She..." I realize I need to think about it for a moment.

In my fanfiction, the hero typically takes the lead. They are also almost always at the fictional sex club. They've tried a variety of positions, toys, and role-playing, but always at his suggestion.

But they're falling for one another. It's obvious to everyone, even to them. Stepping outside of the sex club and their usual roles says it all. And having the heroine take more of a lead is a change in their dynamic. It's showing that she wants to be more to him than a sexual partner.

I reach for the bottom of my dress where it's bunched at my waist.

It's never just been sex between David and me. It's been a friendship that's been building on a bunch of things we have in common—our hometown, our families, a shared desire to make sure everyone around us is cared for, childhood trauma.

We also like each other, respect and admire each other's work, our relationships with others, the way we interact in the community. We also make each other laugh. We love to tease and flirt.

And we definitely have chemistry. And I want him to know that I want all of this to continue, I want to be a part of it, I appreciate that he's not going to let my dad be an issue.

And I'm all in.

I strip my dress up over my head and toss it on the back of the four-wheeler. I'm completely naked, fully exposed, letting it literally all hang out.

"She'd take what she wants," I tell him." And she'd tell him that he's the best she's ever had." I pause. "In every way. Not just the sex."

"Mia," he says gruffly.

I shift forward and take his cock in hand. I lift up, positioning him at my entrance. "And she'd tell him that she's so very, very glad to be with him here like this, and she hopes that it's just the beginning."

"I'm—"

But whatever he was going to say is cut off as I lower myself onto his length.

We both moan. He's big. Perfect. He stretches me, fills me, makes my damn toes actually curl.

"Oh God," I breathe.

"Jesus," he grits out. "Are you okay?"

"I've never been better."

"Well, let's see if we can do something about making the next few minutes even better."

Then he lifts, then lowers me.

And oh my God.

Then he does it again. And again.

I feel absolutely wanton with the summer breeze lifting my

hair, my breasts bouncing, completely filled up and surrounded by David Bennett. And I want this to go on forever.

But it absolutely is not going to; I already feel my orgasm building again.

"Oh my God, David. I'm going to come again."

"That's the idea," he says, his voice now tight.

I pry my eyes open and look down at him.

He looks almost in pain.

"Are *you* okay?" I ask.

"I'm in fucking heaven. And I need you to come. I'm not gonna hold on much longer."

I think about reaching between my legs, circling my clit and finishing this in the next thirty seconds. I'm right on the edge.

But then I have another idea.

A possibly better idea.

I can say and do anything with David. And there's something I really want.

"Can we stand up?" I ask.

He stops. "Stand up?"

"I want you to bend me over the seat and fuck me from behind."

That felt good saying it out loud. It's amazingly liberating to be able to say dirty fantasies out loud to someone.

A moment later, I find out it's even more thrilling when that person gives a deep growl, says 'fuck yes' and lifts you up easily, and has you standing in the grass, bent over seemingly a second later.

"Hold onto that seat. And tell me if I get too rough."

"Okay."

He takes hold of my braid, tipping my head back. "Mia, I will stop at any point. You're in control here. Tell me you understand."

"I am totally okay. Please, David." I reach back and grab his hip, pulling him closer.

I don't have to ask again. He keeps hold of my hair, grips my hip with his other hand, and thrusts deep and hard.

I grip the seat and hold on, arching my back slightly, pressing back, but then giving myself over to David's rhythm and the amazing sensations.

"Jesus. You're perfect. Amazing. *Fuck yes.*"

It's just those words over and over for the next few minutes.

I say similar things between gasps and moans.

And then my orgasm crashes over me and I am clenching around his cock and calling out his name.

"Fuck yes. *Mia!*" He slams into me one more time and then stiffens as he comes, gripping my hip and my hair.

He holds me like that for a few seconds before slumping over my back, his mouth going to my neck. He kisses up the side of my neck to my cheek, then turns my head and seals his mouth over mine.

When he pulls back, he says, "Are you all right? Did I hurt you?"

"If you did, I loved it," I tell him.

That gets a quiet chuckle. "Yeah, I have to remember the chapter with the flogger."

I laugh. "I'm not quite ready for *that.*"

He gives my ass a little tap, then slips out. "You tell me if and when you are. But there's a lot between this and that."

I realize I love that he knows about my writing. He's actually had a deep look into my fantasies, and it seems he's a fan.

He pulls off the condom and ties the end, tossing it into the bucket with the used sparklers, then reaches for my dress. He turns me to face him, pulling my dress over my head and smoothing it over my body.

"Panties?" I ask.

"What panties?"

"My panties. The ones you have in your back pocket." I saw him grab them from the grass and tuck them in his jeans pocket.

"I have no idea what you're talking about."

Got it. He's keeping my panties. I like that.

"Well, I have to thank you," I tell him.

He chuckles. "You do *not* have to thank me. I had a very good time too."

I laugh. "Not that. I can publish the last half of the scene still tonight."

"People are going to love that she's taking more control." He pauses. "I think it's going to be obvious to everyone that he's really falling for her."

My heart flips over. I try not to overreact. Maybe David doesn't realize that I've put a lot of us into those characters. I started writing their story before David rescued me from the tornado but since then, as they've gotten to know each other better, they've taken on the characteristics of each of us and yeah, okay in my mind it's becoming more fanfiction about *us* than about the book series it started from. "You think so?"

He cups my cheek, his thumb running along my jaw. "Yeah."

Oh, God. Something in his eyes tells me he definitely realizes those characters are him and me.

I'm about two seconds away from telling him I love him. I need to get my shit together.

"Thanks for coming out to check on the fireworks for Judy," I tell him. "But I hope you're not this nice to all the people you apprehend. This isn't your typical way of distracting people from their bad behavior, is it?"

He laughs. "I'd have quite the reputation."

"Women would be camping illegally and burning shit down all over this county," I agree.

"Well...thanks," he says with a wink. "And you haven't even tasted my waffles yet."

"Waffles?"

"Tomorrow's breakfast. But tonight, I'll make you a snack after."

I grin. "After what?"

"After we burn a bunch more calories."

Yes, please.

CHAPTER 21

DAVID

IF THE GOAL was to throw my niece an absolutely crazy, over-the-top, packed-with-people birthday party, we succeeded.

If the goal was to prove that a bunch of pink decorations, giggles, make up, and hair accessories would keep me from thinking about laying Mia Hansen out on my mother's picnic table, and covering her with the pink icing and sprinkles from the cupcakes before licking her clean from head to toe, I am completely failing.

I don't need to worry about thinking about all of the things I did to her the other night. My mind is full of a bunch of *new* things I want to do to her.

She looks absolutely beautiful.

And again, it's not how she has her hair down with curls swishing against her shoulders that are left bare by the baby blue sundress she's wearing. It's not her long tan legs underneath the hem of that dress. It's not the simple, pale pink gloss on her lips or the white sandals on her feet or anything else about her physical appearance.

It's her smile. It's her laugh. It's how she jokes and teases with my brothers. It's how comfortable she is around my parents and how much they obviously like her. It's how her sister and her parents obviously adore her, which is evident just in the way they smile at her and watch her when she's not looking. It's the way my nieces lit up when they saw her walk into the room.

It's just the way she fits here.

She's already a part of my life. She knows all of the important people to me, and they all like her and enjoy having her around.

Dating Mia Hansen—doing even more than dating Mia Hansen—would be so fucking easy.

Except for one man.

Scott and Peyton did, in fact, attend the party.

And Scott is now sitting at the picnic table with my father and my uncle Ty. They each have a beer in hand and are chatting and laughing easily. They've known each other for years and Scott fits here as comfortably as Mia does.

I cast one more look at Mia, to remind myself that this is absolutely worth it, then head to the picnic table and take a seat next to Ty.

"Nice," Ty comments when he notices my painted fingernails.

"I see you went for the sapphire blue," I say. He grins and wiggles his fingers, but only one hand is painted.

"You couldn't decide on a color?" I ask Scott, the only one at the table with no paint on the tips of his fingers.

After Mia and Sloan painted the girls' fingernails, they all wanted to practice. Because all of their friends' fingernails were already done, it fell to the adults to be the test subjects.

We all had happily volunteered. Chelsea is having an amazing time. I haven't seen her smile this much in months.

"I got a mani too," Scott says. He holds his hand out and I peer closer.

His nails are shiny. "Clear polish doesn't count," I say.

He chuckles and lifts his beer. "You're just jealous you didn't think of it."

He's right.

I take a long swallow of my cola, then say, "Scott, hey, I've been meaning to tell you, I think the pavilion plans are great. I know the other day we got off on the subject of all the animals and stuff. But I did want to tell you that."

He looks surprised, but nods. "Thanks. I know that spot probably has some nostalgia for you."

Fucker. Yes, I drank and smoked down there. But really? Did he have to bring that up when I was being nice?

He seems to realize what he said and holds up a hand. "I'm sorry. I appreciate it. And it's fine that you didn't say anything. You were busy. We threw a lot at you. That's my fault. I should've called you a long time ago."

I nod. "You should have. It would've been a lot easier." Then I realize I did the same thing. He has apologized. I should just accept it and move on. So I shake my head. "Sorry too. We'll get it taken care of now. It'll be fine."

"Even with the cats? You can get eight cats moved?"

"No. Moving them isn't a good idea. That's their territory. They'll probably just end up back there if we try to relocate them all at once too quickly." I glance at my dad. He just takes another drink of beer. "And one's pregnant. I'm afraid she'll return and have kittens in the work site somewhere and we won't know it. Instead, Mom and Dad are going to take them in."

"All eight?" Scott asks, turning to my dad.

"*Temporarily,*" Dad says.

I chuckle. Eight is a lot of cats. Especially when one of

them is about to turn into five or more. "We're going to work on taming them. Get them fixed. Socialize them. Then get them adopted."

"We?" Scott asks.

"The deal is I have to help," I say. "And they're using my old bedroom as a cat room. It's equipped with kennels, cat toys, and litter boxes now."

"Are we talking about the cats?" Charlie asks as he and Jack join us at the table with drinks.

"Yep," Dad says. "You're going to come help too?"

Charlie grins at me then at Dad. "You've got Chelsea and Ray and Del. They're going to be thrilled to have all those cats. You don't need me."

"How long will socializing take?" Ty asks.

"Could be a few months," I admit. "They've been wild strays for a while. It takes time to win their trust. Prove that they're safe. Get to the point where they'll let you touch them and take care of them. Definitely a while until they're 'family pet ready'."

"Definitely going to need a lot of hands," Charlie says.

"You should ask Mia to help," Jack says. Looking directly at *me*.

I widen my eyes and say, "Why would I do that?"

Has Jack been drinking? Is he about to out me and Mia?

"She's a librarian. Ask her for some research material about taming stray cats and I bet she shows up and helps out. That's what I did about manicures and look at this party." He gestures around the yard at large.

"That's true," Charlie muses. "She's very *hands-on* for a librarian. Or are they all like that?"

He directs the question to Scott.

I might kill my brother.

"She does love to research and try new things," Scott says, nodding.

I almost swallow my soda wrong. I cough. Charlie gives me a huge grin.

"That's very...adventurous of her," he says.

Yes, I'm definitely going to kill him.

"Damn. We really are causing you a problem," Scott says to me, pulling my attention from the kind of research I'm going to need to do to make Charlie's death look like an unfortunate accident.

I shake my head. "It's my job." It is. Moving animals around so that they can live alongside people with everyone safe and happy is a big part of what I do. Even with stray town cats.

Scott and I give each other a long look. We silently acknowledge that we both know what's going on. We are trying to extend olive branches and it is uncomfortable and unusual for us.

But it's nice to be trying.

"But you are relocating the bees, right?" Scott asks. "Next week?"

"Yeah. Monday is the plan," I confirm.

"Bees?" Ty asks. "Like bumblebees?"

"Honeybees," Scott says. "Turns out there are some beehives down there in part of the old shelter. No one really knew what to do. It could've been a huge problem, for obvious reasons, tearing into the space they've taken up. Not just for the workers but also for the bees."

"No kidding," Ty says he looks at me. "You're gonna go in and kill all the bees?"

I look at him with wide eyes. "I am not going to *kill* all the bees. I'm going to remove them. We're going to set them up somewhere else where they'll be safe and won't bother anyone. You don't *kill* honeybees, Ty."

Tyler laughs and shakes his head. "Okay, man. Better you than me."

Scott shrugs. "Well, yeah. It's why people like David are so important."

I give him a surprised look. "Thanks."

"Well, it's true. You keep people, and animals, safe."

The warmth I feel in my chest is unwelcome. I want to get along with Scott. I want him to think that I am good enough for his daughter. But I don't want to start wanting his approval and attention. I'm past all of that. He is just a guy. He's not a hero, he's not a role model, he's just a guy. And I'm a grown man who doesn't have or need a hero or role model anymore.

"So, have you guys seen what they're doing for the girls tonight after we all clear out?" Charlie asks.

"Yeah, we're setting them up for movies here in the backyard," my dad says.

We laugh. It's his backyard. Obviously he knows what's going on.

Charlie looks straight at me. "Yeah. They're putting up a big sheet to project the movie onto like a big movie screen. Then, setting the girls up with pillows, blankets, and sleeping bags. They're stringing up twinkle lights too, making it a whole outdoor movie theater thing. Isn't that a cool, unique idea?"

I widen my eyes at my brother. What the fuck is he doing?

"That sounds cool. Need some help putting the lights up or something?" Ty asks.

"Yeah, I could use some help with that. I think there's probably some poles to string the lights from? What do you think, David? Does that sound right?"

I am going to beat my brother before I kill him.

"Why are you asking me?" I ask. "I'm guessing Mom and Dad have it worked out."

"Oh, I don't know, actually," Dad says. "The idea was Mia and Sloan's."

Hearing her name, and the fact that she loaned our movie idea to them for the birthday party, makes heat arrow through my gut.

Fuck, I like that girl. And now I really want to fucking kiss her. I want to find her, pull her into a secret corner, and kiss the hell out of her.

"Oh well, then why don't you go ask them?" I say to Charlie, trying to keep my voice and expression calm.

"Yeah, they said something about poles and lights. I was hoping maybe you could help."

I narrow my eyes, but nod. "Happy to help. What exactly do you need?"

"Could you go in the house and get the lights?"

"Do you want me to help you put up poles?" Dad asks. "Or I can go in and find the lights. I think they're in the kitchen."

Charlie shakes his head quickly. "We've got it. Go get the lights, David."

"Okay, Jesus." I get up. Things were going good with Scott. I could've used a few more minutes. But maybe it's better in short spurts like this. There's a chance I would've said something sarcastic or rude if we kept talking. Or worse, I would have started trying to impress him.

I head into the kitchen, assuming that strings of lights will be easy to locate.

But I come up short.

Suddenly, Charlie's insistence that I help with the project makes sense.

"Hi," Mia says with a big smile.

It's just her and me in the kitchen.

Okay, but I'm still going to get him back for the "She's very hands-on for a librarian".

"Hi." I cross the floor to where she's standing, crowding close.

The window to my right over the sink looks out over the backyard and if anyone looks in the window, they could see us standing close together. We need to be careful here. But this is the first time I've had a chance to really talk to her.

We've been exchanging glances across the yard. She gave me a cheeky grin when I first arrived, and I did pass close to her and let my hand brush over her ass at one point when we were all dishing up food from my mother's enormous buffet.

But otherwise, as far as anyone at this party knows, we are just like always—we barely know each other and have no reason to really talk.

"Charlie sent me in here to find lights."

She holds up her hand, strings of lights dangling from her fingers. "These lights?"

"I don't care," I put my hand on the front of her throat and start walking her backward. When her back hits the fridge, we are out of line of sight of the window.

"You look amazing," I tell her. "And I have been thinking about what cake frosting would taste like licked off your clit since the moment I arrived."

She sucks in a little breath. "That's interesting because I've been thinking about what cake icing would taste like sucked off your cock since you walked in."

I cover her mouth with mine, kissing her deep and hot. It can't be long, but I fully taste her before lifting my head. "I want you to walk around the rest of this party, thinking about exactly that. And the fact that I am going to swipe a cupcake on my way out of here, and you *will* be seeing that cupcake again later. For a few seconds at least before I dip it down between your pretty legs, paint it over your gorgeous pussy, and then spend the next several minutes making us both very, very happy."

She shivers but gives me a big smile. "There's no chance we can sneak up to your childhood bedroom right now, is there?" Her gaze flickers to something just beyond my shoulder.

I glance over and see extra cupcakes sitting on the counter.

The question is flirty and a little dirty, and I love it. But something strange happens. I feel like she reached in, wrapped her sweet hand around my heart, and squeezed. I am suddenly filled with soft emotions, affection, and delight, and probably, if it wasn't too fucking fast and too damn easy, I'd call it love.

I can imagine pulling her up to my room. I can imagine spending the night in that room with her so we can wake up with the family on Christmas morning. I can imagine tucking our kids into bed in that room when they come to spend the night with Grandma and Grandpa.

Of course, all of that will be *after* we finish fostering the eight cats that are up there right now.

"Not today," I tell her. "But after everyone knows we're together, and we're here for Thanksgiving or Christmas or someone else's birthday, I am absolutely taking you upstairs, locking that door, throwing you on my childhood bed, and finding out if you can stay quiet while I eat your pretty pussy."

She's breathing fast by the time I finish, and I realize that it all hit her the same way it hit me when she says, "Thanksgiving or Christmas?"

I nod. "Maybe even Thanksgiving *and* Christmas."

The front door of the house opens and closes, and I step back quickly. She moves away from the fridge, spinning quickly and opening it, bending over as if she's searching for something. I move to lean back against the counter.

"And all he has is ten, can you believe that?" I ask.

"Only ten? That's crazy," she says, as her mother walks into the room.

"Oh, here you are." Peyton looks from Mia to me. "What are you doing?"

"Just getting David a soda," she says, straightening from the fridge and handing me an orange soda I absolutely don't want.

I hate orange soda. I still pop the top and take a long drink. "Thanks."

Peyton narrows her eyes and watches as Mia swings the door to the fridge shut.

"David couldn't come in and get his own soda from his mother's refrigerator?" she asks.

"Well, I was already in here and closer to the fridge, and he asked if I'd grab him one," Mia says.

It's actually impressive and possibly concerning how quickly and easily that lie rolls off her tongue.

"Why are you in the kitchen?"

Mia holds up the lights. "I'm helping Charlie put up the twinkle lights for the girls' movie night. He sent me in here to find them."

Peyton crosses her arms. "The lights that Delaney swore she already took outside and had on the picnic table with the big sheet that they're going to hang up for the screen?"

Mia shrugs. "I don't know. Charlie sent me in here and here they were."

Peyton suddenly bursts out laughing. "Okay, I realize that your dad is terrible about telling when you're lying to him, which still to this day absolutely amazes me, but you guys are gonna have to work on that if you're not going to tell him."

Mia straightens and looks at me. My eyes are wide as I look from her back to Peyton.

Peyton rolls her eyes. "Seriously? I mean okay, I have an advantage because I read about the deer stand and the camping with the twinkle lights." She looks at me. "That sounded really romantic by the way."

I frown and look at Mia. "Read about it?"

Mia groans. "My mom reads my fanfiction."

I straighten away from the counter. Oh...shit.

"I actually just thought she was writing some *wishes*," Peyton says.

"Mom!"

"Until I read the four-wheeler one. I skimmed it, by the way, when I realized it really was you."

Mia groans. "You found *that* story? Mom. How do you keep doing this?"

"Doing what?" I ask.

Peyton grins. "She started a whole new story. It's still set in the same world, but it's outside the sex club. It's a whole new couple. They've interestingly known each other since childhood. And they've had hot, dirty sex in a deer stand, and in the back of a pickup. With twinkle lights."

I shake my head. "There are *more* stories? And that didn't happen." I look at Mia.

"Stuff happened," she protests.

"Not hot, dirty sex."

"It was pretty hot on my end," Mia says.

"But we didn't do *anything* in the deer stand."

"Okay that..." Mia trails off, then says. "I took artistic freedom with both. It was more what I imagined or wanted or fantasized about what could've happened in both those places."

Peyton is just listening, grinning widely.

I groan and run a hand over my face. "This is your *mom*."

"I love her stuff. I think she needs to submit it to a publisher and see if they'll buy it."

"I started a new username and wrote that story completely

separately from what I usually write. You weren't supposed to find it or know it was me."

"Please. I love that whole fanfiction world, and have things set up so I get notifications for *anyone* publishing there. And your writing style is very distinctive. Plus, a deer stand and the back of a pickup sounded like something you'd like to try. The four-wheeler did surprise me, though."

I look at Mia. "I think I'm gonna need your new username."

And I realize that I will very much like watching this woman blush for the rest of my life.

"Anyway," Peyton says. "You guys are gonna have to be a little less obvious if you don't want Scott to find out."

Now Mia looks a little chagrined. "I don't like keeping it from him, but—"

Peyton holds up both hands. "I get it. You have your reasons. I do think you need to tell him. He would appreciate hearing about it rather than just finding out or suspecting it. He always thinks you're sweet and telling him the truth," Peyton says to Mia. "But eventually, he's going to get suspicious. He is a very good cop."

"We've been talking about it."

"I'm glad to hear that. It seemed to me, judging from the fanfiction, that you guys didn't have a lot of time to be doing anything like talking." Then she gives us a wink and turns and walks out of the kitchen.

And I realize I'm also going to really enjoy having her as a mother-in-law.

And then I realize that *that* thought should have sent shock-waves through my system. I should at least be appalled or amazed that it occurred to me so easily. But as I look over at Mia, I realize that no. I'm not amazed or appalled.

This has happened fast. But it feels right, and I'm tired of just making this up as we go along. I want this to be real.

"Sorry about that," Mia says before I can say anything.

"Sorry that your mom just outed your extra dirty fanfiction or sorry that you haven't told me about it yet?"

She wrinkles her nose and looks absolutely edible. "Sorry about all of that?"

"New username," I say firmly.

"Mia H."

I bark out a laugh. "No way."

She nods. "I kind of thought that maybe people would think it was too obvious. That there is no way I would actually use my real name, so they would never think it was me."

I shake my head and say, "I really like you, Mia H."

She looks surprised but pleased. "I really like you, too.

"I hate that I can't kiss you more right now."

"Me too."

"We'll fix that. Soon."

She nods. "Yes."

"But if you come over tonight, I'll kiss you a lot."

She grins. "Where?"

"All over, sweet girl. All fucking over."

She smiles and turns to leave the kitchen but pauses in the doorway and glances back.

"Maybe you should grab *two* cupcakes on your way out of the party. We wouldn't want to run out of icing."

I watch her sweet ass sashay out my mother's front door.

And make a note to grab three cupcakes.

CHAPTER 22

DAVID

"SO, it's simple. We're going to move the hive into the box," I say, pointing to the wooden box that's already secured in the back of my truck. "I'll seal the box, we'll drive it over to Sally's, unload it in the new location, open the box, and let the bees come out as they want to."

I'm explaining the procedure for taking the hive from the park to Sally Rumkin's backyard to Landon Woods, one of the volunteer firefighters, and Scott.

Sally has agreed to have the hive at the back of her property on the edge of town. It's the best solution. The hive will be nearly a mile from its original spot, and bees operate according to strict rules, but it is possible to teach bees to find their hive that far away. Sally has also had bees before, so it should all be fine.

"That sounds easy," Landon says.

"Well, it *sounds* easy, let's just hope it really is," I tell him. "It can be a little tough on them to move their hive location, but there are some things I'm going to do to make it easier on them. I'm also going to set up a smaller box to hopefully capture any stragglers." I look up at the sky. "This is a good time of day, though. Most of them should be inside." I waited until dusk intentionally.

"Okay, I'm ready," Landon says.

I look at Scott. He nods. "Me too."

"Okay, let's suit up."

We all reach for the sting-proof jumpsuits and start pulling them over our clothes. We've also got boots and helmets with veils on them to protect our faces and heads. They'll zip onto the jumpsuits to keep any bees from sneaking inside.

I help both men with their zippers and then step back to inspect everything.

"Okay, gloves, and we're ready to go."

The rest of the operation goes smoothly enough. I use a smoker to gently encourage the lingering bees into the hive and then seal it. The drive to Sally's is short and uneventful, as is moving the hive from my truck to the spot where Sally is letting the bees make their new home.

The entire thing takes less than an hour, including the setup of the extra box back at the park.

Landon takes off, leaving Scott and me alone.

"So a couple of days and the straggler bees should be rounded up?" Scott asks.

"Right. The queen is definitely with the hive, so getting them over there shouldn't be hard. I don't think they'll be causing any trouble over here."

Scott bends to take his boots off, and as I unzip my jump-suit, he asks, "Hey, can we talk for a minute?"

I tense. We've been talking. About the project. About work. The safe things.

If he's asking specifically to talk when it's just the two of us, that means the topic is not casual.

Shit.

Did he notice something at the party this weekend? Did Peyton or Charlie say something?

Is it just guilt that makes my thoughts immediately jump to Mia and our sneaking around? It could be. I've got a lot of it.

I don't like keeping this secret. Not only because it feels wrong to keep this from the people that we care about, but because I really want people to know that I am with her. Mia is amazing, and the fact that she wants to spend time with me is something I'm very proud of.

I straighten and face Scott. "Of course."

He tosses the boots in the back of my truck.

"A few days ago, when I was talking to Mia and Peyton about this project, your name came up."

I cross my arms, then uncross them, aware that's a very defensive posture. "Okay."

"I came home that day, the first day you showed up, frustrated. But not at you. At myself. As I've said, I realize I should've called you before this. But I didn't because things have been tense between us for a long time. But Peyton and Mia got me talking about it. And, well, thinking about it ever since then." He blows out a breath and rubs the back of his neck. "You came to me once and asked if I thought you should be a cop. I told you no." He meets my gaze.

"Actually, you said I'd be a terrible cop."

"Right." He tucks his hands in his pockets. "I'm sorry I said it that way. I should've talked it out with you instead."

To say I'm shocked by this would be an understatement. But I study him, going over his words before I ask, "So you're sorry for the *way* you said it, but not *what* you said?"

Scott nods. "Yeah. I did not want you to be a cop. And I'm not sorry that I told you that. I always tried to be honest with you. But I think I could've said it differently."

"You're not sure?" I give a short chuckle. "You're not sure

that there was a better way of saying *you would be a terrible cop?"*

He looks a little sheepish. "I wanted you to hear me. You were a headstrong, rebellious young adult at that point. I guess I was afraid that if I wasn't blunt, you might not hear me."

"So you really did think I would be terrible, and you wanted to be *sure* I heard you say that."

His shoulders drop, and his expression softens. "Honestly, it wasn't about you being bad at the job. It was the job being bad for you."

I feel that impact in my chest. My ribs feel tight, and my heart thumps against them as if trying to escape the squeeze. "What do you mean?"

He takes another breath and blows it out. "I wanted you to be happy. I wanted you to do something that would be good for you. Something that would make you happy and proud, but that would spare you pain."

I take that in. "You think being a cop would've been hard on me?"

"For sure. I know you wanted to work in a small town, but, David, it can be hard here, too. When shit goes sideways and bad things happen, we're called in. In a small town, it can be worse because those bad things are happening to people we know and care about." He lifts his hands, then lets them fall. "The last thing I wanted was for you to show up at the scene of a shooting—intentional or accidental—and have it be someone that you knew and cared about. And have it turn out badly."

My chest tightens even further.

I wasn't there when my mother was shot, of course. I never saw the scene. But I had imagined it many times over the years. Of course, I never want to see a scene like that with someone I know.

"And you know that we're also called in for medical emergencies."

I wet my lips, my mouth suddenly dry.

Emergency response includes the fire department, the EMTs, and yes, the cops.

"I didn't want you to have to be the one who responded when someone passed away at home."

My dad had passed away at home. I had been there when it happened. Delaney and my brothers had all been there. That had helped. I was glad I'd been there, but wow, it had sucked.

The hours after are still a blur, even this many years later, but I do remember people in uniforms coming to the house.

"You've had to do that?" My throat feels like I've swallowed sand.

He nods. "Yeah. Of course. We're there to help and support in all kinds of situations, especially in a town like this. And I'm happy to do it. I'm proud to do it. But it's hard. I just didn't think you should have to do that. Not when there were other ways to take care of people and serve the community and be happy. I saw you, David, and I knew that Game and Parks would be perfect for you."

I swallow hard. Then I have to swallow again. "You were protecting me."

"Trying to. And I hated that it made you angry with me. But if it protected you and saved you from some pain, it was worth it."

I swallow again and take a deep breath. "I've spent years thinking that you didn't care. That you quit trying because you were sick of me. And that you talked me out of being a cop because you didn't want to work with me."

I see the pain on his face at my confession, but he takes a deep breath and nods. "I guess I can see that. I'm really damned sorry. I didn't know that. I knew we had tension. I figured you were pissed because I had pushed your family into holding that intervention."

I give a short laugh. "I needed that intervention. If I'd known you were the one pushing for it, I probably would've appreciated it. Eventually."

"So we've had a sincere lack of communication."

"Very much so," I agree nodding. "That really sucks."

"It does. But you ended up where you needed to be. Where we all needed you to be. Sapphire Falls, this whole area, is lucky to have you doing what you do. And you're happy. I'm grateful for that."

I am happy. I can't deny that. "Yeah, I am, Scott. I really am."

He nods, looking relieved, and I realize he needed to hear me say that.

"We've just missed out on working together. Cooperatively anyway," I say. "I'm sorry for that."

"There's a lot of time ahead. We can work together a lot from here on out."

I smile. It's going to take me some time to process all of this fully, but I already feel lighter. "I'd like that, Scott," I clear my throat. "Thank you for this. Whatever made you finally tell me, I really appreciate it."

"Yeah. Of course. I should've said it a long time ago. There was just something about talking to Mia about it that made things click. I suddenly realized there was a lot more to the story that you should know."

Hearing her name makes my heart squeeze.

Mia. The most important thing Scott and I have in common. And it turns out we have a lot of important things in common.

"Let's just make an agreement that going forward we're going to communicate well," Scott says. "When there's something going on, we're going to say it, clearly, and even if it needs to be blunt, we'll talk it all the way through. Not just the basics. We tell each other everything behind it."

And now my stomach cramps.

Communication. Honesty. The full story.

Yeah. We should definitely do that.

Fuck.

CHAPTER 23

MIA

THE SUNSET from the little dock at Judy Turner's private pond is gorgeous. The weather is perfect as well. It was a hot, humid day that is just now starting to slightly cool as the sun drops. The perfect evening for skinny dipping.

I grin.

Skinny dipping has always sounded fun, but it's not something I would do with just anyone. Also, I would never do it in the river because all kinds of stuff lives and floats there.

But a private pond on a friend's property is perfect.

And skinny dipping with only me and David Bennett is exactly how I want to get naked in any situation.

From now on.

I hug my knees to my chest and wrap my arms around them as I watch the sun drop behind the horizon.

Thoughts like that have been seeping into my mind more and more often.

I know it's too fast. But it's just so easy with us. Chelsea's birthday party seemed to illustrate that better than anything.

Our families mix so naturally. Our histories are so similar.

Our lives in this little town we both love are so much alike. Add to all of that the chemistry we have and how much we enjoy being around each other, and it just seems obvious to start thinking about the future. Even in the short time we've been "dating".

I suppose we should talk about that.

But that will lead to a conversation about telling my father. And frankly, I'm not sure how that conversation will go. I watched them together at the birthday party, and they seemed to be getting along. I saw smiles and even some laughter.

But it's a big deal, and I can't just assume David is ready to forgive and forget.

I hear tires crunching on the path leading down to the pond. I quickly scramble to my feet and shrug off the swimsuit cover-up I'm wearing.

Sans the swimming suit.

I tested the water a little bit earlier, and it's nice and warm. So with a giggle, I jump off the end of the dock.

I hit the water, going under slightly. I have my hair pulled up on top of my head, so it's out of my face when I break the surface. I wipe a hand over my eyes and tread water, waiting to see David stride to the end of the dock.

From here, I intend to watch him strip out of his uniform with just enough light left to see all of the essential details before he joins me down here in the water.

The footsteps on the dock definitely sound like boots, but it sounds like he's stomping angrily. I grin. He's probably worked up and turned on. He has to know it's me. My car is parked off to the side for one thing, and at this point, surely he knows when Judy calls him to come out to her property, it will have to do with me.

Hopefully, Judy never has a real issue she needs David for.

Then again, he always shows up right away so even if it's something legit, he'll be here to take care of it for her.

He also has to know that I'm down here, naked, considering my bikini top and bottoms, and the cover-up are lying in plain sight on the dock.

"*Mia?*"

I stop for a second, but then have to start paddling again. But that is not David's voice.

And worse, I know exactly whose voice it is.

"*Dad?*"

My dad comes to the end of the dock and looks down at me. "What the hell are you doing?"

"Swimming," I say, trying to inject confidence in my tone.

Okay, he doesn't know that David was on his way out here to join me.

Oh God, I hope David isn't on his way out here now.

We're going to have to lie our asses off if he shows up. I'm so tired of lying about us.

Having my dad catch me and David skinny-dipping is not an ideal situation, but continuing to lie to my dad about a guy that I have big, serious feelings for is really getting icky.

"You're swimming in Judy's pond? Without permission?"

"How... How do you know I don't have permission?"

"Because she called to report that someone was swimming in her pond without permission." He looks around. "And you're the only one here."

I frown. "Judy called *you?*" I had specifically told Judy to call David again, and I know she has his number.

"I think she called the Game and Parks office. But they knew David was tied up dealing with the bees at the park. When they found out what it was about, they called me. Figured a trespassing situation was right up my alley." He plants his hands on his hips. "I don't think they knew it was my daughter."

I wince.

I knew David had the bee thing. Dammit. I should've done this tomorrow night.

"I didn't think Judy would mind."

"She probably wouldn't have if you'd asked."

"So, what now?"

"Now you get out of her pond. And probably tell her it was you and apologize. I'm going to assume she won't press charges."

I can assure him that she won't. "Okay."

He continues to stand there.

"Um..." I say.

"I'm afraid I'm going to need to escort you to her house," he says. "That's what I would do with anyone else, and I can't play favorites."

I roll my eyes. He's always such a stickler for the rules, and ironically, this reminds me that he and David have a lot in common. "Okay," I say. "But I'm going to need you to turn around. I'm naked."

My dad steps back from the end of the dock as if I said I was going to throw a piranha up on him. "You're naked? What the hell are you doing swimming *naked*?"

Waiting to seduce the Game and Parks guy I was hoping was going to show up is not the right answer here. "It just seemed like fun," I say, happy that's at least not a total lie.

My dad blows out an exasperated breath. "Get up here and get dressed. Then we'll head to Judy's."

Honestly, as I climb the short little wooden ladder and pull on my bikini and cover up, I'm wincing inside for another reason.

My dad doesn't get mad at me very often. He's not frustrated or exasperated or disappointed in me hardly ever. Mostly because I tried very hard not to let that happen. I admire my dad. I think he's amazing. And he's been my hero since I was a little girl. I tried very hard to toe the line and make him proud of me.

This is a tiny infraction. It's nothing serious. It's certainly not going to turn into charges. But I can't deny that the little girl inside me is still feeling very sheepish right now.

"Okay, I'm decent," I say.

He turns. "Swimming naked is not a great idea for a lot of reasons. Not just because somebody you're not expecting might show up. There could be poison ivy or oak around the banks."

I press my lips together and nod. He's right, of course.

"Also, you don't know what kind of bacteria there might be in there. And there could be water snakes. Or underwater branches that could scratch you up. There are certain parts of your body where you don't want scratches, Mia."

I giggle. I can't help it.

Not because scratches on my private parts are funny, but because this is so reminiscent of how David acted when he found me in the field the very first night during the storm. And when he found me in the deer stand. And probably how he would react if he found me out here skinny-dipping, to be honest.

My dad's brows arch. "What's funny?"

"Just that you're maybe overreacting slightly. The chances of me getting scratched by a branch or bitten by a snake out here are slim, right?"

"Slim doesn't mean impossible."

I stifle my laughter and nod. He's not wrong.

But wow, my dad and David really are the same guy in a lot of ways. My mom was absolutely right.

My children are going to either be the most obedient children Sapphire Falls has ever seen or absolute hellions.

Ten minutes later, we're knocking on Judy's front door.

The older woman pulls the door open with a huge smile. "Mia!" Then her eyes land on my dad coming up the steps behind me. "Hello, Scott."

"Evenin', Judy. This is who was trespassing at your pond."

"Oh, I know."

I grimace.

My dad stops beside me. "You know?"

"She figured it out when I showed up soaking wet in my swimsuit," I say quickly, giving Judy a wide-eyed stare.

I really like Judy, and she has been awesome about going along with all of my shenanigans. But I'm not sure how good she is at thinking on her feet or catching subtle please-go-along-with-this hints.

But she nods quickly. "Right. Of course."

"Well, I know you called Game and Parks, but they sent me when David was busy," my dad says. "I wanted to let you know that it was just Mia and nothing to worry about. But..." My dad looks at me expectantly.

"I shouldn't have been out there without permission. I'm really sorry. I will ask next time."

Judy holds up a hand. "No need to ask. You're free to use it anytime. You and David just consider that pond your own."

My breath lodges in my chest.

My dad freezes next to me.

Oh. Crap.

I swear ten seconds of total silence tick past, feeling like a year, before my dad turns and looks down at me. "David? David, who?"

I squeeze my eyes shut and take a deep breath, then turn and meet his gaze. "David Bennett. David was going to meet me out there. At least that was the plan."

"Out at the pond. Where you were swimming. Naked."

I nod.

"And would David have been completely shocked to find you out there like that?"

I shake my head. "Pleasantly surprised, maybe. But..." I swallow hard. "He would've joined me."

"And you know this because you..." My dad trails off.

"We're seeing each other," I fill in.

"Okay then. Things make a lot more sense now." He looks back to Judy. "Have a nice night, Judy." Then he turns on his heel and descends the steps of her porch.

I watch him go, my heart pounding painfully in my chest. I have no idea what to do.

Should I go after him? Let him go? Call my mom? Call David? Call Kyle and Derek, my dad's best friends?

Where will he go? What will he do? Will he want to be alone to process this? Who will he tell first?

My mom. For sure.

But she already knows. Will she tell him that? Will that cause them to fight?

I swallow hard.

Well...my dad now knows about me and David. I guess that's something.

I need to tell David.

I look at Judy. "I'll see you later, Judy."

She looks upset. "I am so sorry. I didn't mean to slip like that."

"It is not your fault. We are the ones who should've told my dad a long time ago. Please don't blame yourself."

Judy reaches out as I start to turn away. "Your dad loves you so much, Mia. This is not a big deal."

"Oh, it's a very big deal. There's history between him and David."

She shrugs. "It doesn't matter. David Bennett is a wonderful man. Having a man like that love his daughter the way David loves you will make your dad happy. He wants you to be happy and safe. David can do that. That's what will matter."

My heart flips over in my chest, hearing her say that David loves me. "Do you know my dad that well?" I ask. Maybe the number of years that Judy has known my dad gives her special insight into him, and I can trust her word.

"I don't need to know your dad. That's how good fathers feel, and yours is exceptional."

Well, she's right about that.

CHAPTER 24

DAVID

MY PHONE RINGS just as I'm pulling clothes on after a shower.

I immediately smile when I see Mia's name pop up. I hit the button to connect it to speakerphone. "Hey, beautiful."

"My dad knows about us."

I feel a cold ball of dread settle in my gut. "What? How? I just saw him a little bit ago."

"I was trespassing and skinny-dipping at Judy's. She tried to call you, but you were busy, and apparently they routed the call to my dad."

My eyes slide shut and my head tips back as I groan. "Well, that's about the worst thing I've ever heard. I missed you skinny dipping, *and* your dad found out about us."

"Yeah. He left me without saying much. I need to go talk to him, but I wanted you to know."

"Thanks. I think maybe we should talk to him together. He and I had a nice moment earlier today."

Fuck. Just when I thought we were making some headway too.

"I have no idea how he's going to react," Mia says. "He and I have never had a falling out like this."

Of course, she's been the perfect daughter. That doesn't surprise me.

I hear a knock on my front door. Frowning, I head in that direction. Very few people come clear out here, and even fewer do it without invitation. Maybe it's one of my brothers. Maybe they found out that Scott found out. Maybe Scott's down at the Come Again getting drunk and ranting about what an asshole I am.

I am carrying the phone with me as I pull the door open.

I am surprised for two seconds and then I blow out a breath. "Well, I think I know how he's going to react," I tell Mia.

"We need to talk," Scott Hansen says from my front porch.

"Dad? Is that you?" Mia calls through the phone. "Dad, please don't do anything to David! I started the whole thing. I went after him! I seduced him!"

"Mia," I cut her off. "Don't take this the wrong way, okay?"

"Take what the wrong way?"

I hang up on her.

"Why couldn't you tell me?" Scott asks.

I step back and motion for him to come in. He shakes his head. "This will be quick. Why did you feel like you couldn't tell me?"

"It started out as just a flirtation. I didn't think anything would happen. So I didn't think it was worth getting you riled up about your daughter seeing a guy you didn't like."

Scott frowns. "I've never not liked you."

I tuck my hands into the pockets of the lounge pants I pulled on. "But we've just now established that. I didn't know that."

"Fair enough." He takes a breath. "You thought it was just a flirtation. But when it got more serious, you still didn't want to tell me? Does Peyton know?"

"Only because she figured it out. We didn't tell her. We didn't tell anyone. Everyone just...figured it out."

Scott shakes his head. "Except the cop."

"To be fair, we tried extra hard to keep it from you."

"Because you thought I wouldn't approve?"

I nod. "And I know you're probably not happy—"

"That's why I'm here," he interrupts. "I'm hurt that I'm the last one to know. But I am here because I need you to hear me say something."

I brace myself. "Okay." I'm going to have to tell Scott that it only matters a little what he thinks and feels. That I'm in love with his daughter and I intend to stay that way for the rest of my life. But I can hear him out first.

"I'm very happy for my daughter to date you," Scott says. "You are a good man. You are an excellent officer. You're a wonderful son. You're a fantastic brother. You are an important part of our community."

I stare at him, stunned.

"Mia needs to be loved hard," Scott goes on. "Fully. She needs people who will love her in a way where there is no question. So I'm here to tell you that I'm glad it's you. But she needs to be loved openly, unabashedly, by someone who isn't afraid to make an ass of himself over her. She can never have a question about how you feel. I need you to do that. To be upfront and out loud and public about it."

My chest is tight with emotion, but I draw myself up straight. "Yes, sir. I can do that."

Scott nods. "I know you can. I'm sorry if I made it so you couldn't to this point."

I stick my hand out to shake his, for the first time in probably nearly a decade. He takes it, but he doesn't shake my hand. He uses it to pull me into a hug.

And as he squeezes me, I feel the rest of the weight that has been on my shoulders lift.

I watch him leave, and then I head for his daughter's house.

She opens the door before I even knock. "Oh my God, you're alive. Please tell me you're not breaking up with me. I will seriously yell at him. I love him so much. And I absolutely respect him. And I really want the two of you to get along. But we'll work this out. Please don't—"

"I'm in love with you," I tell her, cutting her off. "I know it's fast and probably a little nuts, but I am. I have no question about that. I want to date you, I want to be with you constantly, and I want everybody in the entire world to know."

She stands staring at me, her mouth hanging open.

I move in close until I'm almost on top of her and cup her face in my hands. "Your dad and I are good. He loves you very much, and everything is fine. Better than fine. We're...really good. He's happy about us."

Her hands circle my wrists, and she swallows. "Really?"

"Really."

She takes a deep breath and then lets it out. "Okay."

"Well, there is one thing," I say.

She frowns. "What?"

"You haven't told me how you feel yet. And if you'll date me."

Her smile is bright and wide. "Oh my God, yes, I will date you. David, I am madly in love with you. I have never felt this way before. I want to write the dirtiest stories because of you, but I also want to write sweet, sappy love stories because of you. I want to go four-wheeling, and rock climbing, and yes, skinny dipping." Her hands come to my waist, and she hooks her fingers through my belt loops, pulling me close. "I want to do everything. I want to cuddle on the couch with you, and go to family birthday parties with you, and I absolutely positively want you to do very dirty things to me in your childhood bedroom at Christmas."

I stare down at her, my heart feeling like it might burst wide open. "I am up for making all kinds of plans with you, Mia Hansen," I tell her. "But I have to be honest."

"Always," she agrees.

"I'm not really into rock climbing."

It takes her a beat, then she laughs. "Okay, well, I can go rock climbing with Sloan."

"We'll see," I tell her. "Rock climbing is pretty risky. You have to—"

She seals her lips to mine.

And I realize I'm okay with her shutting me up this way. For the rest of our lives.

Then she reaches past me and pushes the front door shut with a nice, hard slam. "Why don't you carry me down the hall to the second room on the left? It will be totally safe. No storms are brewing, and there are no critters or poisonous plants or branches that might scrape up our private parts in there."

"Branches that might—" I start.

"Never mind," she tells me. "Just take me to bed, David."

"You mean have sex *indoors*?"

She grins. "Think you can handle that, Officer Bennett?"

I bend and lift her into my arms and start down the hall. "I'm sure we'll come up with something," I tell her. "Turns out we're pretty good at making it up as we go along."

"OH, hang on, there's one more."

Everyone looks up from their side conversations and gathering up used wrapping paper to where my dad is standing in the doorway. He's holding a flat box wrapped in shiny gold paper with a huge red bow.

"Says it's from you to Mia," he tells David.

I look at David sitting next to me on the couch.

"Oh, yeah. Almost forgot." He glances at me. "Just a little something."

He already got me a beautiful soft cardigan, a pair of "sensible" boots, and a two-person tent since his is really only for one. Though we can certainly sleep close enough that it didn't seem to matter the one time we took it out in the fall.

My dad brings the package over. It's very light. Everyone in the room has stopped what they're doing and is watching me unwrap this last Christmas present.

As I tear the paper off my heart once again expands, and I feel like crying. I've felt like this all day. Just because we're all here like this together. Just because I'm so happy.

We've celebrated four birthdays, Halloween, and Thanksgiving as one big, happy family. But Christmas is my favorite, and being here with our families all blended together, as if we've been doing this forever, is amazing.

I unwrap a flat cardboard box and lift the lid. Inside are a few typed pages.

I lift my puzzled gaze to David's.

"I wrote a new chapter," he tells me.

My eyes widen and I slap the box lid back on the box.

David has been writing in the fanfiction world. He's actually quite good. And very dirty.

It's been fun sharing that part of my life with him, not just having him as my biggest fan, but also reading what he comes up with.

But this is obviously not the time.

He chuckles and leans in, lifting the lid again.

"I want you to read this one right now."

"Are you sure?"

"Trust me."

I do, of course, so I pull out the two pages and start reading. Just not out loud. Just in case.

It only takes me three paragraphs to figure out what's going on.

My hand flies up to cover my mouth, and I look at him with wide eyes.

He slides to the floor next to me. Just like described in the scene.

Shockingly, however, my father strides over and hands David a black velvet ring box.

They exchange a smile, then David turns to me and opens the box.

I assume the ring is gorgeous, but I can't look away from David's face. He looks madly in love and incredibly happy.

God, I hope I get to see that look on his face for the rest of our lives.

"Mia Hansen, will you marry me?"

It's simple, not flowery, and perfectly David Bennett.

I nod. "Yes. Of course."

He pulls me up from the couch, wrapping me in his arms, burying his face in my hair. "I love you so much," he says against my ear.

"I love you, too. I'm so happy right now."

"I intend to keep you that way for a very long time."

I have no doubt that he will.

Everyone swarms around us, hugging us, offering congratulations, declaring they knew it was going to happen like this. Our moms are both crying and hugging one another. My sister is crying harder than anyone.

But it's my dad that I can't stop watching. He stands off to the side, watching everything with an expression of pride and love.

There's no mistaking what he's feeling.

We had a long talk after he found out that David and I were dating. After he went to David and told him how happy he was.

I never doubted that he wanted me to be happy. I just didn't know what he would do if I ever did something that he wasn't expecting or that he might disapprove of.

It turns out he did exactly what he'd always said he would do—love me unconditionally.

I eventually make it to his side.

"You were holding the ring for David?"

"Well, I'm easily the most trustworthy of this bunch," he tells me with a little grin.

I grin up at him. "Does this mean that David asked you for permission to propose?"

He slips an arm around my shoulders and hugs me up against his side. "You and David don't need my permission for anything."

"But he told you he was going to propose?" I'm not surprised.

David and my dad talk several times a day, every single day. I can't even count how many times I've told David something about my dad and he's said, "oh, I know," or I've filled my parents in on some something David's been up to, and my dad's corrected me on a detail or two in my story because he's already heard about it from David.

"He didn't have to tell me. It's been pretty obvious for a long time that you were headed this direction," my dad says. "But I found out for sure about a month ago. Do you remember the day that David rescued that baby deer?"

"Of course." That day had been scary as hell. Someone had called in that they'd seen a baby deer in the river struggling. It had fallen through the ice. David and a couple of other Game and Parks officers had responded as had my dad and the sheriff from the next county.

Of course, David was the one who decided to belly crawl out onto the ice and pull the deer out.

I was so grateful I found out about all of it *after* the fact when both David and the deer were safe and sound.

"When he was getting ready to go out on ice, he pulled the ring out of his pocket. He'd been carrying it around with him constantly. He handed it to me for safekeeping."

"And you just hung onto it after that?" I guess.

My dad chuckles. "Pretty much. Told him he could have it back when he was down on one knee."

That story is so in character for both of them.

I hug him tightly. "I'm really happy, Dad."

"That's very obvious, daughter."

. . .

Iᴛ's ᴊᴜsᴛ before midnight and I'm staring up at David's childhood bedroom ceiling, cuddled up against my *fiancé*, his strong heartbeat under my ear, his big hand on my ass, the ripples of an amazing orgasm just fading, and feeling like life can't get any better.

"So I know tomorrow is Christmas Day," David says. "But…"

I roll my eyes, but I am not a bit surprised by this. "What are you and my dad going to do?"

Neither of them is supposed to be working tomorrow, but that doesn't mean they're not going to be busy with something.

I swear, if we hadn't started dating while David still disliked my dad, I would think he was with me just to get closer to him.

"Well, since the kids are off from school for the next two weeks, some of us were talking that it might be fun to have some activities down at the park. We were thinking like building snow forts, and a snowman building contest. It's also really fun to use paintball guns on the snow because the colors show up amazingly. So we thought we'd meet down at the pavilion and look into setting up a hot chocolate stand and see if we can get a popcorn machine plugged in. I think there are plenty of outlets, but your dad isn't sure. And while we're there—"

I roll toward him and kiss him to shut him up.

His hands are in my hair a moment later, and I feel him getting into the kiss and forgetting all about hot chocolate and snow forts.

I pull back. "It sounds like you, my dad, and your brothers want to build snow forts and play with paintball guns, and you all think that saying you're doing it as a community service for the kids is a good cover-up. Kind of like the water balloon fight a few months ago. And the Punkin' Chunkin' contest in October."

He squeezes my ass. "Don't tell anyone."

I laugh. Everyone knows. And loves it about this group of guys. "Or what?" I ask, wiggling against him.

He growls. "Or I won't deny you orgasms tomorrow night once we're back in our own bed. I'll just give you one hard, fast one and that's it."

I giggle. Of course, denying orgasms sounds like that should be a punishment, but it is so delicious when he does it to me that it is *not* a deterrent. I had to first learn about it in one of the dirty fanfictions we wrote together, but he was very happy to give me a hands-on demonstration after that chapter published.

In fact, we've had a great time exploring a lot of things that we write about in the new fanfiction we're co-writing. It's the most popular thing on the entire site and has been for the past three months since we started.

I'll bring something up as the shy, innocent heroine. He'll answer in his chapter as the broody, alpha hero. And then he'll show me everything in graphic, full detail, real life at home.

He rolls toward me. "You know, it is really hot to be fucking my best friend's daughter."

Yeah, except *that* trope. He wanted to do that in our latest, and I said no.

I shake my head quickly. "No, we're still not doing that."

He chuckles and nuzzles my neck. "Okay, I'll make something else up."

"You know I don't need you to make anything up. I like us just exactly the way we are."

"Me too. Playing prissy and prim librarian with the dirty, rugged Game and Parks officer is always a good time."

"My favorite *non*-fiction of all," I agree as he pulls me over on top of him, and my diamond ring sparkles in the moonlight.

Thank you so much for reading Making It Up! I hope you loved David and Mia's story!

If this is your first trip to Sapphire Falls, I'm so excited that you're here! If you'd like to read about David and Mia's parents (and all their friends) keep scrolling for the list of the entire original series! (you even get to meet David as a little boy!)

If this is a return trip for you, welcome back!  I'm so happy to be back in this little town and I'm thrilled to have you all with me!

Find ALL of my books at **ErinNicholas. com**

And the best place to find out all the news about that (including upcoming books and more!) is right here!
bit.ly/Keep-In-Touch-Erin
Be sure you get those dashes and upper case letters in there!

And this is your personal invitation to my Facebook group, Erin Nicholas's Super Fans where you can get first looks, behind the scenes peeks, and daily fun with fellow romance lovers (including me!)!

ABOUT THE AUTHOR

Erin Nicholas is the New York Times and USA Today bestselling author of over sixty sexy contemporary romances. Her stories have been described as toe-curling, enchanting, steamy and fun. She loves to write about reluctant heroes, imperfect heroines and happily ever afters. She lives in the Midwest with her husband who only wants to read the sex scenes in her books, her kids who will never read the sex scenes in her books, and family and friends who say they're shocked by the sex scenes in her books (yeah, right!).

You can sign up for *all* the Erin news right HERE!

You can also find her here:

facebook.com/ErinNicholasBooks

instagram.com/authorerinnicolle

bookbub.com/authors/erin-nicholas

Digital ebook ISBN: 978-1-967534-07-4

Paperback print ISBN: 978-1-967534-06-7

Editor: Fedora Chen

Cover design: Qamber Designs

Photography: Wander Aguiar

Interior Illustration: Concepts by Canea